A MURDER
OF QUALITY

Carne School kept itself carefully apart from the small Dorset
town it dominated. An ancient foundation, even if its traditions
and ecclesiastical affectations were largely nineteenth century,
Carne prided itself on preserving proper standards and social
distinctions.

But something terrible had happened in this enclosed world.
Murder had been done, and the victim was the wife of a junior
master.

There was an obvious suspect: a local madwoman had
disappeared. Everyone hoped that the whole grisly business
could be cleared up quickly and discreetly.

So Smiley, doing a favour for an old friend, went down to
Dorset to listen, to take sherry and gently persevere; to ask
questions and to think. Carefully, he would uncover layer upon
layer of complexity, open cupboards and reveal skeletons.

ALSO BY JOHN LE CARRÉ

Call for the Dead
The Spy Who Came In from the Cold
The Looking Glass War
A Small Town in Germany
The Naive and Sentimental Lover
Tinker, Tailor, Soldier, Spy*
The Honourable Schoolboy*
Smiley's People*
The Little Drummer Girl
A Perfect Spy
The Russia House
The Secret Pilgrim

*Published in an omnibus edition
  entitled *The Quest for Karla*

le Carré

A MURDER OF QUALITY

The Novel
&
The Screenplay

Hodder & Stoughton

LONDON SYDNEY AUCKLAND TORONTO

A CIP catalogue record is available from
the British Library

ISBN 0-340-55551-3

The Novel copyright © 1962 Le Carré Productions
First published in Great Britain 1962
Foreword to the Novel © 1991 David Cornwell
The Screenplay © Le Carré Productions 1991
Introduction to the Screenplay © Le Carré Productions 1991

This edition first published in Great Britain in 1991

Published by Hodder and Stoughton,
a division of Hodder and Stoughton Ltd,
Mill Road, Dunton Green, Sevenoaks, Kent TN13 2YA.
Editorial Office: 47 Bedford Square, London WC1B 3DP.

Photoset by Rowland Phototypesetting Ltd,
Bury St Edmunds, Suffolk

Printed in Great Britain by Butler and Tanner Ltd,
Frome and London

The publishers would like to thank
Murray Close and Portobello Productions/Thames Television
for permission to reproduce colour photographs.

Contents

THE NOVEL

FOREWORD

The origins of most of my books are by now a mystery to me, even if they were not at the time, but *A Murder of Quality* is clearly set in my memory. It was my second book and I wrote it in the flush of the modest success enjoyed by my first, *Call for the Dead*. I began it in 1961 when I arrived in Bonn ahead of my family to take up a junior post at the British Embassy, and by the time it appeared I had *The Spy Who . . .* in my sights.

I still had a notion in those days of writing a thriller a year and adding a much-needed few hundred pounds to my Foreign Service salary. Or so I told myself, even if my ambitions were secretly larger. I wrote *A Murder of Quality* first in the gloomy *pension* in Bad Godesberg where young British diplomats were stabled while they awaited accommodation, then in the tiny house in the Gringstrasse where we lived with our two children and our au pair. In consequence, I wrote the book lying down, on beds, in notebooks, in the few snatched hours that were left to me by family and diplomatic life.

My sources were extremely present to me, as they will be to the reader. I hated English boarding schools. I found them monstrous and still do, probably because I began my boarding school career at the age of five, at a place called St Martin's, Northwood, and did not end it till I was sixteen, when I flatly refused to return to Westcott House, Sherborne, on the solid grounds that I would take no more of such institutions.

Yet as life would have it, eight years later I was banged up once again, this time at Eton as a junior Modern Languages master.

Eton was not Sherborne at all. Sherborne in my day had been rustic, colonialist, chauvinist, militarist, religious, patriotic and repressive. Boys beat other boys, housemasters beat boys, and even the headmaster turned his hand to beating boys when the crime was held to be sufficiently heinous or school discipline was thought to be slipping. I don't know whether masters beat masters but, in any case, I loathed them, and I loathed their grotesque allegiances most of all. To this day, I can find no forgiveness for their terrible abuse of the charges entrusted to them.

Only adults had nervous breakdowns in those days, so the methods of survival for boys who refused to join the system were animal cunning, 'internal immigration' as the Germans call it, or simply getting the hell out. I practised the first two, then opted for the third and took myself to Switzerland.

But Eton was an English social class of its own. A graduate of Eton is an Etonian first and a citizen second. He enjoys, during his schooling, more personal access to the staff than in any other school I am aware of, and an extremely high standard of teaching. Certainly the system had its barbarisms, but it awarded more privacy, more sovereignty to its pupils, more self-esteem – some would say arrogance – than I had imagined possible. As a young schoolmaster, I had the sensation of embarking on a second, vicarious education of my own, reacting sometimes against it, sometimes for it, but never calmly, never with any sense of integration or acceptance. Probably, since I had not yet begun to write, I had not realised quite how much of an outsider I was anyway, constantly repelled by the very institutions that drew me.

So the components are there for you to dissect as you will: an outrage at my Sherborne schooling, a fascination with the mores of the Etonian class, an attraction to it all, a revulsion from it, a bestiary of frightening adults drawn from the timid chambers of my institutional and largely parentless childhood; and a spiritual brutality towards young minds that in this far-from-perfect story takes the form of bloody violence.

As to poor Stella Rode and her Nonconformism, they came from even further back, from the days when my brother and I spent our Sundays in the chapels and tabernacles of coastal Dorset, listening to the counsel of a far humbler God than He who guided the untroubled conscience of the British ruling classes. I wrote about this world again in *A Perfect Spy*, in which the hells of British private education also find their place. So perhaps by the end of my career I too shall have discovered the truth of the adage that, after all their flailing about and looking for new material and experience, novelists end up writing the same book all through their lives.

Rereading this book now, I find a flawed thriller redeemed by ferocious and quite funny social comment. Most of all I recognise the dankness of those old stone walls that formed the limits of my childhood and left me for the rest of my life with an urge to fight off whatever threatened to enclose me. As to the screenplay – well, let's talk about that later.

Contents

Chapter 1

<u>BLACK CANDLES</u>

The greatness of Carne School has been ascribed by common consent to Edward VI, whose educational zeal is ascribed by history to the Duke of Somerset. But Carne prefers the respectability of the monarch to the questionable politics of his adviser, drawing strength from the conviction that Great Schools, like Tudor Kings, were ordained in Heaven.

And indeed its greatness is little short of miraculous. Founded by obscure monks, endowed by a sickly boy king, and dragged from oblivion by a Victorian bully, Carne had straightened its collar, scrubbed its rustic hands and face and presented itself shining to the courts of the twentieth century. And in the twinkling of an eye, the Dorset bumpkin was London's darling: Dick Whittington had arrived. Carne had parchments in Latin, seals in wax, and Lammas Land behind the Abbey. Carne had property, cloisters and woodworm, a whipping block and a line in the Doomsday Book – then what more did it need to instruct the sons of the rich?

And they came; each Half they came (for terms are not elegant things), so that throughout a whole afternoon the trains would unload sad groups of black-coated boys on to the station platform. They came in great cars that shone with mournful purity. They came to bury poor King Edward, trundling handcarts over the cobbled streets or carrying tuck boxes like little coffins. Some wore gowns, and when they walked they looked like crows, or black angels come for the burying. Some followed singly like undertakers' mutes, and you could hear the clip of their boots as they went. They were always in mourning at Carne; the small boys because they must stay and the big boys because they must leave, the masters because respectability was underpaid; and now, as the Lent Half (as the Easter term was called) drew to its end, the cloud of gloom was as firmly settled as ever over the grey towers of Carne.

Gloom and the cold. The cold was crisp and sharp as flint. It cut the faces of the boys as they moved slowly from the deserted playing fields after the school match. It pierced their black topcoats and turned their stiff, pointed collars into icy rings round their necks. Frozen, they plodded from the field to the long walled road which led to the main tuck shop and the town, the line gradually dwindling into groups, and the groups into pairs. Two boys who looked even colder than the rest crossed the road and made their way along a narrow path which led towards a distant but less populated tuck shop.

'I think I shall die if ever I have to watch one of those beastly rugger games again. The noise is fantastic,' said one. He was tall with fair hair, and his name was Caley.

'People only shout because the dons are watching from the pavilion,' the other rejoined; 'that's why each house has to stand together. So that the house dons can swank about how loud their houses shout.'

'What about Rode?' asked Caley. 'Why does he stand with us and make us shout, then? He's not a house don, just a bloody usher.'

'He's sucking up to house dons all the time. You can see him in the quad between lessons buzzing round the big men. All the junior masters do.' Caley's companion was a cynical red-haired boy called Perkins, Captain of Fielding's house.

'I've been to tea with Rode,' said Caley.

'Rode's hell. He wears brown boots. What was tea like?'

'Bleak. Funny how tea gives them away. Mrs Rode's quite decent, though – homely in a plebby sort of way: doyleys and china birds. Food's good: Women's Institute, but good.'

'Rode's doing Corps next Half. That'll put the lid on it. He's so *keen*, bouncing about all the time. You can tell he's not a gentleman. You know where he went to school?'

'No.'

'Branxome Grammar. Fielding told my Mama, when she came over from Singapore last Half.'

'God. Where's Branxome?'

'On the coast. Near Bournemouth. I haven't been to tea

with anyone except Fielding.' Perkins added after a slight pause, 'You get roast chestnuts and crumpets. You're never allowed to thank him, you know. He says emotionalism is only for the lower classes. That's typical of Fielding. He's not like a don at all. I think boys bore him. The whole house goes to tea with him once a Half, he has us in turn, four at a time, and that's about the only time he talks to most men.'

They walked on in silence for a while until Perkins said:

'Fielding's giving another dinner party tonight.'

'He's pushing the boat out these days,' Caley replied, with disapproval. 'Suppose the food in your house is worse than ever?'

'It's his last Half before he retires. He's entertaining every don and all the wives separately by the end of the Half. Black candles every evening. For mourning. Hells extravagant.'

'Yes. I suppose it's a sort of gesture.'

'My Pater says he's a queer.'

They crossed the road and disappeared into the tuck shop, where they continued to discuss the weighty affairs of Mr Terence Fielding, until Perkins drew their meeting reluctantly to a close. Being a poor hand at science, he was unfortunately obliged to take extra tuition in the subject.

The dinner party to which Perkins had alluded that afternoon was now drawing to a close. Mr Terence Fielding, senior housemaster of Carne, gave himself some more port and pushed the decanter wearily to his left. It was his port, the best he had. There was enough of the best to last the Half – and after that, be damned. He felt a little tired after watching the match, and a little drunk, and a little bored with Shane Hecht and her husband. Shane was so hideous. Massive and enveloping, like a faded Valkyrie. All that black hair. He should have asked someone else. The Snows for instance, but he was too clever. Or Felix D'Arcy, but D'Arcy interrupted. Ah well, a little later he would annoy Charles Hecht, and Hecht would get in a pet and leave early.

Hecht was fidgeting, wanting to light his pipe, but Fielding damn well wouldn't have it. Hecht could have a cigar if he wanted to smoke. But his pipe could stay in his dinner-jacket pocket, where it belonged, or didn't belong, and his athletic profile could remain unadorned.

'Cigar, Hecht?'

'No thanks, Fielding. I say, do you mind if I . . .'

'I can recommend the cigars. Young Havelake sent them from Havana. His father's ambassador there, you know.'

'Yes, dear,' said Shane tolerantly; 'Vivian Havelake was in Charles's troop when Charles was commandant of the Cadets.'

'Good boy, Havelake,' Hecht observed, and pressed his lips together to show he was a strict judge.

'It's amusing how things have changed.' Shane Hecht said this rapidly with a rather wooden smile, as if it weren't really amusing. 'Such a grey world we live in, now.

'I remember before the war when Charles inspected the Corps on a white horse. We don't do that kind of thing now, do we? I've got nothing against Mr Iredale as commandant, nothing at all. What *was* his regiment, Terence, do you know? I'm sure he does it very nicely, whatever they do now in the Corps – he gets on so well with the boys, doesn't he? His wife's such a nice person . . . I wonder why they can never keep their servants. I hear Mr Rode will be helping out with the Corps next Half.'

'Poor little Rode,' said Fielding slowly; 'running about like a puppy, trying to earn his biscuits. He tries so hard; have you seen him cheering at school matches? He'd never seen a game of rugger before he came here, you know. They don't play rugger at grammar schools – it's all soccer. Do you remember when he first came, Charles? It was fascinating. He lay very low at first, drinking us in: the games, the vocabulary, the manners. Then, one day it was as if he had been given the power of speech, and he spoke in our language. It was amazing, like plastic surgery. It was Felix D'Arcy's work of course – I've never seen anything quite like it before.'

'Dear Mrs Rode,' said Shane Hecht in that voice of abstract vagueness which she reserved for her most venomous pronouncements: 'So sweet . . . and such simple taste, don't you think? I mean, whoever would have dreamed of putting those china ducks on the wall? Big ones at the front and little ones at the back. Charming, don't you think? Like one of those teashops. I wonder where she bought them. I must ask her. I'm told her father lives near Bournemouth. It must be so lonely for him, don't you think? Such a vulgar place; no one to talk to.'

Fielding sat back and surveyed his own table. The silver was good. The best in Carne, he had heard it said, and he was inclined to agree. This Half he had nothing but black candles. It was the sort of thing people remembered when you'd gone: 'Dear old Terence – marvellous host. He dined every member of the staff during his last Half, you know, wives too. Black candles, rather touching. It broke his heart giving up his house.' But he must annoy Charles Hecht. Shane would like that. Shane would egg him on because she hated Charles, because within her great ugly body she was as cunning as a snake.

Fielding looked at Hecht and then at Hecht's wife, and she smiled back at him, the slow rotten smile of a whore. For a moment Fielding thought of Hecht pasturing in that thick body: it was a scene redolent of Lautrec . . . yes, that was it! Charles pompous and top-hatted, seated stiffly upon the plush coverlet; she massive, pendulous and bored. The image pleased him: so perverse to consign that fool Hecht from the Spartan cleanliness of Carne to the brothels of nineteenth-century Paris . . .

Fielding began talking, pontificating rather, with an air of friendly objectivity which he knew Hecht would resent.

'When I look back on my thirty years at Carne, I realise I have achieved rather less than a road sweeper.' They were watching him now – 'I used to regard a road sweeper as a person inferior to myself. Now, I rather doubt it. Something is dirty, he makes it clean, and the state of the world is advanced. But I – what have *I* done? Entrenched a ruling class which is distinguished by neither talent, culture, nor wit; kept alive for one more generation the distinctions of a dead age.'

Charles Hecht, who had never perfected the art of not listening to Fielding, grew red and fussed at the other end of the table.

'Don't we teach them, Fielding? What about our successes, our scholarships?'

'I have never taught a boy in my life, Charles. Usually the

boy wasn't clever enough; occasionally, I wasn't. In most boys, you see, perception dies with puberty. In a few it persists, though where we find it we take good care at Carne to kill it. If it survives our efforts the boy wins a scholarship . . . Bear with me, Shane; it's my last Half.'

'Last Half or not, you're talking through your hat, Fielding,' said Hecht, angrily.

'That is traditional at Carne. These successes, as you call them, are the failures, the rare boys who have not learned the lessons of Carne. They have ignored the cult of mediocrity. We can do nothing for them. But for the rest, for the puzzled little clerics and the blind little soldiers, for them the truth of Carne is written on the wall, and they hate us.'

Hecht laughed rather heavily.

'Why do so many come back, then, if they hate us so much? Why do they remember us and come and see us?'

'Because we, dear Charles, are the writing on the wall! The one lesson of Carne they never forget. They come back to read *us*, don't you see? It was from us they learnt the secret of life: that we grow old without growing wise. They realised that nothing happened when we grew up: no blinding light on the road to Damascus, no sudden feeling of maturity.' Fielding put his head back and gazed at the clumsy Victorian moulding on the ceiling, and the halo of dirt round the light rose.

'We just got a little older. We made the same jokes, thought the same thoughts, wanted the same things. Year in, year out, Hecht, we were the same people, not wiser, not better; we haven't had an original thought between us for the last fifty years of our lives. They saw what a trick it all was, Carne and us: our academic dress, our schoolroom jokes, our wise little offerings of guidance. And that's why they come back year after year of their puzzled, barren lives to gaze fascinated at you and me, Hecht, like children at a grave, searching for the secret of life and death. Oh, yes, they have learned *that* from us.'

Hecht looked at Fielding in silence for a moment.

'Decanter, Hecht?' said Fielding, in a slightly conciliatory way, but Hecht's eyes were still upon him.

'If that's a joke . . .' he began, and his wife observed with satisfaction that he was very angry indeed.

'I wish I knew, Charles,' Fielding replied with apparent earnestness. 'I really wish I knew. I used to think it was clever to confuse comedy with tragedy. Now I wish I could distinguish them.' He rather liked that.

They had coffee in the drawing-room, where Fielding resorted to gossip, but Hecht was not to be drawn. Fielding rather wished he had let him light his pipe. Then he recalled his vision of the Hechts in Paris, and it restored him. He had been rather good this evening. There were moments when he convinced himself.

While Shane fetched her coat, the two men stood together in the hall, but neither spoke. Shane returned, an ermine stole, yellow with age, draped over her great white shoulders. She inclined her head to the right, smiled and held out her hand to Fielding, the fingers down.

'Terence, darling,' she said, as Fielding kissed her fat knuckles; 'so kind. And in your last Half. You must dine with us before you go. So sad. So few of us left.' She smiled again, half closing her eyes to indicate emotional disturbance, then followed her husband into the street. It was still bitterly cold and snow was in the air.

Fielding closed and carefully bolted the door behind them – perhaps a fraction earlier than courtesy required – and returned to the dining-room. Hecht's port glass was still about half full. Fielding picked it up and carefully poured the contents back into the decanter. He hoped Hecht wasn't too upset; he hated people to dislike him. He snuffed the black candles and damped their wicks between his forefinger and thumb. Switching on the light, he took from the sideboard a sixpenny notebook, and opened it. It contained his list of dining guests for the remainder of the Half. With his fountain pen he placed a neat tick against the name Hecht. They were done. On Wednesday he would have the Rodes. The husband was quite good value, but she, of course, was hell . . . It was not always the way with married couples. The wives as a rule were so much more sympathetic.

He opened the sideboard and took from it a bottle of brandy and a tumbler. Holding them both in the same hand, he shuffled wearily back to the drawing-room, resting his other hand on the wall as he went. God! He felt old, suddenly; that thin line of pain across the chest, that heaviness in the legs and feet. Such an effort being with people – on stage all the time. He hated to be alone, but people bored him. Being alone was like being tired, but unable to sleep. Some German poet had said that; he'd quoted it once, 'You may sleep but I must dance.' Something like that.

'That's how I am,' thought Fielding. 'That's how Carne is, too; an old satyr dancing to the music.' The music grew faster and their bodies older, but they must dance on – there were young men waiting in the wings. It had been funny once dancing the old dances in a new world. He poured himself some more brandy. He'd be pleased to leave in a way, even though he'd have to go on teaching somewhere else.

But it had its beauty, Carne . . . The Abbey Close in spring . . . the flamingo figures of boys waiting for the ritual of worship . . . the ebb and flow of children, like the seasons of the year, and the old men dying among them. He wished he could paint; he would paint the pageant of Carne in the fallow browns of autumn . . . What a shame, thought Fielding, that a mind so perceptive of beauty had no talent for creation.

He looked at his watch. Quarter to twelve. Nearly time to go out . . . to dance, and not to sleep.

Chapter 2

THE THURSDAY FEELING

I t was Thursday evening and the *Christian Voice* had just been put to bed. This was scarcely a historic event in Fleet Street. The pimply boy from Dispatch who took away the ragged pile of page-proofs showed no more ceremony than was strictly demanded by the eventual prospect of his Christmas bonus. And even in this respect he had learned that the secular journals of Unipress were more provident of material charity than the *Christian Voice*; charity being in strict relationship to circulation.

Miss Brimley, the journal's editor, adjusted the air cushion beneath her and lit a cigarette. Her secretary and sub-editor – the appointment carried both responsibilities – yawned, dropped the aspirin bottle into her handbag, combed out her ginger hair and bade Miss Brimley good night, leaving behind her as usual the smell of strongly scented powder and an empty paper-tissue box. Miss Brimley listened contentedly to the clipping echo of her footsteps as it faded down the corridor. It pleased her to be alone at last, tasting the anticlimax. She never failed to wonder at herself, how every Thursday morning brought the same slight uneasiness as she entered the vast Unipress building and stood a little absurdly on one escalator after the other, like a drab parcel on a luxury liner. Heaven knows, she had run the *Voice* for fourteen years, and there were those who said its layout was the best thing Unipress did. Yet the Thursday feeling never left her, the wakeful anxiety that one day, perhaps today, they wouldn't be ready when the dispatch boy came. She often wondered what would happen then. She had heard of failures elsewhere in that vast combine, of features disapproved and staff rebuked. It was a mystery to her why they kept the *Voice* at all, with its expensive room on the seventh floor and a circulation which, if Miss Brimley knew anything, hardly paid for the paper-clips.

The *Voice* had been founded at the turn of the century by old Lord Landsbury, together with a Nonconformist daily newspaper and the *Temperance Gazette*. But the *Gazette* and the daily were long since dead, and Landsbury's son had woken one morning not long ago to find his whole business and every man and woman of it, every stick of furniture, ink, paper-clips, and galley-pins, bought by the hidden gold of Unipress.

That was three years ago and every day she had waited for her dismissal. But it never came; no directive, no question, no word. And so, being a sensible woman, she continued exactly as before and ceased to wonder.

And she was glad. It was easy to sneer at the *Voice*. Every week it offered humbly and without fanfares evidence of the Lord's intervention in the world's affairs, retold in simple and somewhat unscientific terms the early history of the Jews, and provided over a fictitious signature motherly advice to whomever should write and ask for it. The *Voice* scarcely concerned itself with the fifty-odd millions of the population who had never heard of it. It was a family affair, and rather than abuse those who were not members, it did its best for those who were. For them it was kind, optimistic, and informative. If a million children were dying of the plague in India, you may be sure that the weekly editorial described the miraculous escape from fire of a Methodist family in Kent. The *Voice* did not advise you how to disguise the encroaching wrinkles round your eyes, or control your spreading figure; did not dismay you, if you were old, by its own eternal youth. It was itself middle-aged and middle class, counselled caution to girls and charity to all. Nonconformity is the most conservative of habits and families which took the *Voice* in 1903 continued to take it in 1960.

Miss Brimley was not quite the image of her journal. The fortunes of war and the caprice of Intelligence work had thrown her into partnership with the younger Lord Landsbury, and for the six years of war they had worked together efficiently and inconspicuously in an unnamed building in Knightsbridge. The fortunes of peace rendered both unemployed, but Landsbury had the good sense, as well as the generosity, to offer Miss Brimley a job. The *Voice* had ceased publication during the war, and no one seemed anxious to renew it. At first Miss Brimley had felt a little ashamed at reviving and editing a journal which in no way expressed her own vague deism, but quite soon, as the touching letters came in and the circulation recovered, she developed an affection for her job – and for her readers – which outweighed her earlier misgivings. The *Voice* was her life and its readers her preoccupation. She struggled to answer their odd, troubled questions, sought advice of others where she could not provide it herself, and, in time, under a handful of pseudonyms, became, if not their philosopher, their guide, friend, and universal aunt.

Miss Brimley put out her cigarette, absently tidied the pins, paper-clips, scissors, and paste into the top right-hand drawer of her desk, and gathered together the afternoon mail from her in-tray which, because it was Thursday, she had left untouched. There were several letters addressed to Barbara Fellowship, under which name the *Voice* had, since its foundation, answered both privately and through its published columns the many problems of its correspondents. They could wait until tomorrow. She rather enjoyed the 'problem post', but Friday morning was when she read it. She opened the little filing cabinet at her elbow and dropped the letters into a box file at the front of the compartment. As she did so, one of them fell on its back and she noticed with surprise that the sealed flap was embossed with an elegant blue dolphin. She picked the envelope out of the cabinet and looked at it curiously, turning it over several times. It was of pale grey paper, very faintly lined. Expensive – perhaps hand-made. Beneath the dolphin was a tiny scroll on which she could just discern the legend, *Regem defendere diem videre*. The postmark was Carne, Dorset. That must be the school crest. But why was Carne familiar to her? Miss Brimley was proud of her memory, which was excellent, and she was vexed when it failed her. As a last resort she opened the envelope with her faded ivory paper-knife and read the letter.

Dear Miss Fellowship,
    I don't know if you are a real person but it doesn't matter, because you always give such good, kind answers. It was me who wrote last June about the pastry mix. I am not mad and I know my husband is trying to kill me. Could I please

come and see you as soon as it's convenient? I'm sure you'll believe me, and understand that I am normal. Could it be *as soon as possible* please, I am so afraid of the long nights. I don't know who else to turn to. I could try Mr Cardew at the Tabernacle but he wouldn't believe me and Dad's too sensible. I might as well be dead. There's something not quite right about him. At night sometimes when he thinks I'm asleep he just lies watching the darkness. I know it's wrong to think such wicked things and have fear in our hearts, but I can't help it.

I hope you don't get many letters like this.

Yours faithfully,

Stella Rode (Mrs)

née Glaston

She sat quite still at her desk for a moment, looking at the address in handsome blue engraving at the top of the page: 'North Fields, Carne School, Dorset.' In that moment of shock and astonishment one phrase forced itself upon her mind. 'The value of intelligence depends on its breeding.' That was John Landsbury's favourite dictum. Until you know the pedigree of the information you cannot evaluate a report. Yes, that was what he used to say: 'We are not democratic. We close the door on intelligence without parentage.' And she used to reply: 'Yes, John, but even the best families had to begin somewhere.'

But Stella Rode *had* parentage. It all came back to her now. She was the Glaston girl. The girl whose marriage was reported in the editorial, the girl who won the summer competition; Samuel Glaston's daughter from Branxome. She had a card in Miss Brimley's index.

Abruptly she stood up, the letter still in her hand, and walked to the uncurtained window. Just in front of her was a contemporary window-box of woven white metal. It was odd, she reflected, how she could never get anything to grow in that window-box. She looked down into the street, a slight, sensible figure leaning forward a little and framed by the incandescent fog outside; fog made yellow from the stolen light of London's streets. She could just distinguish the street lamps far below, pale and sullen. She suddenly felt the need for fresh air, and on an impulse quite alien to her usual calm, she opened the window wide. The quick cold and the angry surge of noise burst in on her, and the insidious fog followed. The sound of traffic was constant, so that for a moment she thought it was the turning of some great machine. Then above its steady growl she heard the newsboys. Their cries were like the cries of gulls against a gathering storm. She could see them now, sentinels among the hastening shadows.

It might be true. That had always been the difficulty. Right through the war it was the same restless search. It might be true. It was no use relating reports to probability when there was no quantum of knowledge from which to start. She remembered the first intelligence from France on flying bombs, wild talk of concrete runways in the depths of a forest. You had to resist the dramatic, you had to hold out against it. Yet it might be true. Tomorrow, the day after, those newsboys down there might be shouting it, and Stella Rode *née* Glaston might be dead. And if that was so, if there was the remotest chance that this man was plotting to kill this woman, then she, Ailsa Brimley, must do what she could to prevent it. Besides, Stella Glaston had a claim on her assistance if anyone did: both her father and her grandfather had taken the *Voice*, and when Stella married five years ago Miss Brimley had put a couple of lines about it in the editorial. The Glastons sent her a Christmas card every year. They were one of the original families to subscribe . . .

It was cold at the window, but she remained there, still fascinated by the half hidden shadows joining and parting beneath her, and the useless street lights burning painfully among them. She began to imagine him as one of those shadows, pressing and jostling, his murderer's eyes turned to sockets of dark. And suddenly she was frightened and needed help.

But not the police, not yet. If Stella Rode had wanted that she would have gone herself. Why hadn't she? For love? For fear of looking a fool? Because instinct was not evidence? They wanted fact. But the fact of murder was death. Must they wait for that?

Who would help? She thought at once of Landsbury, but he was farming in Rhodesia. Who else had been with them in the war? Fielding and Jebedee were dead, Steed-Asprey vanished. Smiley – where was he? George Smiley, the cleverest and perhaps the oddest of them all. Of course, Miss Brimley remembered now. He made that improbable marriage and went back to research at Oxford. But he hadn't stayed there . . . The marriage had broken up . . . What *had* he done after that?

She returned to her desk and picked up the S–Z directory. Ten minutes later she was sitting in a taxi, heading for Sloane Square. In her neatly gloved hand she held a cardboard folder containing Stella Rode's card from the index and the correspondence which had passed between them at the time of the summer competition. She was nearly at Piccadilly when she remembered she'd left the office window open. It didn't seem to matter much.

'With other people it's Persian cats or golf. With me it's the *Voice* and my readers. I'm a ridiculous spinster, I know, but there it is. I won't go to the police until I've tried *something*, George.'

'And you thought you'd try me?'

'Yes.'

She was sitting in the study of George Smiley's house in Bywater Street; the only light came from the complicated lamp on his desk, a black spider of a thing shining brightly on to the manuscript notes which covered the desk.

'So you've left the Service?' she said.

'Yes, yes, I have.' He nodded his round head vigorously, as if reassuring himself that a distasteful experience was really over, and mixed Miss Brimley a whisky and soda. 'I had another spell there after . . . Oxford. It's all very different in peacetime, you know,' he continued.

Miss Brimley nodded.

'I can imagine it. More time to be bitchy.' Smiley said nothing, just lit a cigarette and sat down opposite her.

'And the people have changed. Fielding, Steed, Jebedee. All gone.' She said this in a matter-of-fact way as she took from her large sensible handbag Stella Rode's letter. 'This is the letter, George.'

When he had read it, he held it briefly towards the lamp,

his round face caught by the light in a moment of almost comic earnestness. Watching him, Miss Brimley wondered what impression he made on those who did not know him well. She used to think of him as the most forgettable man she had ever met; short and plump, with heavy spectacles and thinning hair, he was at first sight the very prototype of an unsuccessful middle-aged bachelor in a sedentary occupation. His natural diffidence in most practical matters was reflected in his clothes, which were costly and unsuitable, for he was clay in the hands of his tailor, who robbed him.

He had put down the letter on the small marquetry table beside him, and was looking at her owlishly.

'This other letter she sent you, Brim. Where is it?'

She handed him the folder. He opened it and after a moment read aloud Stella Rode's other letter:

Dear Miss Fellowship,

I would like to submit the following suggestion for your 'Kitchen Hints' competition.

Make your basic batch of cake mixture once a month. Cream equal quantities of fat and sugar and add one egg for every six ounces of the mixture. For puddings and cakes, add flour to the required quantity of basic mixture.

This will keep well for a month.

I enclose stamped addressed envelope.

Yours sincerely,

Stella Rode (*née* Glaston)

PS – Incidentally, you can prevent wire wool from rusting by keeping it in a jar of soapy water. Are we allowed two suggestions? If so, please can this be my second?

'She won the competition,' Miss Brimley observed, 'but that's not the point. This is what I want to tell you, George. She's a Glaston, and the Glastons have been reading the *Voice* since it started. Stella's grandfather was old Rufus Glaston, a Lancashire pottery king; he and John Landsbury's father built chapels and tabernacles in practically every village in the Midlands. When Rufus died the *Voice* put out a memorial edition and old Landsbury himself wrote the obituary. Samuel

Glaston took on his father's business, but had to move south because of his health. He ended up near Bournemouth, a widower with one daughter, Stella. She's the last of all that family. The whole lot are as down to earth as you could wish, Stella included, I should think. I don't think any of them is likely to be suffering from delusions of persecution.'

Smiley was looking at her in astonishment.

'My dear Brim, I can't possibly take that in. How on earth do you know all this?'

Miss Brimley smiled apologetically.

'The Glastons are easy – they're almost part of the magazine. They send us Christmas cards, and boxes of chocolates on the anniversary of our foundation. We've got about five hundred families who form what I call our Establishment. They were in on the *Voice* from the start and they've kept up ever since. They write to us, George; if they're worried they write and say so; if they're getting married, moving house, retiring from work, if they're ill, depressed, or angry, they write. Not often, Heaven knows; but enough.'

'How do you remember it all?'

'I don't. I keep a card index. I always write back you see . . . only . . .'

'Yes?'

Miss Brimley looked at him earnestly.

'This is the first time anyone has written because she's frightened.'

'What do you want me to do?'

'I've only had one bright idea so far. I seem to remember Adrian Fielding had a brother who taught at Carne . . .'

'He's a housemaster there, if he hasn't retired.'

'No, he retires this Half – it was in *The Times* some weeks ago, in that little bit on the Court page where Carne always announces itself. It said: "Carne School reassembles today for the Lent Half. Mr T. R. Fielding will retire at the end of the Half, having completed his statutory fifteen years as a housemaster."'

Smiley laughed.

'Really, Brim, your memory is absurd!'

'It was the mention of Fielding . . . Anyway, I thought you could ring him up. You must know him.'

'Yes, yes. I know him. At least, I met him once at Magdalen High Table. But –' Smiley coloured a little.

'But what, George?'

'Well, he's not quite the man his brother was, you know.'

'How could he be?' Miss Brimley rejoined a little sharply. 'But he can tell you something about Stella Rode. And her husband.'

'I don't think I could do that on the telephone. I think I'd rather go and see him. But what's to stop you ringing up Stella Rode?'

'Well, I can't tonight, can I? Her husband will be in. I thought I'd put a letter in the post to her tonight telling her she can come to see me any time. But,' she continued, making a slight, impatient movement with her foot, 'I want to do something *now*, George.'

Smiley nodded and went to the telephone. He rang directory inquiries and asked for Terence Fielding's number. After a long delay he was told to ring Carne School central exchange, who would connect him with whomever he required. Miss Brimley, watching him, wished she knew a little more about George Smiley, how much of that diffidence was assumed, how vulnerable he was.

'The best,' Adrian had said. 'The strongest and the best.'

But so many men learnt strength during the war, learnt terrible things, and put aside their knowledge with a shudder when it ended.

The number was ringing now. She heard the dialling tone and for a moment was filled with apprehension. For the first time she was afraid of making a fool of herself, afraid of becoming involved in unlikely explanations with angular, suspicious people.

'Mr Terence Fielding, please . . .' A pause.

'Fielding, good evening. My name is George Smiley; I knew your brother well in the war. We have in fact met . . . Yes, yes, quite right – Magdalen, was it not, the summer before last? Look, I wonder if I might come and see you on a personal matter . . . it's a little difficult to discuss on the telephone. A friend of mine has received a rather disturbing letter from the wife of a Carne master . . . Well, I – Rode, Stella Rode; her husband . . .'

He suddenly stiffened, and Miss Brimley, her eyes fixed upon him, saw with alarm how his chubby face broke into an expression of pain and disgust. She no longer heard what he was saying. She could only watch the dreadful transformation of his face, the whitening knuckles of his hand clutching the receiver. He was looking at her now, saying something . . . it was too late. Stella Rode was dead. She had been murdered late on Wednesday night. They'd actually been dining with Fielding the night it happened.

Chapter 3

THE NIGHT OF THE MURDER

The seven-five from Waterloo to Yeovil is not a popular
train, though it provides an excellent breakfast. Smiley
had no difficulty in finding a first-class compartment to himself.
It was a bitterly cold day, dark and the sky heavy with snow.
He sat huddled in a voluminous travelling coat of Continental
origin, holding in his gloved hands a bundle of the day's
papers. Because he was a precise man and did not care to be
hurried, he had arrived thirty minutes before the train was
due to depart. Still tired after the stresses of the previous night,
when he had sat up talking with Ailsa Brimley until Heaven
knew what hour, he was disinclined to read. Looking out of
the window on to an almost empty station, he caught sight, to
his great surprise, of Miss Brimley making her way along the
platform, peering in at the windows, a carrier bag in her hand.
He lowered the window and called to her.

'My dear Brim, what are you doing here at this dreadful
hour? You should be in bed.'

She sat down opposite him and began unpacking her bag
and handing him its contents: thermos, sandwiches, and
chocolate.

'I didn't know whether there was a breakfast car,' she
explained; 'and besides, I wanted to come and see you off.
You're such a dear, George, and I wish I could come with
you, but Unipress would go mad if I did. The only time they
notice you is when you're not there.'

'Haven't you seen the papers?' he asked.

'Just briefly, on the way here. They seem to think it wasn't
him, but some madman . . .'

'I know, Brim. That's what Fielding said, wasn't it?' There
was a moment's awkward silence.

'George, am I being an awful ass, letting you go off like this?
I was sure last night, but now I wonder . . .'

'After you left I rang Ben Sparrow of Special Branch. You remember him, don't you? He was with us in the war. I told him the whole story.'

'George! At three in the morning?'

'Yes. He's ringing the Divisional Superintendent at Carne. He'll tell him about the letter, and that I'm coming down. Ben had an idea that a man named Rigby would be handling the case. Rigby and Ben were at police college together.' He looked at her kindly for a moment. 'Besides, I'm a man of leisure, Brim. I shall enjoy the change.'

'Bless you, George,' said Miss Brimley, woman enough to believe him. She got up to go, and Smiley said to her:

'Brim, if you should need any more help or anything, and can't get hold of me, there's a man called Mendel who lives in Mitcham, a retired police inspector. He's in the book. If you get hold of him and mention me, he'll do what he can for you. I've booked a room at the Sawley Arms.'

Alone again, Smiley surveyed uneasily the assortment of food and drink which Miss Brimley had provided. He had promised himself the luxury of breakfast in the restaurant car. He would keep the sandwiches and coffee for later, that would be the best thing; for lunch, perhaps. And he would breakfast properly.

In the restaurant car Smiley read first the less sensational reports on the death of Stella Rode. It appeared that on Wednesday evening Mr and Mrs Rode had been guests at dinner of Mr Terence Fielding, the senior housemaster at Carne and brother of the late Adrian Fielding, the celebrated French scholar who had vanished during the war while specially employed by the War Office. They had left Mr Fielding's house together at about ten to eleven and walked the half mile from the centre of Carne to their house, which stood alone at the edge of the famous Carne playing fields. As they reached their house Mr Rode remembered that he had left at Mr Fielding's house some examination papers which urgently required correction that night. (At this point Smiley remembered that he had failed to pack his dinner-jacket, and that Fielding would almost certainly ask him to dine.) Rode determined to walk back to Fielding's house and collect the papers, therefore, starting back at about five past eleven. It appears that Mrs Rode made herself a cup of tea and sat down in the drawing-room to await his return.

Adjoining the back of the house is a conservatory, the inner door of which leads to the drawing-room. It was there that Rode eventually found his wife when he returned. There were signs of a struggle, and certain inexpensive articles of jewellery were missing from the body. The confusion in the conservatory was terrible. Fortunately there had been a fresh fall of snow on Wednesday afternoon, and detectives from Dorchester were examining the footprints and other traces early on Thursday morning. Mr Rode had been treated for shock at Dorchester Central Hospital. The police wished to interview a woman from the adjacent village of Pylle who was locally known as 'Mad Janie' on account of her eccentric and solitary habits. Mrs Rode, who was well known in Carne for her energetic work on behalf of the International Refugee Year, had apparently shown a charitable interest in her welfare, and she had vanished without trace since the night of the murder. The police were currently of the opinion that the murderer had caught sight of Mrs Rode through the drawing-room window (she had not drawn the curtains) and that Mrs Rode had admitted the murderer at the front door in the belief that it was her husband returning from Mr Fielding's house. The Home Office pathologist had been asked to conduct a post-mortem examination.

The other reports were not so restrained: 'Murder most foul has desecrated the hallowed playing fields of Carne' one article began, and another, 'Science teacher discovers murdered wife in blood-spattered conservatory'. A third screamed, 'Mad woman sought in Carne murder'. With an expression of distaste, Smiley screwed up all the newspapers except the *Guardian* and *The Times* and tossed them on to the luggage rack.

He changed at Yeovil for a local line to Sturminster, Okeford and Carne. It was something after eleven o'clock when he finally arrived at Carne station.

He telephoned the hotel from the station and sent his luggage ahead by taxi. The Sawley Arms was only full at Commemoration and on St Andrew's Day. Most of the year it was empty; sitting like a prim Victorian lady, its slate roof in the mauve of half-mourning, on ill-tended lawns midway between the station and Carne Abbey.

Snow still lay on the ground, but the day was fine and dry, and Smiley decided to walk into the town and arrange to meet the police officer conducting the investigation of the murder. He left the station, with its foretaste of Victorian austerity, and walked along the avenue of bare trees which led towards the great Abbey tower, flat and black against the colourless winter sky. He crossed the Abbey Close, a serene and beautiful square of medieval houses, the roofs snow-covered, the white lawns shaded with pin strokes of grass. As he passed the west door of the Abbey, the soft snow creaking where he trod, the clock high above him struck the half-hour, and two knights on horseback rode out from their little castle over the door, and slowly raised their lances to each other in salute. Then, as if it were all part of the same clockwork mechanism, other doors all round the Close opened too, releasing swarms of black-coated boys who stampeded across the snow towards the Abbey. One boy passed so close that his gown brushed against Smiley's sleeve. Smiley called to him as he ran past:

'What's going on?'

'Sext,' shouted the boy in reply, and was gone.

He passed the main entrance to the school and came at once upon the municipal part of the town, a lugubrious nineteenth-century fairyland in local stone, stitched together by a complexity of Gothic chimneys and crenel windows. Here was the town hall, and beside it, with the flag of St George floating at its masthead, the Carne Constabulary Headquarters, built ninety years ago to withstand the onslaughts of archery and battering rams.

He gave his name to the Duty Sergeant, and asked to see the officer investigating the death of Mrs Rode. The Sergeant, an elderly, inscrutable man, addressed himself to the telephone with a certain formality, as if he were about to perform a difficult conjuring trick. To Smiley's surprise, he was told that Inspector Rigby would be pleased to see him at once, and a police cadet was summoned to show him the way. He was led at a spanking pace up the wide staircase in the centre of the hall, and in a matter of moments found himself before the Inspector.

He was a very short man, and very broad. He could have been a Celt from the tin-mines of Cornwall or the collieries of Wales. His dark grey hair was cut very close; it came to a point in the centre of his brow like a devil's cap. His hands were large and powerful, he had the trunk and stance of a wrestler, but he spoke slowly, with a Dorset burr to his soft voice. Smiley quickly noticed that he had one quality rare among small men: the quality of openness. Though his eyes were dark and bright and the movements of his body swift, he imparted a feeling of honesty and straight dealing.

'Ben Sparrow rang me this morning, sir. I'm very pleased you've come. I believe you've got a letter for me.'

Rigby looked at Smiley thoughtfully over his desk, and decided that he liked what he saw. He had got around in the war and had heard a little, just a very little, of the work of George Smiley's Service. If Ben said Smiley was all right, that was good enough for him – or almost. But Ben had said more than that.

'Looks like a frog, dresses like a bookie, and has a brain I'd give my eyes for. Had a very nasty war. Very nasty indeed.'

Well, he looked like a frog, right enough. Short and stubby, round spectacles with thick lenses that made his eyes big. And his clothes *were* odd. Expensive, mind, you could see that. But his jacket seemed to drape where there wasn't any room for drape. What did surprise Rigby was his shyness. Rigby had expected someone a little brash, a little too smooth for Carne, whereas Smiley had an earnest formality of manner which appealed to Rigby's conservative taste.

Smiley took the letter from his wallet and put it on the desk, while Rigby extracted an old pair of gold-rimmed spectacles from a battered metal case and adjusted the ends carefully over his ears.

'I don't know if Ben explained,' said Smiley, 'but this letter was sent to the correspondence section of a small Nonconformist journal to which Mrs Rode subscribed.'

'And Miss Fellowship is the lady who brought you the letter?'

'No; her name is Brimley. She is the editor of the magazine. Fellowship is just a pen-name for the correspondence column.'

The brown eyes rested on him for a moment.

'When did she receive this letter?'

'Yesterday, the seventeenth. Thursday's the day they go to press, their busy day. The afternoon mail doesn't get opened till the evening, usually. This was opened about six o'clock, I suppose.'

'And she brought it straight to you?'

'Yes.'

'Why?'

'She worked for me during the war, in my department. She was reluctant to go straight to the police – I was the only person she could think of who wasn't a policeman,' he added stupidly. 'Who could help, I mean.'

'May I ask what you yourself, sir, do for a living?'

'Nothing much. A little private research on seventeenth-century Germany.' It seemed a very silly answer.

Rigby didn't seem bothered.

'What's this earlier letter she talks about?'

Smiley offered him the second envelope, and again the big, square hand received it.

'It appears she won this competition,' Smiley explained. 'That was her winning entry. I gather she comes from a family which has subscribed to the magazine since its foundation. That's why Miss Brimley was less inclined to regard the letter as nonsense. Not that it follows.'

'Not that what follows?'

'I meant that the fact that her family had subscribed to a journal for fifty years does not logically affect the possibility that she was unbalanced.'

Rigby nodded, as if he saw the point, but Smiley had an uncomfortable feeling that he did not.

'Ah,' said Rigby, with a slow smile. 'Women, eh?'

Smiley, completely bewildered, gave a little laugh. Rigby was looking at him thoughtfully.

'Know any of the staff, do you, sir?'

'Only Mr Terence Fielding. We met at an Oxford dinner some time ago. I thought I'd call round and see him. I knew his brother pretty well.'

Rigby appeared to stiffen slightly at the mention of Fielding, but he said nothing, and Smiley went on:

'It was Fielding I rang when Miss Brimley brought me the letter. He told me the news. That was last night.'

'I see.'

They looked at one another again in silence. Smiley discomfited and slightly comic, Rigby appraising him, wondering how much to say.

'How long are you staying?' he said at last.

'I don't know,' Smiley replied. 'Miss Brimley wanted to come herself, but she has her paper to run. She attached great importance, you see, to doing all she could for Mrs Rode, even though she was dead. Because she was a subscriber, I mean. I promised to see that the letter arrived quickly in the right hands. I don't imagine there's much else I can do. I shall probably stay on for a day or two just to have a word with Fielding . . . go to the funeral, I suppose. I've booked in at the Sawley Arms.'

'Fine hotel, that.'

Rigby put his spectacles carefully back into their case and dropped the case into a drawer.

'Funny place, Carne. There's a big gap between the Town and Gown, as we say; neither side knows nor likes the other. It's fear that does it, fear and ignorance. It makes it hard in a case like this. Oh, I can call on Mr Fielding and Mr D'Arcy and they say, "Good day, Sergeant," and give me a cup of tea in the kitchen, but I can't get among them. They've got their own community, see, and no one outside it can get in. No gossip in the pubs, no contacts, nothing . . . just cups of tea and bits of seed cake, and being called Sergeant.' Rigby laughed suddenly, and Smiley laughed with him in relief. 'There's a lot I'd like to ask them, a lot of things; who liked the Rodes and who didn't, whether Mr Rode's a good teacher and whether his wife fitted in with the others. I've got all the facts I want, but I've got no clothes to hang on them.' He looked at Smiley expectantly. There was a very long silence.

'If you want me to help, I'd be delighted,' said Smiley at last. 'But give me the facts first.'

'Stella Rode was murdered between about ten past eleven and quarter to twelve on the night of Wednesday the sixteenth. She must have been struck fifteen to twenty times with a cosh or bit of piping or something. It was a terrible murder . . .

27

terrible. There are marks all over her body. At a guess I would say she came from the drawing-room to the front door to answer the bell or something, when she opened the door she was struck down and dragged to the conservatory. The conservatory door was unlocked, see?'

'I see . . . It's odd that he should have known that, isn't it?'

'The murderer may have been hiding there already: we can't tell from the prints just there. He was wearing boots – Wellington boots, size 10½. We would guess from the spacing of the footprints in the garden that he was about six foot tall. When he had got her to the conservatory he must have hit her again and again – mainly on the head. There's a lot of what we call travelled blood in the conservatory, that's to say, blood spurted from an open artery. There's no sign of that anywhere else.'

'And no sign of it on her husband?'

'I'll come to that later, but the short answer is, no.' He paused a moment and continued:

'Now, I said there were footprints, and so there were. The murderer came through the back garden. Where he came from and went to, Heaven alone knows. You see, there are no tracks leading away – not Wellingtons. None at all. Of course, it's possible the outgoing tracks followed the path to the front gate and got lost in all the to-ing and fro-ing later that night. But I don't think we'd have lost them even then.' He glanced at Smiley, then went on:

'He left one thing behind him in the conservatory – an old cloth belt, navy blue, from a cheap overcoat by the look of it. We're working on that now.'

'Was she . . . robbed or anything?'

'No sign of interference. She was wearing a string of green beads round her neck, and they've gone, and it looks as though he tried to get the rings off her finger, but they were too tight.' He paused.

'I need hardly tell you that we've had reports from every corner of the country about tall men in blue overcoats and gumboots. But none of them had wings as far as I know. Or seven-league boots for jumping from the conservatory to the road.'

They paused, while a police cadet brought in tea on a tray.

He put it on the desk, looked at Smiley out of the corner of his eye and decided to let the Inspector pour out. He guided the teapot round so that the handle was towards Rigby and withdrew. Smiley was amused by the immaculate condition of the tray cloth, by the matching china and tea-strainer, laid before them by the enormous hands of the cadet. Rigby poured out the tea and they drank for a moment in silence. There was, Smiley reflected, something devastatingly competent about Rigby. The very ordinariness of the man and his room identified him with the society he protected. The nondescript furniture, the wooden filing cupboards, the bare walls, the archaic telephone with its separate earpiece, the brown frieze round the wall and the brown paint on the door, the glistening linoleum and the faint smell of carbolic, the burbling gas-fire, and the calendar from the Prudential – these were the evidence of rectitude and moderation; their austerity gave comfort and reassurance. Rigby continued:

'Rode went back to Fielding's house for the examination papers. Fielding confirms that, of course. He arrived at Fielding's house at about 11.35, near as Fielding can say. He hardly spent any time there at all – just collected his papers at the door – they were in a small writing-case he uses for carrying exercise books. He doesn't remember whether he saw anyone on the road. He thinks a bicycle overtook him, but he can't be sure. If we take Rode's word for it, he walked straight home. When he got there he rang the bell. He was wearing a dinner-jacket and so he hadn't got his key with him. His wife was expecting him to ring the bell, you see. That's the devil of it. It was a moonlit night, mind, and snow on the ground, so you could see a mighty long way. He called her, but she didn't answer. Then he saw footprints going round to the side of the house. Not just footprints, but blood marks and the snow all churned up where the body had been dragged to the conservatory. But he didn't know it was blood in the moonlight, it just showed up dark, and Rode said afterwards he thought it was the dirty water from the gutters running over on to the path.

'He followed the prints round until he came to the conservatory. It was darker in there and he fumbled for the light switch, but it didn't work.'

'Did he light a match?'

'No, he didn't have any. He's a non-smoker. His wife didn't approve of smoking. He moved forward from the door. The conservatory walls are mainly glass except for the bottom three feet, but the roof is tiled. The moon was high that night, and not much light got in at all, except through the partition window between the drawing-room and the conservatory – but she'd only had the little table light on in the drawing-room. So he groped his way forward, talking all the time, calling Stella, his wife. As he went, he tripped over something and nearly fell. He knelt down and felt with his hands, up and down her body. He realised that his hands were covered in blood. He doesn't remember much after that, but there's a senior master living a hundred yards up the road – Mr D'Arcy his name is, lives with his sister, and he heard him screaming on the road. D'Arcy went out to him. Rode had blood all over his hands and face and seemed to be out of his mind. D'Arcy rang the police and I got there at about one o'clock that morning. I've seen some nasty things in my time, but this is the worst. Blood everywhere. Whoever killed her must have been covered in it. There's an outside tap against the conservatory wall. The tap had been turned on, probably by the murderer to rinse his hands. The boffins have found traces of blood in the snow underneath it. The tap was lagged recently by Rode I gather . . .'

'And fingerprints?' Smiley asked. 'What about them?'

'Mr Rode's were everywhere. On the floor, the walls and windows, on the body itself. But there were other prints; smudges of blood, little more, made with a gloved hand probably.'

'And they were the murderer's?'

'They had been made *before* Rode made his. In some cases Rode's prints were partly superimposed on the glove prints.'

Smiley was silent for a moment.

'These examination papers he went back for. Were they as important as all that?'

'Yes. I gather they were. Up to a point anyway. The marks had to be handed in to Mr D'Arcy by midday on Friday.'

'But why did he take them to Fielding's in the first place?'

'He didn't. He'd been invigilating exams all afternoon and

the papers were handed in to him at six o'clock. He put them in his little case and had them taken to Fielding's by a boy – head boy in Mr Fielding's house, name of Perkins. Rode was on Chapel duty last week, so he didn't have time to return home before dinner.'

'Where did he change then?'

'In the Tutors' Robing Room, next to the Common Room. There are facilities there, mainly for games tutors who live some distance from Carne.'

'The boy who brought this case to Fielding's house – who was he?'

'I can't tell you much more than I've said. His name is Perkins; he's head of Mr Fielding's house. Fielding has spoken to him and confirmed Rode's statement . . . House tutors are very possessive about their boys, you know . . . don't like them to be spoken to by rough policemen.' Rigby seemed to be slightly upset.

'I see,' Smiley said at last, helplessly, and then: 'But how do you explain the letter?'

'It isn't only the letter we've got to explain.'

Smiley looked at him sharply.

'What do you mean?'

'I mean,' said Rigby slowly, 'that Mrs Rode did several pretty queer things in the last few weeks.'

Chapter 4

TOWN AND GOWN

'**M**rs Rode was Chapel, of course,' Rigby continued, 'and we've quite a community in Carne. Truth to tell,' he added with a slow smile, 'my wife belongs to it.

'A couple of weeks ago our Minister called round to see me. It was in the evening, about half past six, I suppose. I was just thinking of going home, see. He walked in here and sat himself down where you're sitting now. He's a big fellow, the Minister, a fine man; comes from up North, where Mrs Rode came from. Cardew, his name is.'

'The Mr Cardew in the letter?'

'That's him. He knew all about Mrs Rode's family before the Rodes ever came here. Glaston's quite a name up North, and Mr Cardew was very pleased when he heard that Stella Rode was Mr Glaston's daughter; very pleased indeed. Mrs Rode came to the Tabernacle regular as clockwork, you can imagine, and they like to see that round here. My wife was pleased as Punch, I can tell you. It was the first time, I suppose, that anyone from the School had done that. Most of the Chapel people here are tradespeople – what we call the locals.' Rigby smiled again. 'It isn't often that Town and Gown come together, so to speak. Not here.'

'How about her husband? Was he Chapel too?'

'Well, he had been, so she told Mr Cardew. Mr Rode was born and bred in Branxome, and all his family were Chapel people. That's how Mr and Mrs Rode first met, I gather – at Branxome Tabernacle. Ever been there, have you? A fine church, Branxome, right up on the hill there, overlooking the sea.'

Smiley shook his head and Rigby's wide brown eyes rested on him thoughtfully for a moment.

'You should,' he said, 'you should go and see that. It seems,' he continued, 'that Mr Rode turned Church of England when he came to Carne. Even tried to persuade his wife to do the same. They're very strong at the School. I heard that from my wife, as a matter of fact. I never let her gossip as a rule, being a policeman's wife and that, but Mr Cardew told her that himself.'

'I see,' said Smiley.

'Well now, Cardew came and saw me. He was all worried and bothered with himself. He didn't know what he should make of it, but he wanted to talk to me as a friend and not as a policeman.' Rigby looked sour, 'When people say that to me, I always know that they want to talk to me as a policeman. Then he told me his story. Mrs Rode had called to see him that afternoon. He'd been out visiting a farmer's wife over in Okeford and didn't come home until half past five or thereabouts, so Mrs Cardew had had to talk to her and hold the fort until the Minister came home. Mrs Rode was white as a sheet, sitting very still by the fire. As soon as the Minister arrived, Mrs Cardew left them alone and Stella Rode started talking about her husband.'

He paused. 'She said Mr Rode was going to kill her. In the long nights. She seemed to have a kind of fixation about being murdered in the long nights. Cardew didn't take it too seriously at first, but thinking about it afterwards, he decided to let me know.'

Smiley looked at him sharply.

'He couldn't make out what she meant. He thought she was out of her mind. He's a down-to-earth man, see, although he's a Minister. I think he was probably a bit too firm with her. He asked her what put this dreadful thought into her head, and she began to weep. Not hysterical, apparently, but just crying quietly to herself. He tried to calm her down, promised to help her any way he could, and asked her again what had given her this idea. She just shook her head, then got up, walked over to the door, still shaking her head in despair. She turned to him, and he thought she was going to say something, but she didn't. She just left.'

'How very curious,' said Smiley, 'that she lied about that in her letter. She went out of her way to say she *hadn't* told Cardew.'

Rigby shrugged his great shoulders.

'If you'll pardon me,' he said, 'I'm in a darned awkward position. The Chief Constable would sooner cut his throat than call in Scotland Yard. He wants an arrest and he wants one quick. We've got enough clues to cover a Christmas tree; footprints, time of the murder, indication of murderer's clothing, and even the weapon itself.'

Smiley looked at him in surprise.

'You've *found* the weapon, then?'

Rigby hesitated. 'Yes, we've found it. There's hardly a soul knows this, sir, and I'll trouble you to remember that. We found it the morning after the murder, four miles north of Carne on the Okeford road, tossed into a ditch. Eighteen inches of what they call coaxial cable. Know what that is, do you? It comes in all sizes, but this piece is about two inches in diameter. It has a copper rod running down the middle and plastic insulation between the rod and the outer cover. There was blood on it: Stella Rode's blood group, and hairs from her head, stuck to the blood. We're keeping that very dark indeed. By the Grace of God, it was found by one of our own men. It pinpoints the line of the murderer's departure.'

'There's no doubt, I suppose, that it *is* the weapon?' Smiley asked lamely.

'We found particles of copper in the wounds on the body.'

'It's odd, isn't it,' Smiley suggested reflectively, 'that the murderer should have carried the weapon so far before getting rid of it? Specially if he was walking. You'd think he'd want to get rid of it as soon as he could.'

'It is odd. Very odd. The Okeford road runs beside the canal for half of those four miles; he could have pitched the cable into the canal anywhere along there. We'd never have been the wiser.'

'Was the cable old?'

'Not particularly. Just standard type. It could have come from almost anywhere.' Rigby hesitated a minute, then burst out:

'Look, sir, this is what I am trying to say. The circumstances of this case demand a certain type of investigation: wide-scale search, detailed laboratory work, mass inquiry. That's what the Chief wants, and he's right. We've no case against the husband at all, and to be frank he's precious little use to us.

He seems a bit lost, a bit vague, contradicting himself on little things that don't matter, like the date of his marriage or the name of his doctor. It's shock, of course, I've seen it before. I know all about your letter, sir, and it's damned odd, but if you can tell me how he could have produced Wellington boots out of a hat and got rid of them afterwards, battered his wife to death without leaving more than a few smudges of blood on himself, and got the weapon four miles from the scene of the crime, all within ten minutes of being at Fielding's house, I'll be grateful to you. We're looking for a stranger, six foot tall, wearing newish Dunlop Wellington boots size 10½, leather gloves and an old blue overcoat stained with blood. A man who travels on foot, who was in the area of North Fields between 11.10 and 11.45 on the night of the murder, who left in the direction of Okeford, taking with him one and a half feet of coaxial cable, a string of green beads and an imitation diamond clip, valued at twenty-three and six. We're looking for a maniac, a man who kills for pleasure or the price of a meal.' Rigby paused, smiled wistfully and added, 'Who can fly fifty feet through the air? But with information like this how else should we spend our time? What else can we look for? I can't put men on to chasing shadows when there's work like that to be done.'

'I understand that.'

'But I'm an old policeman, Mr Smiley, and I like to know what I'm about. I don't like looking for people I can't believe in, and I don't like being cut off from witnesses. I like to meet people and talk to them, nose about here and there, get to know the country. But I can't do that, not at the School. Do you follow me? So we've got to rely on laboratories, tracker dogs, and nation-wide searches, but somehow in my bones I don't think it's altogether one of those cases.'

'I read in the paper about a woman, a Mad Janie . . .'

'I'm coming to that. Mrs Rode was a kindly woman, easy to talk to. I always found her so, anyway. Some of the women at Chapel took against her, but you know what women are. It seems she got friendly with this Janie creature. Janie came begging, selling herbs and charms at the back door; you know the kind of thing. She's queer, talks to birds and all that. She lives in a disused Norman chapel over Pylle. Stella Rode used to give her food and clothes – the poor soul was often as not half-starved. Now Janie's disappeared. She was seen early Wednesday night on the lane towards North Fields and hasn't been seen since. That don't mean a thing. These people come and go in their own way. They'll be all over the neighbourhood for years, then one day they're gone like snow in the fire. They've died in a ditch, maybe, or they've took ill and crept away like a cat. Janie's not the only queer one round here. There's a lot of excitement because we found a spare set of footprints running along the fringe of trees at the far end of the garden. They were a woman's prints by the look of them, and at one point they come quite close to the conservatory. Could be a gypsy or a beggar woman. Could be anything, but I expect it's Janie right enough. I hope to Heaven it was, sir; we could do with an eyewitness, even a mad one.'

Smiley stood up. As they shook hands, Rigby said, 'Good-bye, sir. Ring me any time, any time at all.' He scribbled a telephone number on the pad in front of him, tore off the sheet and gave it to Smiley. 'That's my home number.' He showed Smiley to the door, seemed to hesitate, then he said, 'You're not a Carnian yourself by any chance, are you, sir?'

'Good heavens, no.'

Again Rigby hesitated. 'Our Chief's a Carnian. Ex-Indian Army. Brigadier Havelock. This is his last year. He's very interested in this case. Doesn't like me messing around the school. Won't have it.'

'I see.'

'He wants an arrest quickly.'

'And outside Carne, I suppose?'

'Good-bye, Mr Smiley. Don't forget to ring me. Oh, another thing I should have mentioned. That bit of cable . . .'

'Yes?'

'Mr Rode used a length of the same stuff in a demonstration lecture on elementary electronics. Mislaid it about three weeks ago.'

Smiley walked slowly back to his hotel.

My dear Brim,

As soon as I arrived I handed your letter over to the CID man in charge of the case – it was Rigby, as Ben had supposed: he looks like a mixture of Humpty-Dumpty and a Cornish elf – very short and broad – and I don't think he's anyone's fool.

To begin at the middle – our letter didn't have quite the effect we expected; Stella Rode evidently told Cardew, the local Baptist Minister, two weeks ago, that her husband was trying to kill her in the long nights, whatever they are. As for the circumstances of the murder – the account in the *Guardian* is substantially correct.

In fact, the more Rigby told me, the less likely it became that she was killed by her husband. Almost everything pointed away from him. Quite apart from motive, there is the location of the weapon, the footprints in the snow (which indicate a tall man in Wellingtons), the presence of unidentified glove-prints in the conservatory. Add to that the strongest argument of all: whoever killed her must have been covered in blood – the conservatory was a dreadful sight, Rigby tells me. Of course, there *was* blood on Rode when he was picked up by his colleague in the lane, but only smears which could have resulted from stumbling over the body in the dark. Incidentally, the footprints only go into the garden and not out.

As things stand at the moment, there is, as Rigby points out, only one interpretation – the murderer was a stranger, a tramp, a madman perhaps, who killed her for pleasure or for her jewellery (which was worthless) and made off along the Okeford road, throwing the weapon into a ditch. (But why carry it four miles – and why not throw it into the canal the other side of the ditch? The Okeford road crosses Okemoor, which is all cross-dyked to prevent flooding.) If this interpretation is correct, then I suppose we attribute Stella's letter and her interview with Cardew to a persecuted mind, or the premonition of death, depending on whether we're superstitious. If that is so, it is the most monstrous coincidence I have ever heard of. Which brings me to my final point.

I rather gathered from what Rigby *didn't* say that his Chief Constable was treading on his tail, urging him to scour the country for tramps in bloodstained blue overcoats (you remember the belt). Rigby, of course, has no alternative but to follow the signs and do as his Chief expects – but he is clearly uneasy about something – either something he hasn't told me, or something he just feels in his bones. I think he was sincere when he asked me to tell him anything I found out about the *School* end – the Rodes themselves, the way they fitted in, and so on. Carne's monastery walls are still pretty high, he feels . . .

So I'll just sniff around a bit, I think, and see what goes on. I rang Fielding when I got back from the police station and he's asked me to supper tonight. I'll write again as soon as I have anything to tell you.

George.

Having carefully sealed the envelope, pressing down the corners with his thumbs, Smiley locked his door and made his way down the wide marble staircase, treading carefully on the meagre coconut matting that ran down the centre. There was a red wooden letter box in the hall for the use of residents, but Smiley, being a cautious man, avoided it. He walked to the pillar box at the corner of the road, posted his letter and wondered what to do about lunch. There were, of course, the sandwiches and coffee provided by Miss Brimley. Reluctantly he returned to the hotel. It was full of journalists, and Smiley hated journalists. It was also cold, and he hated the cold. And there was something very familiar about sandwiches in a hotel bedroom.

Chapter 5

CAT AND DOG

I t was just after seven o'clock that evening when George Smiley climbed the steps which led up to the front door of Mr Terence Fielding's house. He rang, and was admitted to the hall by a little plump woman in her middle fifties. To his right a log fire burned warmly on a pile of wood ash and above him he was vaguely aware of a minstrel gallery and a mahogany staircase, which rose in a spiral to the top of the house. Most of the light seemed to come from the fire, and Smiley could see that the walls around him were hung with a great number of paintings of various styles and periods, and the chimney-piece was laden with all manner of *objets d'art*. With an involuntary shudder, he noticed that neither the fire nor the pictures quite succeeded in banishing the faint smell of school – of polish bought wholesale, of cocoa and community cooking. Corridors led from the hall, and Smiley observed that the lower part of each wall was painted a dark brown or green according to the inflexible rule of school decorators. From one of these corridors the enormous figure of Mr Terence Fielding emerged.

He advanced on Smiley, massive and genial, with his splendid mane of grey hair falling anyhow across his forehead, and his gown billowing behind him.

'Smiley? Ah! You've met True, have you – Miss Truebody, my housekeeper? Marvellous this snow, isn't it? Pure Bruegel! Seen the boys skating by the Eyot? Marvellous sight! Black suits, coloured scarves, pale sun; all there, isn't it, all there! Bruegel to the life. Marvellous!' He took Smiley's coat and flung it on to a decrepit deal chair with a rush seat which stood in the corner of the hall.

'You like that chair – you recognise it?'

'I don't think I do,' Smiley replied in some confusion.

'Ah, you should, you know, you should! Had it made in

Provence before the war. Little carpenter I knew. Place it now? Facsimile of Van Gogh's yellow chair; some people recognise it.' He led the way down a corridor and into a large comfortable study adorned with Dutch tiles, small pieces of Renaissance sculpture, mysterious bronzes, china dogs and unglazed vases; and Fielding himself towering magnificent among them.

As senior housemaster of Carne, Fielding wore, in place of the customary academic dress, a wonderful confection of heavy black skirts and legal bib, like a monk in evening dress. All this imparted a suggestion of clerical austerity in noted contrast to the studied flamboyance of his personality. Evidently conscious of this, he sought to punctuate the solemnity of his uniform and give to it a little of his own temperament, by adorning it with flowers carefully chosen from his garden. He had scandalised the tailors of Carne, whose frosted windows carried the insignia of royal households, by having buttonholes let into his gown. These he would fill according to his mood with anything from hibernia to bluebells. This evening he wore a rose, and from its freshness Smiley deduced that he had this minute put it into place, having ordered it specially.

'Sherry wine or Madeira?'

'Thank you; a glass of sherry.'

'Tart's drink, Madeira,' Fielding called, as he poured from a decanter, 'but boys like it. Perhaps that's why. They're frightful flirts.' He handed Smiley a glass and added, with a dramatic modification of his voice:

'We're all rather subdued at the moment by this dreadful business. We've never had anything quite like it, you know. Have you seen the evening papers?'

'No, I'm afraid I haven't. But the Sawley Arms is packed with journalists of course.'

'They've really gone to town. They've got the Army out in Hampshire, playing about with mine-detectors. God knows what they expect to find.'

'How have the boys taken it?'

'They adore it! My own house has been particularly fortunate, of course, because the Rodes were dining here that night. Some oaf from the police even wanted to question one of my boys.'

'Indeed,' said Smiley innocently. 'What on earth about?'

'Oh, God knows,' Fielding replied abruptly, and then, changing the subject, he asked, 'You knew my brother well, didn't you? He talked about you, you know.'

'Yes, I knew Adrian very well. We were close friends.'

'In the war, too?'

'Yes.'

'Were you in his crowd, then?'

'What crowd?'

'Steed-Asprey, Jebedee. All those people.'

'Yes.'

'I never really heard how he died. Did you?'

'No.'

'We didn't see much of one another in later years, Adrian and I. Being a fraud, I can't afford to be seen beside the genuine article,' Fielding declared, with something of his earlier panache. Smiley was spared the embarrassment of a reply by a quiet knock at the door, and a tall red-haired boy came timidly into the room.

'I've called the Adsum, sir, if you're ready, sir.'

'Damn,' said Fielding, emptying his glass. 'Prayers.' He turned to Smiley.

'Meet Perkins, my head prefect. Musical genius, but a problem in the schoolroom. That right, Tim? Stay here or come as you like. It only lasts ten minutes.'

'Rather less tonight, sir,' said Perkins. 'It's the Nunc Dimittis.'

'Thank God for small mercies,' Fielding declared, tugging briefly at his bib, as he led Smiley at a spanking pace out into the corridor and across the hall, with Perkins stalking along behind them. Fielding was speaking all the time without bothering to turn his head:

'I'm glad you've chosen this evening to come. I never entertain on Fridays as a rule because everyone else does, though none of us quite knows what to do about entertaining at the moment. Felix D'Arcy will be coming tonight, but that's hardly entertaining. D'Arcy's a professional. Incidentally, we normally dress in the evening, but it doesn't matter.'

Smiley's heart sank. They turned a corner and entered another corridor.

'We have prayers at all hours here. The Master's revived

the seven Day Hours for the Offices: Prime, Terce, Sext and so on. A surfeit during the Half, abstinence during the holidays, that's the system, like games. Useful in the house for roll-calls, too.' He led the way down yet another corridor, flung open a double door at the end of it and marched straight into the dining-room, his gown filling gracefully behind him. The boys were waiting for him.

'More sherry? What did you think of prayers? They sing quite nicely, don't they? One or two good tenors. We tried some plainsong last Half; quite good, really quite good. D'Arcy will be here soon. He's a frightful toad. Looks like a Sickert model fifty years after – all trousers and collar. However, you're lucky his sister isn't accompanying him. She's worse!'

'What's his subject?' They were back in Fielding's study.

'Subject! I'm afraid we don't have subjects here. None of us has read a word on any subject since we left University.' He lowered his voice and added darkly, 'That's if we *went* to University. D'Arcy teaches French. D'Arcy is Senior Tutor by election, bachelor by profession, sublimated pansy by inclination . . .' he was standing quite still now, his head thrown back and his right hand stretched out towards Smiley, '. . . and his subject is other people's shortcomings. He is principally, however, self-appointed majordomo of Carne protocol. If you wear a gown on a bicycle, reply incorrectly to an invitation, make a fault in the *placement* of your dinner guests or speak of a colleague as "Mister", D'Arcy will find you out and admonish you.'

'What are the duties of Senior Tutor, then?' Smiley asked, just for something to say.

'He's the referee between the classics and the scientists; arranges the timetable and vets the exam. results. But principally, poor man, he must reconcile the Arts with the Sciences.' He shook his head sagely. 'And it takes a better man than D'Arcy to do that. Not, mind you,' he added wearily, 'that it makes the least difference who wins the extra hour on Friday evenings. Who cares? Not the boys, poor dears, that's certain.'

Fielding talked on, at random and always in superlatives, sometimes groping in the air with his hand as if to catch the more elusive metaphors; now of his colleagues with caustic derision, now of boys with compassion if not with understanding; now of the Arts with fervour – and the studied bewilderment of a lonely disciple.

'Carne isn't a school. It's a sanatorium for intellectual lepers. The symptoms began when we came down from University; a gradual putrefaction of our intellectual extremities. From day to day our minds die, our spirits atrophy and rot. We watch the process in one another, hoping to forget it in ourselves.' He paused, and looked reflectively at his hands.

'In me the process is complete. You see before you a dead soul, and Carne is the body I live in.' Much pleased by this confession, Fielding held out his great arms so that the sleeves of his gown resembled the wings of a giant bat; 'the Vampire of Carne', he declared, bowing deeply. '*Alcoholique et poète!*' A bellow of laughter followed this display.

Smiley was fascinated by Fielding, by his size, his voice, the wanton inconstancy of his temperament, by his whole big-screen style; he found himself attracted and repelled by this succession of contradictory poses; he wondered whether he was supposed to take part in the performance, but Fielding seemed so dazzled by the footlights that he was indifferent to the audience behind them. The more Smiley watched, the more elusive seemed the character he was trying to comprehend: changeful but sterile, daring but fugitive; colourful, unbounded, ingenuous, yet deceitful and perverse. Smiley began to wish he could acquire the material facts of Fielding – his means, his ambitions and disappointments.

His reverie was interrupted by Miss Truebody. Felix D'Arcy had arrived.

No candles, and a cold supper admirably done by Miss Truebody. Not claret, but hock, passed round like port. And at last, at long last, Fielding mentioned Stella Rode.

They had been talking rather dutifully of the Arts and the Sciences. This would have been dull (for it was uninformed) had not D'Arcy constantly been goaded by Fielding, who seemed anxious to exhibit D'Arcy in his worst light. D'Arcy's judgements of people and problems were largely coloured by what he considered 'seemly' (a favourite word) and by an effeminate malice towards his colleagues. After a while Fielding

43

asked who was replacing Rode during his absence, to which D'Arcy said, 'No one,' and added unctuously:

'It was a terrible shock to the community, this affair.'

'Nonsense,' Fielding retorted. 'Boys love disaster. The further we are from death the more attractive it seems. They find the whole affair most exhilarating.'

'The publicity has been most unseemly,' said D'Arcy, 'most. I think that has been prominent in the minds of many of us in the Common Room.' He turned to Smiley:

'The press, you know, is a constant worry here. In the past it could never have happened. Formerly our great families and institutions were not subjected to this intrusion. No, indeed not. But today all that is changed. Many of us are compelled to subscribe to the cheaper newspapers for this very reason. One Sunday newspaper mentioned no fewer than four of Hecht's old boys in one edition. All of them in an unseemly context, I may say. And of course such papers never fail to mention that the boy is a Carnian. You know, I suppose, that we have the young Prince here. (I myself have the honour to supervise his French studies.) The young Sawley is also at Carne. The activity of the press during his parents' divorce suit was deplorable. Quite deplorable. The Master wrote to the Press Council, you know. I drafted the letter myself. But on this tragic occasion they have excelled themselves. We even had the press at Compline last night, you know, waiting for the Special Prayer. They occupied the whole of the two rear pews on the west side. Hecht was doing Chapel Duty and tried to have them removed.' He paused, raised his eyebrows in gentle reproach and smiled. 'He had no business to, of course, but that never stopped the good Hecht.' He turned to Smiley, 'One of our *athletic* brethren,' he explained.

'Stella was too common for you, Felix, wasn't she?'

'Not at all,' said D'Arcy quickly. 'I would not have you say that of me, Terence. I am by no means discriminatory in the matter of class; merely of manners. I grant you, in that particular field, I found her wanting.'

'In many ways she was just what we needed,' Fielding continued, addressing Smiley and ignoring D'Arcy. 'She was everything we're forced to ignore – she was red-brick, council estates, new towns, the very antithesis of Carne!' He turned suddenly to D'Arcy and said, 'But to you, Felix, she was just bad form.'

'Not at all; merely unsuitable.'

Fielding turned to Smiley in despair.

'Look,' he said. 'We talk academic here, you know, wear academic dress and hold high table dinners in the Common Room; we have long graces in Latin that none of us can translate. We go to the Abbey and the wives sit in the hencoop in their awful hats. But it's a charade. It means nothing.'

D'Arcy smiled wanly.

'I cannot believe, my dear Terence, that anyone who keeps such an excellent table as yourself can have so low an opinion of the refinements of social conduct.' He looked to Smiley for support and Smiley dutifully echoed the compliment. 'Besides, we know Terence of old at Carne. I am afraid we are accustomed to his roar.'

'I know why you disliked that woman, Felix. She was honest, and Carne has no defence against that kind of honesty.'

D'Arcy suddenly became very angry indeed.

'Terence, I will not have you say this. I simply will not have it. I feel I have a certain duty at Carne, as indeed we all have, to restore and maintain those standards of behaviour which suffered so sadly in the war. I am sensible that this determination has made me on more than one occasion unpopular. But such comment or advice as I offer is never – I beg you to notice this – is *never* directed against personalities, only against behaviour, against unseemly lapses in conduct. I will acknowledge that more than once I was compelled to address Rode on the subject of his wife's conduct. That is a matter quite divorced from personalities, Terence. I will not have it said that I disliked Mrs Rode. Such a suggestion would be disagreeable at all times, but under the present tragic circumstances it is deplorable. Mrs Rode's own . . . background and education did not naturally prepare her for our ways; that is quite a different matter. It does, however, illustrate the point that I wish to emphasise, Terence: it was a question of enlightenment, not of criticism. Do I make myself clear?'

'Abundantly,' Fielding answered dryly.

'Did the other wives like her?' Smiley ventured.

'Not entirely,' D'Arcy replied crisply.

'The wives! My God!' Fielding groaned, putting his hand to his brow. There was a pause.

'Her clothes, I believe, were a source of distress to some of them. She also frequented the public laundry. This, too, would not make a favourable impression. I should add that she did not attend our church . . .'

'Did she have any close friends among the wives?' Smiley persisted.

'I believe young Mrs Snow took to her.'

'And you say she was dining here the night she was murdered?'

'Yes,' said Fielding quietly, 'Wednesday. And it was Felix and his sister who took in poor Rode afterwards . . .' He glanced at D'Arcy.

'Yes, indeed,' said D'Arcy abruptly. His eyes were on Fielding, and it seemed to Smiley that something had passed between them. 'We shall never forget, never . . . Terence, if I may talk shop for just one moment, Perkins's construe is abysmal; I declare I have never seen work like it. Is he unwell? His mother is a most cultured woman, a cousin of the Samfords, I am told.'

Smiley looked at him and wondered. His dinner-jacket was faded, green with age. Smiley could almost hear him saying it had belonged to his grandfather. The skin of his face was so unlined that he somehow suggested fatness without being fat. His voice was pitched on one insinuating note, and he smiled all the time, whether he was speaking or not. The smile never left his smooth face, it was worked into the malleable fabric of his flesh, stretching his lips across his perfect teeth and opening the corners of his red mouth, so that it seemed to be held in place by the invisible fingers of his dentist. Yet D'Arcy's face was far from unexpressive; every mark showed. The smallest movement of his mouth or nose, the quickest glance or frown, were there to read and interpret. And he wanted to change the subject. Not away from Stella Rode (for he returned to discussing her himself a moment later), but away from the particular evening on which she died, away from the precise narration of events. And what was more, there was not a doubt in Smiley's mind that Fielding had seen it too, that in that look which passed between them was a pact of fear, a warning perhaps, so that from that moment Fielding's manner changed, he grew sullen and preoccupied, in a way that puzzled Smiley long afterwards.

D'Arcy turned to Smiley and addressed him with cloying intimacy.

'*Do* forgive my deplorable descent into Carne gossip. You find us a little cut off, here, do you not? We are often held to be cut off, I know. Carne is a "Snob School", that is the cry. You may read it every day in the gutter press. And yet, despite the claims of the *avant-garde*,' he said, glancing slyly at Fielding, 'I may say that *no one* could be less of a snob than Felix D'Arcy.' Smiley noticed his hair. It was very fine and ginger, growing from the top and leaving his pink neck bare.

'Take poor Rode, for instance. I certainly don't hold Rode's background against him in any way, poor fellow. The grammar schools do a splendid job, I am sure. Besides, he settled down here very well. I told the Master so. I said to him that Rode had settled down well; he does Chapel duty quite admirably – that was the very point I made. I hope I have played my part, what is more, in helping him to fit in. With careful instruction, such people can, as I said to the Master, learn our customs and even our manners; and the Master agreed.'

Smiley's glass was empty and D'Arcy, without consulting Fielding, filled it for him from the decanter. His hands were polished and hairless, like the hands of a girl.

'But,' he continued, 'I must be honest. Mrs Rode did not adapt herself so willingly to our ways.' Still smiling, he sipped delicately from his glass. He wants to put the record straight, thought Smiley.

'She would never really have fitted in at Carne; that is my opinion – though I am sure I never voiced it while she was alive. Her background was against her. The fault was not hers – it was her background which, as I say, was unfortunate. Indeed, if we may speak frankly and in confidence, I have reason to believe it was her past that brought about her death.'

'Why do you say that?' asked Smiley quickly, and D'Arcy replied with a glance at Fielding, 'It appears she was expecting to be attacked.'

*   *   *

'My sister is devoted to dogs,' D'Arcy continued. 'You may know that already perhaps. King Charles spaniels are her *forte*. She took a first at the North Dorset last year and was commended at Cruft's shortly afterwards for her "Queen of Carne". She sells to America, you know. I dare say there are few people in the country with Dorothy's knowledge of the breed. The Master's wife found occasion to say the very same thing a week ago. Well, the Rodes were our neighbours, as you know, and Dorothy is not a person to neglect her neighbourly duties. Where duty is concerned, you will not find her discriminatory, I assure you. The Rodes also had a dog, a large mongrel, quite an intelligent animal, which they brought with them. (I have little idea where they came from, but that is another matter.) They appeared quite devoted to the dog, and I have no doubt they were. Rode took it with him to watch the football until I had occasion to advise him against it. The practice was giving rise to unseemly humour among the boys. I have found the same thing myself when exercising Dorothy's spaniels.

'I shall come to the point presently. Dorothy uses a vet called Harriman, a superior type of person who lives over toward Sturminster. A fortnight ago she sent for him. "Queen of Carne" was coughing badly and Dorothy asked Harriman to come over. A bitch of her quality is not to be taken lightly, I assure you.'

Fielding groaned, and D'Arcy continued, oblivious:

'I happened to be at home, and Harriman stayed for a cup of coffee. He is, as I say, a superior type of person. Harriman made some reference to the Rodes' dog and then the truth came out; Mrs Rode had had the dog destroyed the previous day. She said it had bitten the postman. Some long and confused story; the Post Office would sue, the police had been round, and I don't know what else. And, anyway, she said, the dog couldn't really protect, it could only warn. She had said so to Harriman, "It wouldn't do any good."'

'Wasn't she upset about losing the dog?' asked Smiley.

'Oh, indeed, yes. Harriman said she was in tears when she arrived. Mrs Harriman had to give her a cup of tea. They suggested she should give the dog another chance, put it in kennels for a while, but she was adamant, quite adamant.

Harriman was most perplexed. So was his wife. When they discussed it afterwards they agreed that Mrs Rode's behaviour had not been quite normal. Not normal at all, in fact. Another curious fact was the condition of the dog: it had been maltreated, seriously so. Its back was marked as if from beatings.'

'Did Harriman follow up this remark she made? About not doing any good? What did Harriman make of it?' Smiley was watching D'Arcy intently.

'She repeated it to Mrs Harriman, but she wouldn't explain it. However, I think the explanation is obvious enough.'

'Oh?' said Fielding.

D'Arcy put his head on one side and plucked coyly at the lobe of his ear.

'We all have a little of the detective in us,' he said. 'Dorothy and I talked it over after the – death. We decided that Stella Rode had formed some unsavoury association before coming to Carne, which had recently been revived . . . possibly against her will. Some violent ruffian – an old admirer – who would resent the improvement in her station.'

'How badly was the postman bitten by the dog?' Smiley asked.

D'Arcy turned to him again.

'That is the extraordinary thing. That is the very crux of the story, my dear fellow: the postman hadn't been bitten at all. Dorothy inquired. Her whole story was an absolute string of lies from beginning to end.'

They rose from the table and made their way to Fielding's study, where Miss Truebody had put the coffee. The conversation continued to wander back and forth over Wednesday's tragedy. D'Arcy was obsessed with the indelicacy of it all – the persistence of journalists, the insensitivity of the police, the uncertainty of Mrs Rode's origin, the misfortune of her husband. Fielding was still oddly silent, sunk in his own thoughts, from which he occasionally emerged to glance at D'Arcy with a look of hostility. At exactly a quarter to eleven D'Arcy pronounced himself tired, and the three of them went into the great hall, where Miss Truebody produced a coat for Smiley and a coat and muffler and cap for D'Arcy. Fielding accepted D'Arcy's thanks with a sullen nod. He turned to Smiley:

'That business you rang me about. What was it exactly?'

'Oh – a letter from Mrs Rode just before she was murdered,' said Smiley vaguely, 'the police are handling it now, but they do not regard it as . . . significant. Not significant at all. She seems to have had a sort of' – he gave an embarrassed grin – 'persecution complex. Is that the expression? However, we might discuss it some time. You must dine with me at the Sawley before I go back. Do you come to London at all? We might meet in London perhaps, at the end of the Half.'

D'Arcy was standing in the doorway, looking at the new fall of snow which lay white and perfect on the pavement before him.

'Ah,' he said, with a little knowing laugh, 'the long nights, eh, Terence, the long nights.'

Chapter 6

HOLLY FOR THE DEVIL

'What are the long nights?' Smiley asked, as he and D'Arcy walked briskly away from Fielding's house through the new snow towards the Abbey Close.

'We have a proverb that it always snows at Carne in the long nights. That is the traditional term here for the nights of Lent,' D'Arcy replied. 'Before the Reformation the monks of the Abbey kept a vigil during Lent between the Offices of Compline and Lauds. You may know that already perhaps. As there is no longer a religious order attached to the Abbey, the custom has fallen into disuse. We continue to observe it, however, by the saying of Compline during Lent. Compline was the last of the Canonical Day Hours and was said before retiring for the night. The Master, who has a great respect for traditions of this kind, has reintroduced the old words for our devotions. Prime was the dawn Office, as you are no doubt aware. Terce was at the third hour of daylight – that is to say at 9.0 a.m. Thus we no longer refer to Morning Prayer, but to Terce. I find it delightful. Similarly, during Advent and Lent we say Sext at midday in the Abbey.'

'Are all these services compulsory?'

'Of course. Otherwise it would be necessary to make arrangements for those boys who did not attend. That is not desirable. Besides, you forget that Carne is a religious foundation.'

It was a beautiful night. As they crossed the Close, Smiley looked up at the tower. It seemed smaller and more peaceful in the moonlight. The whiteness of the new snow lit the very sky itself; the whole Abbey was so sharply visible against it that even the mutilated images of saints were clear in every sad detail of their defacement, wretched figures, their purpose lost, with no eyes to see the changing world.

They reached the cross-roads to the south of the Abbey.

'The parting of the ways, I fear,' said D'Arcy, extending his hand.

'It's a beautiful night,' Smiley replied quickly, 'let me come with you as far as your house.'

'Gladly,' said D'Arcy dryly.

They turned down North Fields Lane. A high stone wall ran along one side; and on the other the great expanse of playing fields, twenty or more rugby pitches, bordered the road for over half a mile. They walked this distance in silence, until D'Arcy stopped and pointed with his stick past Smiley towards a small house on the edge of the playing fields.

'That's North Fields, the Rodes' house. It used to belong to the head groundsman, but the school added a wing a few years ago, and now it's a staff house. My own house is rather larger, and lies farther up the road. Happily, I am fond of walking.'

'Was it along here that you found Stanley Rode that night?'

There was a pause, then D'Arcy said: 'It was nearer to my house, about a quarter of a mile farther on. He was in a terrible condition, poor fellow, terrible. I am myself unable to bear the sight of blood. If I had known how he would look when I brought him into the house, I do not think I could have done it. Mercifully, my sister Dorothy is a most competent woman.'

They walked on in silence, until Smiley said: 'From what you were saying at dinner, the Rodes were a very ill-assorted couple.'

'Precisely. If her death had happened any other way, I would describe it as providential: a blessed release for Rode. She was a thoroughly mischievous woman, Smiley, who made it her business to hold her husband up to ridicule. I believe it was intentional. Others do not. I do, and I have my reasons. She took pleasure in deriding her husband.'

'And Carne too, no doubt.'

'Just so. This is a critical moment in Carne's development. Many public schools have conceded to the vulgar clamour for change – change at any price. Carne, I am pleased to say, has not joined these Gadarene swine. That makes it more important than ever that we protect ourselves from within as well as from without.' He spoke with surprising vehemence.

52

'But was she really such a problem? Surely her husband could have spoken to her?'

'I never encouraged him to do so, I assure you. It is not my practice to interfere between man and wife.'

They reached D'Arcy's house. A high laurel hedge entirely concealed the house from the road, except for two multiple chimney-stacks which were visible over the top of it, confirming Smiley's impression that the house was large and Victorian.

'I am not ashamed of the Victorian taste,' said D'Arcy as he slowly opened the gate; 'but then, I am afraid we are not close to the modern idiom at Carne. This house used to be the rectory for North Fields Church, but the church is now served by a priest-in-charge from the Abbey. The vicarage is still within the school's gift, and I was fortunate enough to receive it. Good night. You must come for sherry before you go. Do you stay long?'

'I doubt it,' Smiley replied, 'but I am sure you have enough worries at the moment.'

'What do you mean?' D'Arcy said sharply.

'The press, the police and all the attendant fuss.'

'Ah yes, just so. Quite so. Nevertheless, our community life must continue. We always have a small party in the middle of the Half, and I feel it is particularly important that we should do so on this occasion. I will send a note to the Sawley tomorrow. My sister would be charmed. Good night.' He clanged the gate to, and the sound was greeted by the frantic barking of dogs from somewhere behind the house. A window opened and a harsh female voice called:

'Is that you, Felix?'

'Yes, Dorothy.'

'Why do you have to make such a bloody noise? You've woken those dogs again.' The window closed with a significant thud, and D'Arcy, without so much as a glance in Smiley's direction, disappeared quickly into the shadow of the house.

Smiley set off along the road again, back towards the town. After walking for about ten minutes he stopped and looked again towards the Rodes' house a hundred yards across the playing fields. It lay in the shadow of a small coppice of fir trees, dark and secret against the white fields. A narrow lane led towards the house; there was a brick pillar-box on one corner and a small oak sign-post, quite new, pointed along the lane, which must, he decided, lead to the village of Pylle. The legend upon the sign was obscured by a film of snow, and Smiley brushed it away with his hand, so that he could read the words 'North Fields', done in a contrived suburban Gothic script which must have caused D'Arcy considerable discomfort. The snow in the lane was untrodden; obviously more had fallen recently. There could not be much traffic between Pylle and Carne. Glancing quickly up and down the main road he began making his way along the lane. The hedge rose high on either side, and soon Smiley could see nothing but the pale sky above him, and the straggling willow wands reaching towards it. Once he thought he heard the sound of a footstep, close behind him, but when he stopped he heard nothing but the furtive rustle of the laden hedges. He grew more conscious of the cold: it seemed to hang in the still damp of the sunken road, to clutch and hold him like the chill air of an empty house. Soon the hedge on his left gave way to a sparse line of trees, which Smiley judged to belong to the coppice he had seen from the road. The snow beneath the trees was patchy, and the bare ground looked suddenly ugly and torn. The lane took him in a gradual curve to the left and, quite suddenly the house stood before him, gaunt and craggy in the moonlight. The walls were brick and flint, half obscured by the mass of ivy which grew in profusion across them, tumbling over the porch in a tangled mane.

He glanced towards the garden. The coppice which bordered the lane encroached almost as far as the corner of the house, and extended to the far end of the lawn, screening the house from the playing fields. The murderer had reached the house by a path which led across the lawn and through the trees to the lane at the farthest end of the garden. Looking carefully at the snow on the lawn, he was able to discern the course of the path. The white glazed door to the left of the house must lead to the conservatory . . . And suddenly he knew he was afraid – afraid of the house, afraid of the sprawling dark garden. The knowledge came to him like an awareness of pain. The ivy walls seemed to reach forward and hold him, like an old woman cosseting an unwilling child. The house was large, yet dingy, holding to itself unearthly shapes, black and oily in the sudden contrasts of moonlight. Fascinated despite his fear, he moved towards it. The shadows broke and reformed, darting swiftly and becoming still, hiding in the abundant ivy, or merging with the black windows.

He observed in alarm the first involuntary movement of panic. He was afraid, then suddenly the senses joined in one concerted cry of terror, where sight and sound and touch could no longer be distinguished in the frenzy of his brain. He turned round and ran back to the gate. As he did so, he looked over his shoulder towards the house.

A woman was standing in the path, looking at him, and behind her the conservatory door swung slowly on its hinges.

For a second she stood quite still, then turned and ran back towards the conservatory. Forgetting his fear, Smiley followed. As he reached the corner of the house he saw to his astonishment that she was standing at the door, rocking it gently back and forth in a thoughtful, leisurely way, like a child. She had her back to Smiley, until suddenly she turned to him and spoke, with a soft Dorset drawl, and the childish lilt of a simpleton:

'I thought you was the Devil, Mister, but you'm got no wings.'

Smiley hesitated. If he moved forward, she might take fright again and run. He looked at her across the snow, trying to make her out. She seemed to be wearing a bonnet or shawl over her head, and a dark cape over her shoulders. In her hand she held a sprig of leaves, and these she gently waved back and forth as she spoke to him.

'But you'm carn't do nothin', Mister, 'cos I got the holly fer to hold yer. So you do bide there, Mister, for little Jane can hold yer.' She shook the leaves vehemently towards him and began laughing softly. She still had one hand upon the door, and as she spoke her head lolled to one side.

'You bide away from little Jane, Mister, however pretty she'm do be.'

'Yes, Jane,' said Smiley softly, 'you're a very pretty girl, I can see that; and that's a pretty cape you're wearing, Jane.'

Evidently pleased with this, she clutched the lapels of her cape and turned slowly round, in a child's parody of a fine lady.

As she turned, Smiley saw the two empty sleeves of an overcoat swinging at her sides.

'There's some do laugh at Janie,' she said, a note of petulance in her voice, 'but there's not many seen the Devil fly, Mister. But Janie seed 'im, Janie seed 'im. Silver wings like fishes 'e done 'ad, Janie saw.'

'Where did you find that coat, Janie?'

She put her hands together and shook her head slowly from side to side.

'He'm a bad one. Ooh, he'm a bad one, Mister,' and she laughed softly. 'I seed 'im flying, riding on the wind,' she laughed again, 'and the moon be'ind 'im, lightin' up the way! They'm close as sisters, moon and Devil.'

On an impulse Smiley seized a handful of ivy from the side of the house and held it out to her, moving slowly forward as he did so.

'Do you like flowers, Janie? Here are flowers for Janie; pretty flowers for pretty Janie.' He had nearly reached her when with remarkable speed she ran across the lawn, disappeared into the trees and ran off down the lane. Smiley let her go. He was drenched in sweat.

As soon as he reached the hotel he telephoned Detective Inspector Rigby.

Chapter 7

KING ARTHUR'S CHURCH

The coffee lounge of the Sawley Arms resembles nothing so much as the Tropical Plants Pavilion at Kew Gardens. Built in an age when cactus was the most fashionable of plants and bamboo its indispensable companion, the lounge was conceived as the architectural image of a jungle clearing. Steel pillars, fashioned in segments like the trunk of a palm tree, supported a high glass roof whose regal dome replaced the African sky. Enormous urns of bronze or green-glazed earthenware contained all that was elegant and prolific in the cactus world, and between them very old residents could relax on sofas of spindly bamboo, sipping warm coffee and re-living the discomforts of safari.

Smiley's efforts to obtain a bottle of whisky and a syphon of soda at half past eleven at night were not immediately rewarded. It seemed that, like carrion from the carcass, the journalists had gone. The only sign of life in the hotel was the night porter, who treated his request with remote disapproval and advised him to go to bed. Smiley, by no means naturally persistent, discovered a half-crown in his overcoat pocket and thrust it a little irritably into the old man's hand. The result, though not magical, was effective, and by the time Rigby had made his way to the hotel, Smiley was seated in front of a bright gas fire in the coffee lounge with glasses and a whisky bottle before him.

Smiley retold his experiences of the evening with careful accuracy.

'It was the coat that caught my eye. It was a heavy overcoat like a man's,' he concluded. 'I remembered the blue belt and . . .' He left the sentence unfinished. Rigby nodded, got up and walked briskly across the lounge and through the swing doors to the porter's desk. Ten minutes later, he returned.

'I think we'd better go and pull her in,' he said simply. 'I've sent for a car.'

'We?' asked Smiley.

'Yes, if you wouldn't mind. What's the matter? Are you frightened?'

'Yes,' he replied. 'Yes, I am.'

The village of Pylle lies to the south of North Fields, upon a high spur which rises steeply from the flat, damp pastures of the Carne valley. It consists of a handful of stone cottages and a small inn where you may drink beer in the landlord's parlour. Seen from Carne playing fields, the village could easily be mistaken for an outcrop of rock upon a tor, for the hill on which it stands appears conical from the northern side. Local historians claim that Pylle is the oldest settlement in Dorset, that its name is Anglo-Saxon for harbour, and that it served the Romans as a port when all the lowlands around were covered by the sea. They will tell you, too, that King Arthur rested there after seven months at sea, and paid homage to Saint Andrew, the patron saint of sailors, on the site of Pylle Church, where he burned a candle for each month he had spent afloat; and that in the church, built to commemorate his visit and standing to this day lonely and untended on the hillside, there is a bronze coin as witness to his visit – the very one King Arthur gave to the verger before he set sail again for the Isle of Avalon.

Inspector William Rigby, himself a keen local historian, gave Smiley a somewhat terse précis of Pylle's legendary past as he drove cautiously along the snow-covered lanes.

'These small, out-of-the-way villages are pretty strange places,' he concluded. 'Often only three or four families, all so inbred you can no more sort them out than a barnful of cats. That's where your village idiots come from. They call it the Devil's Mark; I call it incest. They hate to have them in the village, you know – they'll drive them away at any price, like trying to wash away their shame, if you follow me.'

'I follow you.'

'This Jane's the religious sort. There's one or two of them turn that way. The villagers at Pylle are all Chapel now, see, so there's been no use for King Arthur's Church since Wesley.

It's empty, falling to bits. There's a few from the valley go up to see it, for its history, like, but no one cares for it, or didn't, not till Janie moved in.'

'Moved in?'

'Yes. She's taken to cleaning the church out night and day, bringing in wild flowers and such. That's why they say she's a witch.'

They passed Rode's house in silence and after turning a sharp bend began climbing the long steep hill that led to Pylle village. The snow in the lane was untouched and apart from occasional skidding they progressed without difficulty. The lower slopes of the hill were wooded, and the lane dark, until suddenly they emerged to find themselves on a smooth plateau, where a savage wind blew the fine snow like smoke across the fields, whipping it against the car. The snow had risen in drifts to one side of the lane, and the going became increasingly difficult.

Finally Rigby stopped the car and said:

'We'll walk from here, sir, if you don't mind.'

'How far is it?'

'Short and sour, I'd say. That's the village straight ahead.'

Through the windscreen, Smiley could discern behind the drifting veils of blown snow two low buildings about a quarter of a mile away. As he looked, a tall, muffled figure advanced towards them along the lane.

'That's Ted Mundy,' said Rigby with satisfaction, 'I told him to be here. He's the sergeant from Okeford.' He leaned out of the car window and called merrily:

'Hullo, Ted there, you old buzzard, how be?' Rigby opened the back door of the car and the sergeant climbed in. Smiley and Mundy were briefly introduced.

'There's a light in the church,' said Mundy, 'but I don't know whether Janie's there. I can't ask no one in the village, see, or I'd have the whole lot round me. They thought she'd gone for good.'

'Does she sleep there then, Ted? She got a bed there or something?' Rigby asked, and Smiley noticed with pleasure that his Dorset accent was more pronounced when he spoke to Mundy.

'So they say, Bill. I couldn't find no bed when I looked in

there Saturday. But I tell you an odd thing, Bill. It seems Mrs Rode used to come up here sometimes, to the chapel, to see Janie.'

'I heard about that,' said Rigby shortly. 'Now which way's the church, Ted?'

'Over the hill,' said Mundy. 'Outside the village, in a paddock.' He turned to Smiley. 'That's quite common round here, sir, as I expect you know.' Mundy spoke very slowly, choosing his words. 'You see, when they had the plague they left their dead in the villages and moved away; not far though, on account of their land and the church. Terrible it was, terrible.' Somehow Mundy managed to imply that the Black Death was a fairly recent disaster in those parts, if not actually within living memory.

They got out of the car, forcing the doors against the strong wind, and made their way towards the village, Mundy leading and Smiley in third place. The driven snow, fine and hard, stung their faces. It was an unearthly walk, high on that white hill on such a night. The curve of the bleak hill's crest and the moaning of the wind, the snow cloud which sped across the moon, the dismal, unlit cottages so cautiously passed, belonged to another corner of the world.

Mundy led them sharply to the left, and Smiley guessed that by avoiding the centre of the village he hoped to escape the notice of its inhabitants. After about twenty minutes' walking, often through deep snow, they found themselves following a low hedge between two fields. In the furthest corner of the right-hand field they saw a pale light glimmering across the snow, so pale that at first Smiley had to look away from it, then run his eyes back along the line of that distant hedge to make sure he was not deceived. Rigby stopped, beckoning to the others.

'I'll take over now,' he said. He turned to Smiley. 'I'd be obliged, sir, if you'd stand off a little. If there's any trouble we don't want you mixed up in it, do we?'

'Of course.'

'Ted Mundy, you come up by me.'

They followed the hedge until they came to a stile. Through the gap in the hedge they saw the church clearly now, a low building more like a tithe barn than a church. At one end a pale glow, like the uncertain light of a candle, shone dimly through the leaded windows.

'She's there,' said Mundy, under his breath, as he and Rigby moved forward, Smiley following some distance behind.

They were crossing the field now, Rigby leading, and the church drawing ever closer. New sounds disturbed the moaning of the storm: the parched creak of a door, the mutter of a crumbling roof, the incessant sigh of wind upon a dying house. The two men in front of Smiley had stopped, almost in the shadow of the church wall, and were whispering together. Then Mundy walked quietly away, disappearing round the corner of the church. Rigby waited a moment, then approached the narrow entrance in the rear wall, and pushed the door.

It opened slowly, creaking painfully on its hinges. Then he disappeared into the church. Smiley was waiting outside when suddenly above all the sounds of night he heard a scream, so taut and shrill and clear that it seemed to have no source, but to ride everywhere upon the wind, to mount the ravaged sky on wings; and Smiley had a vision of Mad Janie as he had seen her earlier that night, and he heard again in her demented cry the dreadful note of madness. For a moment he waited. The echo died. Then slowly, terrified, he walked through the snow to the open doorway.

Two candles and an oil lamp on the bare altar shed a dim light over the tiny chapel. In front of the altar, on the sanctuary step, sat Jane, looking vaguely towards them. Her vacuous face was daubed with stains of green and blue, her filthy clothes were threaded with sprigs of evergreen and all about her on the floor were the bodies of small animals and birds.

The pews were similarly decorated with dead creatures of all kinds; and on the altar, broken twigs and little heaps of holly leaves. Between the candles stood a crudely-fashioned cross. Stepping forward past Rigby, Smiley walked quickly down the aisle, past the lolling figure of Jane, until he stood before the altar. For a moment he hesitated, then turned and called softly to Rigby.

On the cross, draped over its three ends like a crude diadem, was a string of green beads.

Chapter 8

<u>FLOWERS FOR STELLA</u>

He woke with the echo of her scream in his ears. He had meant to sleep late, but his watch said half past seven. He put on his bedside lamp, for it was still half-dark, and peered owlishly round the room. There were his trousers, flung over the chair, the legs still sodden from the snow. There were his shoes; he'd have to buy another pair. And there beside him were the notes he had made early that morning before going to sleep, transcriptions from memory of some of Mad Jane's monologue on the journey back to Carne, a journey he would never forget. Mundy had sat with her in the back. She spoke to herself as a child does, asking questions and then in the patient tones of an adult for whom the reply is self-evident, providing the answer.

One obsession seemed to fill her mind: she had seen the devil. She had seen him flying on the wind, his silver wings stretched out behind him. Sometimes the recollection amused her, sometimes inflated her with a sense of her own importance or beauty, and sometimes it terrified her, so that she moaned and wept and begged him to go away. Then Mundy would speak kindly to her, and try to calm her. Smiley wondered whether policemen grew accustomed to the squalor of such things, to clothes that were no more than stinking rags wound round wretched limbs, to puling imbeciles who clutched and screamed and wept. She must have been living on the run for nights on end, finding her food in the fields and dustbins since the night of the murder . . . What had she done that night? What had she seen? Had she killed Stella Rode? Had she seen the murderer, and fancied *him* to be the devil flying on the wind? Why should she think that? If Janie did not kill Stella Rode, what had she seen that so frightened her that for three long winter nights she prowled in terror like an animal in the forest? Had the devil within taken hold of Janie and given power to her arm as she struck down Stella? Was that the devil who rode upon the wind?

But the beads and the coat and the footprints which were not hers – what of them? He lay there thinking, and achieving nothing. At last it was time to get up: it was the morning of the funeral.

As he was getting out of bed the telephone rang. It was Rigby. His voice sounded strained and urgent. 'I want to see you,' he said. 'Can you call round?'

'Before or after the funeral?'

'Before, if possible. What about now?'

'I'll be there in ten minutes.'

Rigby looked, for the first time since Smiley had met him, tired and worried.

'It's Mad Janie,' he said. 'The Chief thinks we should charge her.'

'What for?'

'Murder,' Rigby replied crisply, pushing a thin file across the table. 'The old fool's made a statement . . . a sort of confession.'

They sat in silence while Smiley read the extraordinary statement. It was signed with Mad Janie's mark – J. L. – drawn in a childish hand in letters an inch high. The constable who had taken it down had begun by trying to condense and simplify her account, but by the end of the first page he had obviously despaired. At last Smiley came to the description of the murder:

'So I tells my darling, I tells her: "You are a naughty creature to go with the devil," but her did not hearken, see, and I took angry with her, but she paid no call. I can't abide them as go with devils in the night, and I told her. She ought to have had holly, mister, there's the truth. I told her, mister, but she never would hearken, and that's all Janie's saying, but she drove the devil off, Janie did, and there's one will thank me, that's my darling and I took her jewels for the saints I did, to pretty out the church, and a coat for to keep me warm.'

Rigby watched him as he slowly replaced the statement on the desk.

'Well, what do you think of it?'

Smiley hesitated. 'It's pretty good nonsense as it stands,' he replied at last.

'Of course it is,' said Rigby, with something like contempt. 'She saw something, Lord knows what, when she was out on the prowl; stealing, I shouldn't wonder. She may have robbed the body, or else she picked up the beads where the murderer dropped them. We've traced the coat. Belonged to a Mr Jardine, a baker in Carne East. Mrs Jardine gave it to Stella Rode last Wednesday morning for the refugees. Janie must have pinched it from the conservatory. That's what she meant by "a coat for to keep me warm". But she no more killed Stella Rode than you or I did. What about the footprints, the glove-marks in the conservatory? Besides, she's not strong enough, Janie isn't, to heave that poor woman forty feet through the snow. This is a man's work, as anyone can see.'

'Then what exactly . . . ?'

'We've called off the search, and I'm to prepare a case against one Jane Lyn of the village of Pylle for the wilful murder of Stella Rode. I wanted to tell you myself before you read it all over the papers. So that you'd know how it was.'

'Thanks.'

'In the meantime, if there's any help I can give you, we're still willing.' He hesitated, seemed about to say something, then to change his mind.

As he made his way down the wide staircase Smiley felt useless and very angry, which was scarcely the right frame of mind in which to attend a funeral.

It was an admirably conducted affair. Neither the flowers nor the congregation exceeded what was fitting to the occasion. She was not buried at the Abbey, out of deference perhaps to her simplicity of taste, but in the parish churchyard not far from North Fields. The Master was detained that day, as he was on most days, and had sent instead his wife, a small, very vague woman who had spent a long time in India. D'Arcy was much in evidence, fluttering here and there before the ceremony like an anxious beadle; and Mr Cardew had come to guide poor Stella through the unfamiliarities of High Anglican procedure. The Hechts were there, Charles all in black, scrubbed and shining, and Shane in dramatic weeds, and a hat with a very broad brim.

Smiley, who, like the others, had arrived early in anticipation of the unwholesome public interest which the ceremony might arouse, found himself a seat near the entrance of the church. He watched each new arrival with interest, waiting for his first sight of Stanley Rode.

Several tradesmen arrived, pressed into bulging serge and black ties, and formed a small group south of the aisle, away from the staff and their wives. Soon they were joined by other members of the town community, women who had known Mrs Rode at the Tabernacle; and then by Rigby, who looked straight at Smiley and gave no sign. Then on the stroke of three a tall old man walked slowly through the doorway, looking straight before him, neither knowing nor seeing any-one. Beside him was Stanley Rode.

It was a face which at first sight meant nothing to Smiley, seeming to have neither the imprint of temperament nor the components of character; it was a shallow, ordinary face, inclining to plumpness, and lacking quality. It matched his short, ordinary body and his black, ordinary hair; it was suitably compressed into an expression of sorrow. As Smiley watched him turn into the centre aisle and take his place among the principal mourners, it occurred to him that Rode's very walk and bearing successfully conveyed something entirely alien to Carne. If it is vulgar to wear a pen in the breast pocket of your jacket, to favour Fair Isle pullovers and brown ties, to bob a little and turn your feet out as you walk, then Rode beyond a shadow of doubt was vulgar, for though he did not now commit these sins, his manner implied them all.

They followed the coffin into the churchyard and gathered round the open grave. D'Arcy and Fielding were standing together, seemingly intent upon the service. The tall, elderly figure who had entered the churchyard with Rode was now visibly moved, and Smiley guessed that he was Stella's father, Samuel Glaston. As the service ended, the old man walked quickly away from the crowd, nodding briefly to Rode, and disappeared into the church. He seemed to struggle as he went, like a man walking against a strong wind.

The little group moved slowly away from the graveside, until only Rode remained, an oddly stiff figure, taut and constrained, his eyes wide but somehow sightless, his mouth set in a strict, pedagogic line. Then, as Smiley watched, Rode seemed to wake from a dream; his body suddenly relaxed and he too walked slowly but quite confidently away from the grave towards the small group which by now had reassembled at the churchyard gate. As he did so, Fielding, at the edge of the group, caught sight of him approaching and, to Smiley's astonishment, walked deliberately and quite quickly away with an expression of strong distaste. It was not the calculated act of a man wishing to insult another, for it attracted the notice neither of Rode nor of anyone else standing by. Terence Fielding, for once, appeared to be in the grip of a genuine emotion, and indifferent to the impression he created.

Reluctantly Smiley approached the group. Rode was rather to one side, the D'Arcys were there, and three or four members of the staff. No one was talking much.

'Mr Rode?' he inquired.

'That's right, yes.' He spoke slowly, a trace of an accent carefully avoided.

'I'm representing Miss Brimley of the *Christian Voice*.'

'Oh, yes.'

'She was most anxious that the journal should be represented. I thought you would like to know that.'

'I saw your wreath; very kind, I am sure.'

'Your wife was one of our most loyal supporters,' Smiley continued. 'We regarded her almost as one of the family.'

'Yes, she was very keen on the *Voice*.' Smiley wondered whether Rode was always as impassive as this, or whether bereavement had made him listless.

'When did you come?' Rode asked suddenly.

'Yesterday.'

'Making a week-end of it, eh?'

Smiley was so astonished that for a moment he could think of nothing to say. Rode was still looking at him, waiting for an answer.

'I have one or two friends here . . . Mr Fielding . . .'

'Oh, Terence.' Smiley was convinced that Rode was not on Christian-name terms with Fielding.

'I would like, if I may,' Smiley ventured, 'to write a small obituary for Miss Brimley. Would you have any objection?'

'Stella would have liked that.'

'If you are not too upset, perhaps I could call round tomorrow for one or two details?'

'Certainly.'

'Eleven o'clock?'

'It will be a pleasure,' Rode replied, almost pertly, and they walked together to the churchyard gate.

Chapter 9

THE MOURNERS

I t was a cheap trick to play on a man who had suddenly lost his wife. Smiley knew that. As he gently unlatched the gate and entered the drive, where two nights ago he had conducted his strange conversation with Jane Lyn, he acknowledged that in calling on Rode under any pretext at such a time he was committing a thoroughly unprincipled act. It was a peculiarity of Smiley's character that throughout the whole of his clandestine work he had never managed to reconcile the means to the end. A stringent critic of his own motives, he had discovered after long observation that he tended to be less a creature of intellect than his tastes and habits might suggest; once in the war he had been described by his superiors as possessing the cunning of Satan and the conscience of a virgin, which seemed to him not wholly unjust.

He pressed the bell and waited.

Stanley Rode opened the door. He was very neatly dressed, very scrubbed.

'Oh hullo,' he said, as if they were old friends. 'I say, you haven't got a car, have you?'

'I'm afraid I left it in London.'

'Never mind.' Rode sounded disappointed. 'Thought we might have gone out for a drive, had a chat as we went. I get a bit fed-up, kicking around here on my own. Miss D'Arcy asked me to stay over at their place. Very good people they are, very good indeed; but somehow I didn't wish it, not yet.'

'I understand.'

'Do you?' They were in the hall now, Smiley was getting out of his overcoat, Rode waiting to receive it. 'I don't think many do – the loneliness I mean. Do you know what they've done, the Master and Mr D'Arcy? They meant it well, I know. They've farmed out all my correcting – my exam. correcting, you understand. What am I supposed to do here, all on my own? I've no teaching, nothing; they've all taken a hand. You'd think they wanted to get rid of me.'

Smiley nodded vaguely. They moved towards the drawing-room, Rode leading the way.

'I know they did it for the best, as I said. But after all, I've got to spend the time somehow. Simon Snow got some of my division to correct. Have you met him by any chance? Sixty-one per cent he gave one boy – sixty-one. The boy's an absolute fool; I told Fielding at the beginning of the Half that he wouldn't possibly get his remove. Perkins his name is, a nice enough boy; head of Fielding's house. He'd have been lucky to get thirty per cent . . . sixty-one, Snow gave him. I haven't seen the papers yet, of course, but it's impossible, quite impossible.'

They sat down.

'Not that I don't want the boy to get on. He's a nice enough boy, nothing special, but well-mannered. Mrs Rode and I meant to have him here to tea this Half. We would have done, in fact, if it hadn't been for . . .' There was a moment's silence. Smiley was going to speak when Rode stood up and said:

'I've a kettle on the stove, Mr . . .'

'Smiley.'

'I've a kettle on the stove, Mr Smiley. May I make you a cup of coffee?' That little stiff voice with the corners carefully defined, like a hired morning suit, thought Smiley.

Rode returned a few minutes later with a tray and measured their coffee in precise quantities, according to their taste.

Smiley found himself continually irritated by Rode's social assumptions, and his constant struggle to conceal his origin. You could tell at the time, from every word and gesture, what he was; from the angle of his elbow as he drank his coffee, from the swift, expert pluck at the knee of his trouser leg as he sat down.

'I wonder,' Smiley began, 'whether perhaps I might now . . .'

'Go ahead, Mr Smiley.'

'We are, of course, largely interested in Mrs Rode's association with . . . our Church.'

'Quite.'

'You were married at Branxome, I believe.'

'Branxome Hill Tabernacle; fine church.' D'Arcy wouldn't have liked the way he said that; cocksure lad on a motor-bike. Pencils in the outside pocket.

'When was that?'

'September, fifty-one.'

'Did Mrs Rode engage in charitable work in Branxome? I know she was very active here.'

'No, not at Branxome, but a lot here. She had to look after her father at Branxome, you see. It was refugee relief she was keen on here. That didn't get going much until late 1956 – the Hungarians began it, and then this last year . . .'

Smiley peered thoughtfully at Rode from behind his spectacles, forgot himself, blinked, and looked away.

'Did she take a large part in the social activities of Carne? Does the staff have its own Women's Institute and so on?' he asked innocently.

'She did a bit, yes. But, being Chapel, she kept mainly with the Chapel people from the town . . . you should ask Mr Cardew about that; he's the Minister.'

'But may I say, Mr Rode, that she took an active part in school affairs as well?'

Rode hesitated.

'Yes, of course,' he said.

'Thank you.'

There was a moment's silence, then Smiley continued: 'Our readers will, of course, remember Mrs Rode as the winner of our Kitchen Hints competition. Was she a good cook, Mr Rode?'

'Very good, for plain things, not fancy.'

'Is there any little fact that you would specially like us to include, anything she herself would like to be remembered by?'

Rode looked at him with expressionless eyes. Then he shrugged.

'No, not really. I can't think of anything. Oh, you could say her father was a magistrate up North. She was proud of that.'

Smiley finished his coffee and stood up.

'You've been very patient with me, Mr Rode. We're most

grateful, I assure you. I'll take care to send you an advance copy of our notice . . .'

'Thanks. I did it for her, you see. She liked the *Voice*; always did. Grew up with it.'

They shook hands.

'By the way, do you know where I can find old Mr Glaston? Is he staying in Carne or has he returned to Branxome?'

'He was up here yesterday. He's going back to Branxome this afternoon. The police wanted to see him before he left.'

'I see.'

'He's staying at the Sawley.'

'Thank you. I might try and see him before I go.'

'When do you leave, then?'

'Quite soon, I expect. Good-bye, then, Mr Rode. Incidentally –' Smiley began.

'Yes?'

'If ever you're in London and at a loose end, if ever you want a chat . . . and a cup of tea, we're always pleased to see you at the *Voice*, you know. Always.'

'Thanks. Thanks very much, Mr –'

'Smiley.'

'Thanks, that's very decent. No one's said that to me for a long time. I'll take you up on that one day. Very good of you.'

'Good-bye.' Again they shook hands; Rode's was dry and cool. Smooth.

He returned to the Sawley Arms, sat himself at a desk in the empty residents' lounge and wrote a note to Mr Glaston:

Dear Mr Glaston,
   I am here on behalf of Miss Brimley of the *Christian Voice*. I have some letters from Stella which I think you would like to see. Forgive me for bothering you at this sad moment: I understand you are leaving Carne this afternoon and wondered if I might see you before you left.

He carefully sealed the envelope and took it to the reception desk. There was no one there, so he rang the bell and waited. At last a porter came, an old turnkey with a grey, bristly face, and after examining the envelope critically for a long time,

71

he agreed, against an excessive fee, to convey it to Mr Glaston's room. Smiley stayed at the desk, waiting for his answer.

Smiley himself was one of those solitaries who seem to have come into the world fully educated at the age of eighteen. Obscurity was his nature, as well as his profession. The byways of espionage are not populated by the brash and colourful adventurers of fiction. A man who, like Smiley, has lived and worked for years among his country's enemies learns only one prayer: that he may never, never be noticed. Assimilation is his highest aim, he learns to love the crowds who pass him in the street without a glance; he clings to them for his anonymity and his safety. His fear makes him servile – he could embrace the shoppers who jostle him in their impatience, and force him from the pavement. He could adore the officials, the police, the bus conductors, for the terse indifference of their attitudes.

But this fear, this servility, this dependence, had developed in Smiley a perception for the colour of human beings: a swift, feminine sensitivity to their characters and motives. He knew mankind as a huntsman knows his cover, as a fox the wood. For a spy must hunt while he is hunted, and the crowd is his estate. He could collect their gestures and their words, record the interplay of glance and movement, as a huntsman can record the twisted bracken and the broken twig, or as a fox detects the signs of danger.

Thus, while he waited patiently for Glaston's reply and recalled the crowded events of the last forty-eight hours, he was able to order and assess them with detachment. What was the cause of D'Arcy's attitude to Fielding, as if they were unwilling partners to a shabby secret? Staring across the neglected hotel gardens towards Carne Abbey, he was able to glimpse behind the lead roof of the Abbey the familiar battlements of the school: keeping the new world out and the old world secure. In his mind's eye he saw the Great Court now, as the boys came out of Chapel: the black-coated groups in the leisured attitudes of eighteenth-century England. And he remembered the other school beside the police station: Carne High School; a little tawdry place like a porter's lodge in an empty graveyard, as detached from the tones of Carne as its brick and flint from the saffron battlements of School Hall.

Yes, he reflected, Stanley Rode had made a long, long journey from the Grammar School at Branxome. And if he killed his wife, then the motive, Smiley was sure, and even the means, were to be found in that hard road to Carne.

'It was kind of you to come,' said Glaston; 'kind of Miss Brimley to send you. They're good people at the *Voice*; always were.' He said this as if 'good' were an absolute quality with which he was familiar.

'You'd better read the letters, Mr Glaston. The second one will shock you, I'm afraid, but I'm sure you'll agree that it would be wrong of me not to show it to you.' They were sitting in the lounge, the mammoth plants like sentinels beside them.

He handed Glaston the two letters, and the old man took them firmly and read them. He held them a good way from him to read, thrusting his strong head back, his eyes half closed, the crisp line of his mouth turned down at the corners. At last he said:

'You were with Miss Brimley in the war, were you?'

'I worked with John Landsbury, yes.'

'I see. That's why she came to you?'

'Yes.'

'Are you Chapel?'

'No.'

He was silent for a while, his hands folded on his lap, the letters before him on the table.

'Stanley was Chapel when they married. Then he went over. Did you know that?'

'Yes.'

'Where I come from in the North, we don't do that. Chapel was something we'd stood up for and won. Almost like the Vote.'

'I know.'

His back was as straight as a soldier's. He looked stern rather than sad. Quite suddenly, his eyes turned towards Smiley, and he looked at him long and carefully.

'Are you a schoolmaster?' he asked, and it occurred to

Smiley that in his day Samuel Glaston had been a very shrewd man of business.

'No . . . I'm more or less retired.'

'Married?'

'I was.'

Again the old man fell silent, and Smiley wished he had left him alone.

'She was a great one for chatter,' he said at last.

Smiley said nothing.

'Have you told the police?'

'Yes, but they knew already. That is, they knew that Stella thought her husband was going to murder her. She'd tried to tell Mr Cardew . . .'

'The Minister?'

'Yes. He thought she was overwrought and . . . deluded.'

'Do you think she wasn't?'

'I don't know. I just don't know. But from what I have heard of your daughter I don't believe she was unbalanced. *Something* roused her suspicions, something frightened her very much. I don't believe we can just disregard that. I don't believe it was a coincidence that she was frightened before she died. And therefore I don't believe that the beggar-woman murdered her.'

Samuel Glaston nodded slowly. It seemed to Smiley that the old man was trying to show interest, partly to be polite, and partly because if he did not it would be a confession that he had lost interest in life itself.

Then, after a long silence, he carefully folded up the letters and gave them back. Smiley waited for him to speak, but he said nothing.

After a few moments Smiley got up and walked quietly from the room.

Chapter 10

LITTLE WOMEN

Shane Hecht smiled, and drank some more sherry. 'You must be dreadfully important,' she said to Smiley, 'for D'Arcy to serve decent sherry. What are you, *Almanach de Gotha*?'

'I'm afraid not. D'Arcy and I were both dining at Terence Fielding's on Friday night and D'Arcy asked me for sherry.'

'Terence is *wicked*, isn't he? Charles loathes him. I'm afraid they see Sparta in *quite* different ways . . . Poor Terence. It's his last Half, you know.'

'I know.'

'So sweet of you to come to the funeral yesterday. I hate funerals, don't you? Black is so insanitary. I always remember King George V's funeral. Lord Sawley was at Court in those days, and gave Charles two tickets. So kind. I always think it's *spoilt* us for ordinary funerals in a way. Although I'm never quite *sure* about funerals, are you? I have a suspicion that they are largely a lower-class recreation; cherry brandy and seed cake in the parlour. I think the tendency of people like ourselves is for a *quiet* funeral these days; no flowers, just a short obituary and a memorial service later.' Her small eyes were bright with pleasure. She finished her sherry and held out her empty glass to Smiley.

'Would you mind, dear? I hate sherry, but Felix is so mean.'

Smiley filled her glass from the decanter on the table.

'Dreadful about the murder, wasn't it? That beggar-woman must be mad. Stella Rode was such a nice person, I always thought . . . and so *unusual*. She did such clever things with the same dress . . . But she had such curious friends. All for Hans the woodcutter and Pedro the fisherman, if you know what I mean.'

'Was she popular at Carne?'

Shane Hecht laughed gently: 'No one is popular at Carne . . . but she wasn't easy to like . . . She would wear black crêpe on Sundays . . . Forgive me, but do the lower classes always do that? The townspeople liked her, I believe. They adore anyone who betrays Carne. But then she was a Christian Scientist or something.'

'Baptist, I understand,' said Smiley unthinkingly.

She looked at him for a moment with unfeigned curiosity. 'How sweet,' she murmured. 'Tell me, what *are* you?'

Smiley made some facetious reply about being unemployed, and realised that it was only by a hair's-breadth that he had avoided explaining himself to Shane Hecht like a small boy. Her very ugliness, her size and voice, coupled with the sophisticated malice of her conversation, gave her the dangerous quality of command. Smiley was tempted to compare her with Fielding, but for Fielding other people scarcely existed. For Shane Hecht they did exist: they were there to be found wanting in the minute tests of social behaviour, to be ridiculed, cut off and destroyed.

'I read in the paper that her father was quite well off. From the North. Second generation. Remarkable really how *unspoilt* she was . . . so natural . . . You wouldn't think she *needed* to go to the launderette or to make friends with beggars . . . Though, of course, the Midlands are different, aren't they? Only about three good families between Ipswich and Newcastle. Where did you say you came from, dear?'

'London.'

'How nice. I went to tea with Stella once. Milk in first and Indian. So different,' and she looked at Smiley suddenly and said, 'I'll tell you something. She almost aroused an admiration in me, I found her so insufferable. She was one of those tiresome little snobs who think that only the humble are virtuous.' Then she smiled and added, 'I even agreed with Charles about Stella Rode, and that's saying something. If you're a student of mankind, do go and have a look at him, the contrast is riveting.' But at that moment they were joined by D'Arcy's sister, a bony, virile woman with untidy grey hair and an arrogant, hunting mouth.

'Dorothy darling,' Shane murmured; 'such a lovely party. So *kind*. And so *exciting* to meet somebody from London, don't you think? We were talking about poor Mrs Rode's funeral.'

'Stella Rode may have been damn' bad form, Shane, but she did a lot for my refugees.'

'Refugees?' asked Smiley innocently.

'Hungarians. Collecting for them. Clothes, furniture, money. One of the few wives who *did* anything.' She looked sharply at Shane Hecht, who was smiling benignly past her towards her husband: 'Busy little creature, she was; didn't mind rolling her sleeves up, going from door to door. Got her little women on to it too at the Baptist chapel and brought in a mass of stuff. You've got to hand it to them, you know. They've got *spirit*. Felix, more sherry!'

There were about twenty in the two rooms, but Smiley, who had arrived a little late, found himself attached to a group of about eight who stood nearest the door: D'Arcy and his sister; Charles and Shane Hecht; a young mathematician called Snow and his wife; a curate from the Abbey and Smiley himself, bewildered and mole-like behind his spectacles. Smiley looked quickly round the room, but could see no sign of Fielding.

'. . . Yes,' Dorothy D'Arcy continued, 'she was a good little worker, very . . . right to the end. I went over there on Friday with that parson man from the tin tabernacle – Cardew – to see if there was any refugee stuff to tidy up. There wasn't a thing out of place – every bit of clothing she had was all packed up and addressed; we just had to send it off. She was a damn' good little worker, I will say. Did a splendid job at the bazaar, you know.'

'Yes, darling,' said Shane Hecht sweetly. 'I remember it well. It was the day I presented her to Lady Sawley. She wore such a *nice* little hat – the one she wore on Sundays, you know. And *so* respectful. She called her "my lady".' She turned to Smiley and breathed: 'Rather feudal, don't you think, dear? I always like that: so few of us left.'

The mathematician and his wife were talking to Charles Hecht in a corner and a few minutes later Smiley managed to extricate himself from the group and join them.

Ann Snow was a pretty girl with a rather square face and a turned-up nose. Her husband was tall and thin, with an agreeable stoop. He held his sherry glass between straight, slender fingers as if it were a chemical retort and when he spoke he seemed to address the sherry rather than his listener; Smiley remembered them from the funeral. Hecht was looking pink and rather cross, sucking at his pipe. They talked in a desultory way, their conversation dwarfed by the exchanges of the adjoining group. Hecht eventually drifted away from them, still frowning and withdrawn, and stood ostentatiously alone near the door.

'Poor Stella,' said Ann Snow after a moment's silence. 'Sorry,' she added. 'I can't get her out of my mind yet. It seems mad, just mad. I mean why should she *do* it, that Janie woman?'

'Did you like Stella?' Smiley asked.

'Of course we did. She was sweet. We've been here four Halves now, but she was the only person here who's ever been *kind* to us.' Her husband said nothing, just nodded at his sherry. 'Simon wasn't a boy at Carne, you see – most of the staff were – so we didn't know anyone and no one was really interested. They all pretended to be terribly pleased with us, of course, but it was Stella who really . . .'

Dorothy D'Arcy was descending on them. 'Mrs Snow,' she said crisply, 'I've been meaning to talk to you. I want you to take over Stella Rode's job on the refugees.' She cast an appraising look in Simon's direction: 'The Master's very keen on refugees.'

'Oh, my goodness!' Ann Snow replied, aghast. 'I couldn't possibly, Miss D'Arcy, I . . .'

'Couldn't? Why couldn't you? You helped Mrs Rode with her stall at the bazaar, didn't you?'

'So that's where she got her clothes from,' breathed Shane Hecht behind them. Ann was fumbling on:

'But . . . well I haven't quite got Stella's nerve, if you understand what I mean; and besides, she was a Baptist: all the locals helped her and gave her things, and they all liked her. With me it would be different.'

'Lot of damn' nonsense,' declared Miss D'Arcy, who spoke to all her juniors as if they were grooms or erring children; and Shane Hecht beside her said: 'Baptists are the people who don't like private pews, aren't they? I do so agree – one feels that if one's paid one simply has to go.'

The curate, who had been talking cricket in a corner, was

startled into mild protest: 'Oh, come, Mrs Hecht, the private pew had many advantages . . .' and embarked on a diffuse apologia for ancient custom, to which Shane listened with every sign of the most assiduous interest. When at last he finished she said: 'Thank you, William dear, so sweet,' turned her back on him and added to Smiley in a stage whisper: 'William Trumper – one of Charles's old pupils – such a triumph when he passed his Certificate.'

Smiley, anxious to dissociate himself from Shane Hecht's vengeance on the curate, turned to Ann Snow, but she was still at the mercy of Miss D'Arcy's charitable intentions, and Shane was still talking to him:

'The only Smiley I ever heard of married Lady Ann Sercombe at the end of the war. She left him soon afterwards, of course. A very curious match. I understand he was quite unsuitable. She was Lord Sawley's cousin, you know. The Sawleys have been connected with Carne for four hundred years. The present heir is a pupil of Charles; we often dine at the Castle. I never did hear what became of Ann Sercombe . . . she went to Africa, you know . . . or was it India? No, it was America. So tragic. One doesn't talk about it at the Castle.' For a moment the noise in the room stopped. For a moment, no more, he could discern nothing but the steady gaze of Shane Hecht upon him, and knew she was waiting for an answer. And then she released him as if to say: 'I could crush you, you see. But I won't, I'll let you live,' and she turned and walked away.

He contrived to take his leave at the same time as Ann and Simon Snow. They had an old car and insisted on running Smiley back to his hotel. On the way there, he said:

'If you have nothing better to do, I would be happy to give you both dinner at my hotel. I imagine the food is dreadful.'

The Snows protested and accepted, and a quarter of an hour later they were all three seated in a corner of the enormous dining-room of the Sawley Arms, to the great despondency of three waiters and a dozen generations of Lord Sawley's forebears, puffy men in crumbling pigment.

'We really got to know her our second Half,' Ann Snow ran on. 'Stella didn't do much mixing with the other wives –

she'd learnt her lesson by then. She didn't go to coffee parties and things, so it was really luck that we did meet. When we first came there wasn't a staff house available for us: we had to spend the first Half in a hotel. We moved in to a little house in Bread Street at the end of our second Half. Moving was chaos – Simon was examining for the scholarships and we were terribly broke, so we had to do everything we possibly could for ourselves. It was a wet Thursday morning when we moved. The rain was simply teeming down; but none of our good pieces would get in through the front door, and in the end Mulligan's just dumped me on the doorstep and let me sort it out.' She laughed, and Smiley thought what an agreeable child she was. 'They were absolutely foul. They would have just driven off, I think, but they wanted a cheque as soon as they'd done the delivery, and the bill was pounds more than the estimate. I hadn't got the cheque-book, of course. Simon had gone off with it. Mulligan's even threatened to take all the stuff away again. It was monstrous. I think I was nearly in tears.' She nearly is now, thought Smiley. 'Then out of the blue Stella turned up. I can't think how she even knew we were moving – I'm sure no one else did. She'd brought an overall and an old pair of shoes and she'd come to help. When she saw what was going on she didn't bother with the men at all, just went to a phone and rang Mr Mulligan himself. I don't know what she said to him, but she made the foreman talk to him afterwards and there was no more trouble after that. She was terribly happy – happy to *help*. She was that sort of person. They took the door right out and managed to get everything in. She was marvellous at helping without managing. The rest of the wives,' she added bitterly, 'are awfully good at managing, but don't help at all.'

Smiley nodded, and discreetly filled their glasses.

'Simon's leaving,' Ann said, suddenly confidential. 'He's got a grant and we're going back to Oxford. He's going to do a DPhil and get a University job.'

They drank to his success, and the conversation turned to other things until Smiley asked: 'What's Rode himself like to work with?'

'He's a good schoolmaster,' said Simon, slowly, 'but tiring as a colleague.'

'Oh, he was *quite* different from Stella,' said Ann; 'terribly Carne-minded. D'Arcy adopted him and he got the bug. Simon says all the grammar school people go that way – it's the fury of the convert. It's sickening. He even changed his religion when he got to Carne. Stella didn't, though; she wouldn't dream of it.'

'The Established Church has much to offer Carne,' Simon observed, and Smiley enjoyed the dry precision of his delivery.

'Stella can't exactly have hit it off with Shane Hecht,' Smiley probed gently.

'Of *course* she didn't!' Ann declared angrily. 'Shane was horrid to her, always sneering at her because she was honest and simple about the things she liked. Shane hated Stella – I think it was because Stella didn't *want* to be a lady of quality. She was quite happy to be herself. That's what really worried Shane. Shane likes people to compete so that she can make fools of them.'

'So does Carne,' said Simon, quietly.

'She was awfully good at helping out with the refugees. That was how she got into real trouble.' Ann Snow's slim hands gently rocked her brandy glass.

'Trouble?'

'Just before she died. Hasn't anyone told you? About her frightful row with D'Arcy's sister?'

'No.'

'Of course, they wouldn't have done. Stella never gossiped.'

'Let me tell you,' said Simon. 'It's a good story. When the Refugee Year business started, Dorothy D'Arcy was fired with charitable enthusiasm. So was the Master. Dorothy's enthusiasms always seem to correspond with his. She started collecting clothes and money and packing them off to London. All very laudable, but there was a perfectly good town appeal going, launched by the Mayor. That wasn't good enough for Dorothy, though: the school must have its own appeal; you can't mix your charity. I think Felix was largely behind it. Anyway, after the thing had been going for a few months the refugee centre in London apparently wrote to Dorothy and asked whether anyone would be prepared to accommodate a refugee couple. Instead of publicising the letter, Dorothy wrote straight back and said she would put them up herself. So far so good. The couple turned up, Dorothy and Felix pointed a proud finger at them and the local press wrote it all up as an example of British humanity.

'About six weeks later, one afternoon, these two turned up on Stella's doorstep. The Rodes and the D'Arcys are neighbours, you see, and anyway Stella had tried to take an interest in Dorothy's refugees. The woman was in floods of tears and the husband was shouting blue murder, but that didn't worry Stella. She had them straight into the drawing-room and gave them a cup of tea. Finally, they managed to explain in basic English that they had run away from the D'Arcys because of the treatment they received. The girl was expected to work from morning till night in the kitchen, and the husband was acting as unpaid kennel-boy for those beastly spaniels that Dorothy breeds. The ones without noses.'

'King Charles,' Ann prompted.

'It was about as awful as it could be. The girl was pregnant and he was a fully qualified engineer, so neither of them were exactly suited to domestic service. They told Stella that Dorothy was away till the evening – she'd gone to a dog show. Stella advised them to stay with her for the time being, and that evening she went round and told Dorothy what had happened. She had quite a nerve, you see. Although it wasn't nerve really. She just did the simple thing. Dorothy was furious, and demanded that Stella should return "her refugees" immediately. Stella replied that she was sure that they wouldn't come, and went home. When Stella got home she rang up the refugee people in London and asked their advice. They sent a woman down to see Dorothy and the couple, and the result was that they returned to London the following day . . . You can imagine what Shane Hecht would have made of that story.'

'Didn't she ever find out?'

'Stella never told anyone except us, and we didn't pass it on. Dorothy just let it be known that the refugees had gone to some job in London, and that was that.'

'How long ago did this happen?'

'They left exactly three weeks ago,' said Ann to her husband. 'Stella told me about it when she came to supper the night you were in Oxford for your interview. That was three weeks ago tonight.' She turned to Smiley:

'Poor Simon's been having an awful time. Felix D'Arcy unloaded all Rode's exam. correcting on to him. It's bad enough doing one person's correction – two is frantic.'

'Yes,' replied Simon reflectively. 'It's been a bad week. And rather humiliating in a way. Several of the boys who were up to me for science last Half are now in Rode's forms. I'd regarded one or two of them as practically unteachable, but Rode seems to have brought them on marvellously. I corrected one boy's paper – Perkins – sixty-one per cent for elementary science. Last Half he got fifteen per cent in a much easier paper. He only got his remove because Fielding raised hell. He was in Fielding's house.'

'Oh I know – a red-haired boy, a prefect.'

'Good Lord,' cried Simon. 'Don't say you know him?'

'Oh, Fielding introduced us,' said Smiley vaguely. 'Incidentally – no one else ever mentioned that incident to you about Miss D'Arcy's refugees, did they? Confirmed it, as it were?'

Ann Snow looked at him oddly. 'No. Stella told us about it, but of course Dorothy D'Arcy never referred to it at all. She must have *hated* Stella, though.'

He saw them to their car, and waited despite their protests while Simon cranked it. At last they drove off, the car bellowing down the silent street. Smiley stood for a moment on the pavement, an odd, lonely figure peering down the empty road.

Chapter 11

A COAT TO KEEP HER WARM

A dog that had not bitten the postman; a devil that rode upon the wind; a woman who knew that she would die; a little, worried man in an overcoat standing in the snow outside his hotel, and the laborious chime of the Abbey clock telling him to go to bed.

Smiley hesitated, then with a shrug crossed the road to the hotel entrance, mounted the step and entered the cheap, yellow light of the residents' hall. He walked slowly up the stairs.

He detested the Sawley Arms. That muted light in the hall was typical: inefficient, antiquated and smug. Like the waiters in the dining-room and the lowered voices in the residents' lounge, like his own hateful bedroom with its blue and gilt urns, and the framed tapestry of a Buckinghamshire garden.

His room was bitterly cold; the maid must have opened the window. He put a shilling in the meter and lit the gas. The fire bubbled grumpily and went out. Muttering, Smiley looked around for some paper to write on, and discovered some, much to his surprise, in the drawer of the writing desk. He changed into his pyjamas and dressing-gown and crawled miserably into bed. After sitting there uncomfortably for some minutes he got up, fetched his overcoat and spread it over the eider-down. A coat for to keep her warm . . .

How did her statement read? 'There's one will thank me, that's my darling and I took her jewels for the saints I did, and a coat for to keep me warm . . .' The coat had been given to Stella last Wednesday for the refugees. It seemed reasonable to assume from the way the statement read that Janie had taken the coat from the outhouse at the same time as she took the beads from Stella's body. But Dorothy D'Arcy had been round there on Friday morning – of course she had, with Mr Cardew – she was talking about it at her party that very

84

evening: 'There wasn't a thing out of place – every bit of clothing she had was all packed up and addressed – a damn' good little worker, I will say . . .' Then why hadn't Stella packed the overcoat? If she packed everything else, why not the overcoat too?

Or had Janie stolen the coat earlier in the day, before Stella made her parcel? If that was so, it went some way to weakening the case against her. But it was not so. It was not so because it was utterly improbable that Janie should steal a coat in the afternoon and return to the house the same evening.

'Start at the beginning,' Smiley muttered, a little sententiously, to the crested paper on his lap. 'Janie stole the coat at the same time as she stole the beads – that is, after Stella was dead. Therefore either the coat was not packed with the other clothes, or . . .'

Or what? *Or somebody else, somebody who was not Stella Rode, packed up the clothes after Stella had died and before Dorothy D'Arcy and Mr Cardew went round to North Fields on Friday morning. And why the devil, thought Smiley, should anyone do that?*

It had been one of Smiley's cardinal principles in research, whether among the incunabula of an obscure poet or the laboriously gathered fragments of intelligence, not to proceed beyond the evidence. A fact, once logically arrived at, should not be extended beyond its natural significance. Accordingly he did not speculate with the remarkable discovery he had made, but turned his mind to the most obscure problem of all: motive for murder.

He began writing:

'Dorothy D'Arcy – resentment after refugee fiasco. As a motive for murder – definitely thin.' Yet why did she seem to go out of her way to sing Stella's praises?

'Felix D'Arcy – resented Stella Rode for not observing Carne's standards. As a motive for murder – ludicrous.

'Shane Hecht – hatred.

'Terence Fielding – in a sane world, no conceivable motive.'

Yet was it a sane world? Year in year out they must share the same life, say the same things to the same people, sing the same hymns. They had no money, no hope. The world changed, fashion changed; the women saw it second-hand in the glossy papers, took in their dresses and pinned up their hair, and hated their husbands a little more. Shane Hecht – did she kill Stella Rode? Did she conceal in the sterile omniscience of her huge body not only hatred and jealousy, but the courage to kill? Was she frightened for her stupid husband, frightened of Rode's promotion, of his cleverness? Was she really so angry when Stella refused to take part in the rat race of gentility?

Rigby was right – it was impossible to know. You had to be ill, you had to be sick to understand, you had to be there in the sanatorium, not for weeks, but for years, had to be one in the line of white beds, to know the smell of their food and the greed in their eyes. You had to hear it and see it, to be part of it, to know their rules and recognise their transgressions. This world was compressed into a mould of anomalous conventions: blind, pharisaical but real.

Yet some things were written plain enough: the curious bond which tied Felix D'Arcy and Terence Fielding despite their mutual dislike; D'Arcy's reluctance to discuss the night of the murder; Fielding's evident preference for Stella Rode rather than her husband; Shane Hecht's contempt for everyone.

He could not get Shane out of his mind. If Carne were a rational place, and somebody had to die, then Shane Hecht should clearly be the one. She was a depository of other people's secrets, she had an infallible sense of weakness. Had she not found even Smiley out? She had taunted him with his wretched marriage, she had played with him for her own pleasure. Yes, she was an admirable candidate for murder.

But why on earth should Stella die? Why and how? Who tied up the parcel after her death? And why?

He tried to sleep, but could not. Finally, as the Abbey clock chimed three, he put the light on again and sat up. The room was much warmer and at first Smiley wondered if someone had switched on the central heating in the middle of the night, after it had been off all day. Then he became aware of the sound of rain outside; he went to the window and parted the curtains. A steady rain was falling; by tomorrow the snow would be washed away. Two policemen walked slowly down the road; he could hear the squelch of their boots as they trod in the melting snow. Their wet capes glistened in the arc of the street lamp.

And suddenly he seemed to hear Rigby's voice: 'Blood everywhere. Whoever killed her must have been covered in it.' And then Mad Janie calling to him across the moonlit snow: 'Janie seed 'im . . . silver wings like fishes . . . flying on the wind . . . there's not many seen the devil fly . . .' Of course: the parcel! He remained a long time at the window, watching the rain. Finally, content at last, he climbed back into bed and fell asleep.

He tried to telephone Miss Brimley throughout the morning. Each time she was out and he left no message. Eventually, at about midday, he spoke to her:

'George, I'm terribly sorry – some missionary is in London – I had to go for an interview and I've got a Baptist Conference this afternoon. They've both got to be in this week. Will first thing tomorrow do?'

'Yes,' said Smiley. 'I'm sure it will.' There was no particular hurry. There were one or two ends he wanted to tie up that afternoon, anyway.

Chapter 12

UNCOMFORTABLE WORDS

H e enjoyed the bus. The conductor was a very surly man with a great deal to say about the bus company, and why it lost money. Gently encouraged by Smiley, he expanded wonderfully so that by the time they arrived at Sturminster he had transformed the Directors of the Dorset and General Traction Company into a herd of Gadarene swine charging into the abyss of voluntary bankruptcy. The conductor directed Smiley to the Sturminster kennels, and when he alighted in the tiny village, he set out confidently towards a group of cottages which stood about a quarter of a mile beyond the church, on the Okeford road.

He had a nasty feeling he wasn't going to like Mr Harriman. The very fact that D'Arcy had described him as a superior type of person inclined Smiley against him. Smiley was not opposed to social distinctions but he liked to make his own.

A notice stood at the gate: '*Sturminster Kennels, proprietor, C. J. Reid-Harriman, Veterinary Surgeon. Breeder of Alsatian and Labrador Dogs. Boarding.*'

A narrow path led to what seemed to be a backyard. There was washing everywhere, shirts, underclothes, and sheets, most of it khaki. There was a rich smell of dog. There was a rusted hand-pump with a dozen or so dog leads draped over it, and there was a small girl. She watched him sadly as he picked his way through the thick mud towards the door. He pulled on the bell-rope and waited. He tried again, and the child said:

'It doesn't work. It's bust. It's been bust for years.'

'Is anyone at home?' Smiley asked.

'I'll see,' she replied coolly, and after another long look at him she walked round the side of the house and disappeared from view. Then Smiley heard from inside the house the sound of someone approaching, and a moment later the door opened.

'Good day to you.' He had sandy hair and a moustache. He wore a khaki shirt and a khaki tie of a lighter shade; old Service dress trousers and a tweed jacket with leather buttons.

'Mr Harriman?'

'Major,' he replied lightly. 'Not that it matters, old boy. What can we do for you?'

'I'm thinking of buying an Alsatian,' Smiley replied, 'as a guard dog.'

'Surely. Come in, won't you. Lady wife's out. Ignore the child: she's from next door. Just hangs around; likes the dogs.' He followed Harriman into the living-room and they sat down. There was no fire.

'Where are you from?' Harriman asked.

'I'm staying at Carne at the moment; my father lives over at Dorchester. He's getting on and he's nervous, and he wants me to find him a good dog. There's a gardener to look after it in the daytime, feed it and exercise it and so on. The gardener doesn't live in at night, of course, and it's at night that the old man gets so worried. I've been meaning to get him a dog for some time – this recent business at Carne rather brought it home to me.' Harriman ignored the hint.

'Gardener good chap?'

'Yes, very.'

'You don't want anything brilliant,' said Harriman. 'You want a good, steady type. I'd take a bitch if I were you.' His hands were dark brown, his wrists too. His handkerchief was tucked into his cuff. Smiley noticed that his wrist-watch faced inwards, conforming with the obscure rites of the military *demi-monde* from which he seemed to come.

'What will it do, a dog like that? Will it attack, or what?'

'Depends how she's trained, old boy; depends how she's trained. She'll warn, though; that's the main thing. Frighten the fellers away. Shove a notice up, "Fierce Dog", let her sniff at the tradesmen a bit and the word will get around. You won't get a burglar within a mile of the place.'

They walked out into the garden again, and Harriman led the way to an enclosure with half a dozen Alsatian puppies yapping furiously at them through the wire.

'They're good little beasts, all of them,' he shouted. 'Game as hell.' He unlocked the door and finally emerged with a plump bitch puppy chewing fiercely at his jacket.

'This little lady might do you,' he said. 'We can't show her – she's too dark.'

Smiley pretended to hesitate, allowed Harriman to persuade him and finally agreed. They went back into the house.

'I'd like to pay a deposit,' said Smiley, 'and collect her in about ten days. Would that be all right?' He gave Harriman a cheque for five pounds and again they sat down, Harriman foraging in his desk for inoculation certificates and pedigrees. Then Smiley said:

'It's a pity Mrs Rode didn't have a dog, isn't it? I mean, it might have saved her life.'

'Oh, she *had* a dog, but she had it put down just before she was killed,' said Harriman. 'Damned odd story between ourselves. She was devoted to the beast. Odd little mongrel, bit of everything, but she loved it. Brought it here one day with some tale about it biting the postman, got me to put it down – said it was dangerous. It wasn't anything of the sort. Some friends of mine in Carne made inquiries. No complaints anywhere. Postman liked the brute. Damned silly sort of lie to tell in a small community. Bound to be found out.'

'Why on earth did she tell it then?'

Harriman made a gesture which particularly irritated Smiley. He ran his forefinger down the length of his nose, then flicked either side of his absurd moustache very quickly. There was something shamefaced about the whole movement, as if he were assuming the ways of senior officers, and fearful of rebuke.

'She was trouble,' he said crisply. 'I can spot 'em. I've had a few in the regiment, wives who are trouble. Little simpering types. Butter-wouldn't-melt, holier-than-thou. Arrange the flowers in the church and all that – pious as you please. I'd say she was the hysterical kind, self-dramatising, weeping all over the house for days on end. Anything for a bit of drama.'

'Was she popular?' Smiley offered him a cigarette.

'Shouldn't think so. Thanks. She wore black on Sundays, I gather. Typical. We used to call them "crows" out East, the ones who wore black – Sunday virgins. They were OD mostly

– other denominations. Not C of E – some were Romans, mind . . . I hope I'm not . . .'

'Not at all.'

'You never know, do you? Can't stand 'em myself; no prejudice, but I don't like Romans – that's what my old father used to say.'

'Did you know her husband?'

'Not so well, poor devil, not so well.'

Harriman, Smiley reflected, seemed to have a great deal more sympathy for the living than the dead. Perhaps soldiers were like that. He wouldn't know.

'He's terribly cut up, I hear. Dreadful shock – fortunes of war, eh?' he added and Smiley nodded. 'He's the other type. Humble origin, good officer qualities, credit to the mess. Those are the ones that cut up most, the ones women get at.'

They walked along the path to the gate. Smiley said goodbye, and promised to return in a week or so to collect the puppy. As he walked away Harriman called to him:

'Oh – incidentally . . .'

Smiley stopped and turned round.

'I'll pay that cheque in, shall I, and credit you with the amount?'

'Of course,' said Smiley. 'That will do very well,' and he made his way to the bus stop pondering on the strange byways of the military mind.

The same bus took him back to Carne, the same conductor railed against his employers, the same driver drove the entire distance in second gear. He got out at the station and made his way to the red-brick Tabernacle. Gently opening the Gothic door, made of thickly-varnished ochre pine, he stepped inside. An elderly woman in an apron was polishing the heavy brass chandelier which hung over the centre aisle. He waited a moment, then tiptoed up to her and asked for the Minister. She pointed towards the vestry door. Obeying her mimed directions, he crossed to it, knocked and waited. A tall man in a clerical collar opened the door.

'I'm from the *Christian Voice*,' said Smiley quietly. 'Can I have a word with you?'

Mr Cardew led him through the side entrance and into a

small vegetable garden, carefully tilled, with bright yellow paths running between the empty beds. The sun shone through the crisp air. It was a cold, beautiful day. They crossed the garden and entered a paddock. The ground was hard despite last night's rain, and the grass short. They strolled side by side, talking as they went.

'This is Lammas Land, belonging to the School. We hold our fêtes here in the summer. It's very practical.'

Cardew seemed a little out of character. Smiley, who had a rather childish distrust of clergymen, had expected a Wesleyan hammer, a wordy, forbidding man with a taste for imagery.

'Miss Brimley, our editor, sent me,' Smiley began. 'Mrs Rode subscribed to our journal; her family has taken it since it began. She was almost a part of the family. We wanted to write an obituary about her work for the Church.'

'I see.'

'I managed to have a word with her husband; we wanted to be sure to strike the right note.'

'What did he say?'

'He said I should speak to you about her work – her refugee work particularly.'

They walked on in silence for a while, then Cardew said, 'She came from up North, near Derby. Her father used to be a man of substance in the North – though money never altered him.'

'I know.'

'I've known the family for years, off and on. I saw her old father before the funeral.'

'What may I say about her work for the Church, her influence on the Chapel community here? May I say she was universally loved?'

'I'm afraid,' said Cardew, after a slight pause, 'that I don't hold much with that kind of writing, Mr Smiley. People are never universally loved, even when they're dead.' His North Country accent was strong.

'Then what may I say?' Smiley persisted.

'I don't know,' Cardew replied evenly. 'And when I don't know, I usually keep quiet. But since you're good enough to ask me, I've never met an angel, and Stella Rode was no exception.'

'But was she not a leading figure in refugee work?'

'Yes. Yes, she was.'

'And did she not encourage others to make similar efforts?'

'Of course. She was a good worker.'

They walked on together in silence. The path across the field led downwards, then turned and followed a stream which was almost hidden by the tangled gorse and hawthorn on either side. Beyond the stream was a row of stark elm trees, and behind them the familiar outline of Carne.

'Is that all you wanted to ask me?' said Cardew suddenly.

'No,' replied Smiley. 'Our editor was very worried by a letter she received from Mrs Rode just before her death. It was a kind of . . . accusation. We put the matter before the police. Miss Brimley reproaches herself in some way for not having been able to help her. It's illogical, perhaps, but there it is. I would like to be able to assure her that there was no connexion between Stella Rode's death and this letter. That is another reason for my visit . . .'

'Whom did the letter accuse?'

'Her husband.'

'I should tell your Miss Brimley,' said Cardew slowly, and with some emphasis, 'that she has nothing whatever for which to reproach herself.'

Chapter 13

THE JOURNEY HOME

It was Monday evening. At about the time that Smiley returned to his hotel after his interview with Mr Cardew, Tim Perkins, the Head of Fielding's house, was taking his leave of Mrs Harlowe, who taught him the 'cello. She was a kindly woman, if neurotic, and it distressed her to see him so worried. He was quite the best pupil that Carne had sent her, and she liked him.

'You played foully today, Tim,' she said as she wished him good-bye at the door, 'quite foully. You needn't tell me – you've only got one more Half and you still haven't got three passes in A Level and you've got to get your remove, and you're in a tizz. We won't practise next Monday if you don't want – just come and have buns and we'll play some records.'

'Yes, Mrs Harlowe.' He strapped his music-case on to the carrier of his bicycle.

'Lights working, Tim?'

'Yes, Mrs Harlowe.'

'Well, don't try and beat the record tonight, Tim. You've plenty of time till Boys' Tea. Remember the lane's still quite slippery from the snow.'

Perkins said nothing. He pushed the bicycle on to the gravel path and started towards the gate.

'Haven't you forgotten something, Tim?'

'Sorry, Mrs Harlowe.'

He turned back and shook hands with her in the doorway. She always insisted on that.

'Look, Tim, what *is* the matter? Have you done something silly? You can tell me, can't you? I'm not Staff, you know.'

Perkins hesitated, then said:

'It's just exams, Mrs Harlowe.'

'Are your parents all right? No trouble at home?'

'No, Mrs Harlowe; they're fine.' Again he hesitated, then: 'Good night, Mrs Harlowe.'

'Good night.'

She watched him close the gate behind him and cycle off down the narrow lane. He would be in Carne in a quarter of an hour; it was downhill practically all the way.

Usually he loved the ride home. It was the best moment of the week. But tonight he hardly noticed it. He rode fast, as he always did; the hedge raced against the dark sky and the rabbits scuttled from the beam of his lamp, but tonight he hardly noticed them.

He would have to tell somebody. He should have told Mrs Harlowe; he wished he had. She'd know what to do. Mr Snow would have been all right, but he wasn't up to him for science any longer, he was up to Rode. That was half the trouble. That and Fielding.

He could tell True – yes, that's who he'd tell, he'd tell True. He'd go to Miss Truebody tonight after evening surgery and he'd tell her the truth. His father would never get over it, of course, because it meant failure and perhaps disgrace. It meant not getting to Sandhurst at the end of next Half, it meant more money they couldn't afford . . .

He was coming to the steepest part of the hill. The hedge stopped on one side and instead there was a marvellous view of Sawley Castle against the night sky, like a backcloth for *Macbeth*. He loved acting – he wished the Master let them act at Carne.

He leant forward over the handlebars and allowed himself to gather speed to go through the shallow ford at the bottom of the hill. The cold air bit into his face, and for a moment he almost forgot . . . Suddenly he braked; felt the bike skid wildly beneath him.

Something was wrong; there was a light ahead, a flashing light, and a familiar voice calling to him urgently across the darkness.

Chapter 14

THE QUALITY OF MERCY

The Public Schools Committee for Refugee Relief (Patroness: Sarah, Countess of Sawley) has an office in Belgrave Square. It is not at all clear whether this luxurious situation is designed to entice the wealthy or encourage the dispossessed – or, as some irreverent voices in Society whispered, to provide the Countess of Sawley with an inexpensive *pied-à-terre* in the West End of London. The business of assisting refugees has been suitably relegated to the south of the river, to one of those untended squares in Kennington which are part of London's architectural schizophrenia. York Gardens, as the square is called, will one day be discovered by the world, and its charm lost, but go there now, and you may see real children playing hopscotch in the road, and their mothers, shod in bedroom slippers, abusing them from doorways.

Miss Brimley, dispatched on her way by Smiley's telephone call the previous morning, had the rare gift of speaking to children as if they were human beings, and thus discovered without difficulty the dilapidated, unnamed house which served the Committee as a collecting centre. With the assistance of seven small boys, she pulled on the bell and waited patiently. At last she heard the clatter of feet descending an uncarpeted staircase, and the door was opened by a very beautiful girl. They looked at one another with approval for a moment.

'I'm sorry to be a nuisance,' Miss Brimley began, 'but a friend of mine in the country has asked me to make some inquiries about a parcel of clothes that was sent up a day or two ago. She's made rather a stupid mistake.'

'Oh, goodness, how awful,' said the girl pleasantly. 'Would you like to come in? Everything's frightfully chaotic, I'm afraid, and there's nothing to sit on, but we can give you powdered coffee in a mug.'

Miss Brimley followed her in, closing the door firmly on the seven children, who were edging gently forward in her wake. She was in the hall, and everywhere she looked there were parcels of every kind, some wrapped in jute with smart labels, some in brown paper, torn and clumsy, some in crates and laundry baskets, old suitcases and even an antiquated cabin trunk with a faded yellow label on it which read: 'Not wanted on voyage.'

The girl led the way upstairs to what was evidently the office, a large room containing a deal table littered with correspondence, and a kitchen chair. An oil stove sputtered in one corner, and an electric kettle was steaming in a melancholy way beside it. 'I'm sorry,' said the girl as they entered the room, 'but there just isn't anywhere to talk downstairs. I mean, one can't talk on one leg like the Incas. Or isn't it Incas? Perhaps it's Afghans. However did you find us?'

'I went to your West End office first,' Miss Brimley replied, 'and they told me I should come and see you. I think they were rather cross. After that I relied on children. They always know the way. You are Miss Dawney, aren't you?'

'Lord, no. I'm the sort of daily help. Jill Dawney's gone to see the Customs people at Rotherhithe – she'll be back at tea time if you want to see her.'

'Gracious, my dear, I'm sure I shan't keep you two minutes. A friend of mine who lives in Carne – ('Goodness! How grand,' said the girl) she's a sort of cousin really, but it's simpler to call her a friend, isn't it? – gave an old grey dress to the refugee people last Thursday and now she's convinced she left her brooch pinned to the bodice. I'm sure she hasn't done anything of the sort, mind you – she's a scatter-brain creature – but she rang me yesterday morning in a dreadful state and made me promise to come round at once and ask. I couldn't come yesterday, unfortunately – tied to my little paper from dawn till dusk. But I gather you're a bit behind, so it won't be too late?'

'Gosh, no! We're miles behind. That's all the stuff downstairs, waiting to be unpacked and sorted. It comes from the voluntary reps. at each school – sometimes boys and sometimes staff – and they put all the clothes together and send them up in big parcels, either by train or ordinary mail, usually by train. We sort them here before sending abroad.'

'That's what I gathered from Jane. As soon as she realised she'd made this mistake she got hold of the woman doing the collecting and sending, but of course it was too late. The parcel had gone.'

'How frantic . . . Do you know when the parcel was sent off?'

'Yes. On Friday morning.'

'From Carne? Train or post?'

Miss Brimley had been dreading this question, but she made a guess:

'Post, I believe.'

Darting past Miss Brimley, the girl foraged among the pile of papers on her desk and finally produced a stiff-backed exercise book with a label on it marked 'Ledger'. Opening it at random, she whisked quickly back and forth through the pages, licking the tip of one finger now and then in a harassed sort of way.

'Wouldn't have arrived till yesterday at the earliest,' she said. 'We certainly won't have opened it yet. Honestly, I don't know how we shall *ever* cope, and with Easter coming up we shall just get worse and worse. On top of that, half our stuff is rotting in the Customs sheds – hullo, here we are!' She pushed the ledger over to Miss Brimley, her slim finger pointing to a pencilled entry in the central column: 'Carne, parcel post, 27 lb.'

'I wonder,' said Miss Brimley, 'whether you would mind awfully if we had a quick look inside?'

They went downstairs to the hall.

'It's not quite as hideous as it looks,' the girl called over her shoulder. 'All the Monday lot will be nearest the door.'

'How do you know where they come from if you can't read the postmark?' asked Miss Brimley as the girl began to forage among the parcels.

'We issue volunteer reps. with our printed labels. The labels have an originator's number on. In other cases we just ask them to write the name of the school in capitals on the outside. You see, we simply can't allow covering letters; it would be *too* desperate. When we get a parcel all we have to do is send off a printed card acknowledging with thanks receipt of a parcel of such and such a date weighing so and so much.

People who aren't reps. won't send parcels to this address, you see – they'll send to the advertised address in Belgrave Square.'

'Does the system work?'

'No,' replied the girl, 'it doesn't. The reps. either forget to use our labels or they run out and can't be bothered to tell us. Ten days later they ring up in a rage because they haven't had an acknowledgement. Reps. change, too, without letting us know, and the packing and labelling instructions don't get passed on. Sometimes the boys will suddenly decide to do it themselves, and no one tells them the way to go about it. Lady Sarah gets as mad as a snake if parcels turn up at Head Office – they all have to be carted over here for repacking and inventories.'

'I see.' Miss Brimley watched anxiously as the girl foraged among the parcels, still talking.

'Did you say your friend actually *taught* at Carne? She must be terribly grand. I wonder what the Prince is like: he looks rather soft in his photographs. My cousin went to Carne – he's an utter wet. Do you know what he told me? During Ascot week they all . . . Hello! Here we are!' The girl stood up, a large square parcel in her arms, and carried it to a table which stood in the shadow of the staircase. Miss Brimley, standing beside her as she began carefully to untie the stout twine, looked curiously at the printed label. In its top left-hand corner was stamped the symbol which the Committee had evidently allocated to Carne: C4. After the four the letter B had been written in with ballpoint pen.

'What does the B mean?' asked Miss Brimley.

'Oh, that's a local arrangement at Carne. Miss D'Arcy's the rep. there, but they've done so well recently that she coopted a friend to help with dispatch. When we acknowledge we always mention whether it was A or B. B must be terribly keen, whoever she is.'

Miss Brimley forbore from inquiring what proportion of the parcels from Carne had originated from Miss D'Arcy, and what proportion from her anonymous assistant.

The girl removed the string and turned the parcel upside down in order to liberate the overlap of wrapping paper. As she did so Miss Brimley caught sight of a faint brown smudge, no more, about the size of a shilling, near the join. It was consistent with her essential rationalism that she should search for any explanation other than that which so loudly presented itself. The girl continued the work of unwrapping, saying suddenly: 'I say, Carne was where they had that dreadful murder, wasn't it – that master's wife who got killed by the gypsy? It really *is* awful, isn't it, how much of that kind of thing goes on? Hm! Thought as much,' she remarked, suddenly interrupting herself. She had removed the outer paper, and was about to unwrap the bundle inside when her attention was evidently arrested by the appearance of the inner parcel.

'What?' Miss Brimley said quickly.

The girl laughed. 'Oh, only the packing,' she said. 'The C4Bs are usually so neat – quite the best we get. This is quite different. Not the same person at all. Must be a stand-in. I thought so from the outside.'

'How can you be so sure?'

'Oh, it's like handwriting. We can tell.' She laughed again, and without more ado removed the last wrapping. 'Grey dress, you said, didn't you? Let's see.' With both hands she began picking clothes from the top of the pile and laying them to either side. She was nearly half-way through when she exclaimed, 'Well, *honestly*! They must be having a brain-storm,' and drew from the bundle of partworn clothes a transparent plastic mackintosh, a very old pair of leather gloves, and a pair of rubber overshoes.

Miss Brimley was holding the edge of the table very tightly. The palms of her hands were throbbing.

'Here's a cape. Damp, too,' the girl added in disgust, and tossed the offending articles on to the floor beside the table. Miss Brimley could only think of Smiley's letter: 'Whoever killed her must have been covered in blood.' Yes, and whoever killed her wore a plastic cape and a hood, rubber overshoes and those old leather gloves with the terra-cotta stains. Whoever killed Stella Rode had not chanced upon her in the night, but had plotted long ahead, had waited. 'Yes,' thought Miss Brimley, 'had waited for the long nights.'

The girl was talking to her again: 'I'm afraid it really isn't here.'

'No, my dear,' Miss Brimley replied, 'I see that. Thank you.

You've been very sweet.' Her voice faltered for a moment, then she managed to say: 'I think, my dear, you should leave the parcel exactly as it is now, the wrapping and everything in it. Something very dreadful has happened, and the police will want to . . . know about it and see the parcel . . . You must trust me, my dear – things aren't quite what they seem . . .' And somehow she escaped to the comforting freedom of York Gardens and the large-eyed wonder of its waiting children.

She went to a telephone box. She got through to the Sawley Arms and asked a very bored receptionist for Mr Smiley. Total silence descended on the line until the Trunks operator asked her to put in another three and sixpence. Miss Brimley replied sharply that all she had so far had for her money was a three-minute vacuum; this was followed by the unmistakable sound of the operator sucking her teeth, and then, quite suddenly, by George Smiley's voice.

'George, it's Brim. A plastic mackintosh, a cape, rubber overshoes, and some leather gloves that look as though they're stained with blood. Smudges on some of the wrapping paper too by the look of it.'

A pause.

'Handwriting on the outside of the parcel?'

'None. The Charity organisers issue printed labels.'

'Where is the stuff now? Have you got it?'

'No. I've told the girl to leave everything exactly as it is. It'll be all right for an hour or two . . . George, are you there?'

'Yes.'

'Who did it? Was it the husband?'

'I don't know. I just don't know.'

'Do you want me to do anything – about the clothes, I mean? Phone Sparrow or anything?'

'No. I'll see Rigby at once. Good-bye, Brim. Thanks for ringing.'

She put back the receiver. He sounded strange, she thought. He seemed to lose touch sometimes. As if he'd switched off.

She walked north-west towards the Embankment. It was long after ten o'clock – the first time she'd been late for Heaven knows how long. She had better take a taxi. Being a frugal woman, however, she took a bus.

Ailsa Brimley did not believe in emergencies, for she enjoyed a discipline of mind uncommon in men and even rarer in women. The greater the emergency, the greater her calm. John Landsbury had remarked upon it: 'You have sales resistance to the dramatic, Brim; the rare gift of contempt for what is urgent. I know of a dozen people who would pay you five thousand a year for telling them every day that what is important is seldom urgent. Urgent equals ephemeral, and ephemeral equals unimportant.'

She got out of the bus, carefully putting the ticket in the rubbish compartment. As she stood in the warm sunlight of the street she caught sight of the hoardings advertising the first edition of the evening papers. If it hadn't been for the sun, she might never have looked; but the sun dazzled her and made her glance downwards. And so she did see; she read it in the plump black of the wet newsprint, in the prepacked hysteria of Fleet Street: 'All-night search for missing Carne boy.'

Chapter 15

THE ROAD TO FIELDING

S miley put down the receiver and walked quickly past the reception desk towards the front door. He must see Rigby at once. Just as he was leaving the hotel he heard his name called. Turning, he saw his old enemy, the night porter, braving the light of day, beckoning to him like Charon with his grey hand.

'They've been on to you from the police station,' he observed with undisguised pleasure. 'Mr Rigby wants you, the Inspector. You're to go there at once. At once, see?'

'I'm on my way there now,' Smiley replied irritably, and as he pushed his way through the swing doors he heard the old man repeat; 'At once, mind; they're waiting for you.'

Making his way through the Carne streets, he reflected for the hundredth time on the obscurity of motive in human action: there is no true thing on earth. There is no constant, no dependable point, not even in the purest logic or the most obscure mysticism; least of all in the motives of men when they are moved to act violently.

Had the murderer, now so near discovery, found contentment in the meticulous administration of his plans? For now it was clear beyond a doubt; this was a murder devised to the last detail, even to the weapon inexplicably far from the place of its use; a murder with clues cast to mislead, a murder planned to look unplanned, a murder for a string of beads. Now the mystery of the footprints was solved: having put the overshoes into the parcel, the murderer had walked down the path to the gate, and his own prints had been obscured by the subsequent traffic of feet.

Rigby looked tired.

'You've heard the news, sir, I suppose?'

'What news?'

'About the boy, the boy in Fielding's house, missing all night?'

'No.' Smiley felt suddenly sick. 'No, I've heard nothing.'

'Good Lord, I thought you knew! Half past eight last night Fielding rang us here. Perkins, his head boy, hadn't come back from a music lesson with Mrs Harlowe, who lives over to Longemede. We put out an alert and started looking for him. They sent a patrol car along the road he should have come back on – he was cycling, you see. The first time they didn't see anything, but on the way back the driver stopped the car at the bottom of Longemede Hill, just where the water-splash is. It occurred to him the lad might have taken a long run at the water-splash from the top of the hill, and come to grief in the dip. They found him half in the ditch, his bike beside him. Dead.'

'Oh, my dear God.'

'We didn't let on to the press at first. The boy's parents are in Singapore. The father's an Army officer. Fielding sent them a telegram. We've got on to the War Office, too.'

They were silent for a moment, then Smiley asked, 'How did it happen?'

'We've closed the road and we've been trying to reconstruct the accident. I've got a detective over there now, just having a look. Trouble is, we couldn't do much till the morning. Besides, the men trampled everywhere; you can't blame them. It looks as though he must have fallen near the bottom of the hill and hit his head on a stone: his right temple.'

'How did Fielding take it?'

'He was very shaken. Very shaken indeed. I wouldn't have believed it, to be quite honest. He just seemed to . . . give up. There was a lot that had to be done – telegraph the parents, get in touch with the boy's uncle at Windsor, and so on. But he just left all that to Miss Truebody, his housekeeper. If it hadn't been for her, I don't know how he'd have managed. I was with him for about half an hour, then he just broke down, completely, and asked to be left alone.'

'How do you mean, broke down?' Smiley asked quickly.

'He cried. Wept like a child,' said Rigby evenly. 'I'd never have thought it.'

Smiley offered Rigby a cigarette and took one himself.

'I suppose,' he ventured, 'it was an accident?'

'I suppose so,' Rigby replied woodenly.

'Perhaps,' said Smiley, 'before we go any farther, I'd better give you my news. I was on my way to see you when you rang. I've just heard from Miss Brimley.' And in his precise, rather formal way he related all that Ailsa Brimley had told him, and how he had become curious about the contents of the parcel.

Smiley waited while Rigby telephoned to London. Almost mechanically, Rigby described what he wanted done: the parcel and its contents were to be collected and arrangements made to subject them immediately to forensic examination; the surfaces should be tested for fingerprints. He would be coming up to London himself with some samples of a boy's handwriting and an examination paper; he would want the opinion of a handwriting expert. No, he would be coming by train on the 4.25 from Carne, arriving at Waterloo at 8.05. Could a car be sent to the station to collect him? There was silence, then Rigby said testily, 'All right, I'll take a ruddy taxi,' and rang off rather abruptly. He looked at Smiley angrily for a moment, then grinned, plucked at his ear and said:

'Sorry, sir; getting a bit edgy.' He indicated the far wall with his head and added, 'Fighting on too many fronts, I suppose. I shall have to tell the Chief about that parcel, but he's out shooting at the moment – only pigeon, with a couple of friends, he won't be long – but I haven't mentioned your presence here in Carne, as a matter of fact, and if you don't mind I'll . . .'

'Of course,' Smiley cut in quickly. 'It's much simpler if you keep me out of it.'

'I shall tell him it was just a routine inquiry. We shall have to mention Miss Brimley later . . . but there's no point in making things worse, is there?'

'No.'

'I shall have to let Janie go, I suppose . . . She was right, wasn't she? Silver wings in the moonlight.'

'I wouldn't – no, I wouldn't let her go, Rigby,' said Smiley with unaccustomed vehemence. 'Keep her with you as long as you can possibly manage. No more accidents, for heaven's sake. We've had enough.'

'Then you don't believe Perkins's death was an accident?'

105

'Good Lord, no,' cried Smiley suddenly, 'and nor do you, do you?'

'I've put a detective on to it,' Rigby replied coolly. 'I can't take the case myself. I shall be needed on the Rode murder. The Chief will have to call the Yard in now; there'll be hell to pay, I can tell you. He thought it was all over bar the shouting.'

'And in the meantime?'

'In the meantime, sir, I'm going to do my damnedest to find out who killed Stella Rode.'

'If,' said Smiley slowly, 'if you find fingerprints on that mackintosh, which I doubt, will you have anything . . . local . . . to compare them with?'

'We've got Rode's, of course, and Janie's.'

'But not Fielding's?'

Rigby hesitated.

'As a matter of fact, we have,' he said at last. 'From long ago. But nothing to do with this kind of thing.'

'It was during the war,' said Smiley. 'His brother told me. Up in the North. It was hushed up, wasn't it?'

Rigby nodded. 'So far as I heard, only the D'Arcys knew; and the Master, of course. It happened in the holidays – some Air Force boy. The Chief was very helpful . . .'

Smiley shook hands with Rigby and made his way down the familiar pine staircase. He noticed again the vaguely institutional smell of floor polish and carbolic soap, like the smell at Fielding's house.

He walked slowly back towards the Sawley Arms. At the point where he should have turned left to his hotel, however, he hesitated, then seemed to change his mind. Slowly, almost reluctantly, he crossed the road to the Abbey Close, and walked along the southern edge towards Fielding's house. He looked worried, almost frightened.

Chapter 16

A TASTE FOR MUSIC

Miss Truebody opened the door. The rims of her eyes were pink, as though she had been weeping.

'I wonder if I might see Mr Fielding? To say good-bye.'

She hesitated: 'Mr Fielding's very upset. I doubt whether he'll want to see anyone.' He followed her into the hall and watched her go to the study door. She knocked, inclined her head, then gently turned the handle and let herself in. It was a long time before she returned. 'He'll be out shortly,' she said, without looking at him. 'Will you take off your coat?' She waited while he struggled out of his overcoat, then took it from him and hung it beside the Van Gogh chair. They stood together in silence, both looking towards the study door.

Then, quite suddenly, Fielding was standing in the half-open doorway, unshaven and in his shirt-sleeves. 'For Christ's sake,' he said thickly. 'What do you want?'

'I just wanted to say good-bye, Fielding, and to offer you my condolences.'

Fielding looked at him hard for a moment; he was leaning heavily against the doorway. 'Well, good-bye. Thank you for calling.' He waved one hand vaguely in the air. 'You needn't have bothered really, need you?' he added rudely. 'You could have sent me a card, couldn't you?'

'I could have done, yes; it just seemed so very tragic, when he was so near success.'

'What do you mean? What the devil do you mean?'

'I mean in his work . . . the improvement. Simon Snow was telling me all about it. Amazing really, the way Rode brought him on.'

A long silence, then Fielding spoke: 'Good-bye, Smiley. Thanks for coming.' He was turning back into the study as Smiley called:

'Not at all . . . not at all. I suppose poor Rode must have

been bucked with those exam. results, too. I mean it was more or less a matter of life and death for Perkins, passing that exam., wasn't it? He wouldn't have got his remove next Half if he'd failed in science. They might have superannuated him, I suppose, even though he was head of the house; then he couldn't have sat for the Army. Poor Perkins, he had a lot to thank Rode for, didn't he? And you, too, Fielding, I'm sure. You must have helped him wonderfully . . . both of you did, you and Rode; Rode and Fielding. His parents ought to know that. They're rather hard up, I gather; the father's in the Army, isn't he, in Singapore? It must have been a great effort keeping the boy at Carne. It will comfort them to know how much was done for him, won't it, Fielding?'

Smiley was very pale. 'You've heard the latest, I suppose,' he continued. 'About that wretched gypsy woman who killed Stella Rode? They've decided she's fit to plead. I suppose they'll hang her. That'll be the third death, won't it? You know, I'll tell you an odd thing – just between ourselves, Fielding. I don't believe she did it. Do you? I don't believe she did it at all.'

He was not looking at Fielding. He had clasped his little hands tightly behind his back, and he stood with his shoulders bowed and his head inclined to one side, as though listening for an answer.

Fielding seemed to feel Smiley's words like a physical pain. Slowly he shook his head:

'No,' he said; 'no. Carne killed them; it was Carne. It could only happen here. It's the game we play: the exclusion game. Divide and rule!' He looked Smiley full in the face, and shouted: 'Now for God's sake go! You've got what you want, haven't you? You can pin me on your little board, can't you?' And then, to Smiley's distress, he began sobbing in great uncontrollable gulps, holding his hand across his brow. He appeared suddenly grotesque, stemming the childish tears with his chalky hand, his cumbersome feet turned inwards. Gently, Smiley coaxed him back into the study, gently sat him before the dead fire. Then he began talking to him softly and with compassion.

'If what I think is true, there isn't much time,' he began. 'I want you to tell me about Tim Perkins – about the exam.'

Fielding, his face buried in his hands, nodded.

'He would have failed, wouldn't he? He would have failed and not got his remove; he'd have had to leave.' Fielding was silent. 'After the exam. that day, Rode gave him the writing-case to bring here, the case that contained the papers; Rode was doing chapel duty that week and wouldn't be going home before dinner, but he wanted to correct the papers that night, after his dinner with you.'

Fielding took his hands from his face and leant back in his chair, his great head tilted back, his eyes closed. Smiley continued:

'Perkins came home, and that evening he brought the case to you, as Rode told him to, for safe keeping. Perkins, after all, was head of your house, a responsible boy . . . He gave you the case and you asked him how he'd done in the exam.'

'He wept,' said Fielding suddenly. 'He wept as only a child can.'

'And after breaking down he told you he had cheated? That he had looked up the answers and copied them on to his paper. Is that right? And after the murder of Stella Rode he remembered what else he had seen in the suitcase?'

Fielding was standing up. 'No! Don't you see? Tim wouldn't have cheated to save his life! That's the whole point, the whole bloody irony of it,' he shouted. 'He never cheated at all. *I* cheated for him.'

'But you couldn't! You couldn't copy his handwriting!'

'He wrote with a ball-pen. It was only formulae and diagrams. When he'd gone, and left me alone with the case, I looked at his paper. It was hopeless – he'd only done two out of seven questions. So I cheated for him. I just cribbed them from the science book, and wrote them with blue ballpoint, the kind we all use. Abbots' sell them. I copied his hand as best I could. It only needed about three lines of figures. The rest was diagrams.'

'Then it was you who opened the case? You who saw . . .'

'Yes. It was me, I tell you, not Tim! He couldn't cheat to save his life! But Tim paid for it, don't you see? When the marks were published. Tim must have known something was wrong with them. After all, he'd only attempted two questions

109

out of seven and yet he'd got sixty-one per cent. But he knew *nothing* else, *nothing!*'

For a long time neither spoke. Fielding was standing over Smiley, exultant with the relief of sharing his secret, and Smiley was looking vaguely past him, his face drawn in deep concentration.

'And of course,' he said finally, 'when Stella was murdered, you knew who had done it.'

'Yes,' replied Fielding. 'I knew that Rode had killed her.'

Fielding poured himself a brandy and gave one to Smiley. He seemed to have recovered his self-control. He sat down and looked at Smiley thoughtfully for a time.

'I've got no money,' he said at last. 'None. Nobody knows that except the Master. Oh, they know I'm more or less broke, but they don't know *how* broke. Long ago I made an ass of myself. I got into trouble. It was in the war, when staff was impossible. I had a boys' house and was practically running the school – D'Arcy and I. We were running it together, and the Master running us. Then I made an ass of myself. It was during the holidays. I was up North at the time, giving a course of talks at an RAF educational place. And I stepped out of line. Badly. They pulled me in. And along came D'Arcy wearing his country overcoat and bringing the Master's terms: Come back to Carne, my dear fellow, and we'll say no more about it; go on running your house, my dear fellow, and giving of your wisdom. There's been no publicity. We know it will never happen again, my dear fellow, and we're dreadfully hard up for staff. Come back as a temporary. So I did, and I've been one ever since, going cap in hand to darling D'Arcy every December asking for my contract to be renewed. And, of course – no pension. I shall have to teach at a crammer's. There's a place in Somerset where they'll take me. I'm seeing their Headmaster in London on Thursday. It's a sort of breaker's yard for old dons. The Master had to know, because he gave me a reference.'

'That was why you couldn't tell anyone? Because of Perkins?'

'In a way, yes. I mean they'd want to know all sorts of things. I did it for Tim, you see. The Governors wouldn't have liked that much . . . inordinate affection . . . It looks bad, doesn't it? But it wasn't that kind of affection, Smiley, not any more. You never heard him play the 'cello. He wasn't marvellous, but just sometimes he would play so beautifully, with a kind of studious simplicity, that was indescribably good. He was an awkward boy, and when he played well it was such a surprise. You should have heard him play.'

'You didn't want to drag him into it. If you told the police what you had seen it would ruin Tim too?'

Fielding nodded. 'In the whole of Carne, he was the one thing I loved.'

'Loved?' asked Smiley.

'For God's sake,' said Fielding in an exhausted voice, 'why not?'

'His parents wanted him to go to Sandhurst; I didn't, I'm afraid. I thought that if I could keep him here another Half or two I might be able to get him a music scholarship. That's why I made him Head of House: I wanted his parents to keep him on because he was doing so well.' Fielding paused. 'He was a rotten Head of House,' he added.

'And what exactly was in the writing-case,' Smiley asked, 'when you opened it that evening to look at Tim's exam. paper?'

'A sheet of transparent plastic . . . it may have been one of those pack-away cape things – an old pair of gloves, and a pair of home-made galoshes.'

'Home-made?'

'Yes. Hacked from a pair of Wellington boots, I should think.'

'That's all?'

'No. There was a length of heavy cable, I presumed for demonstrating something in his science lessons. It seemed natural enough in winter to carry waterproofs about. Then, after the murder, I realised how he had done it.'

'Did you know,' he asked Smiley, '*why* he had done it?'

Fielding seemed to hesitate: 'Rode's a guinea-pig,' he began, 'the first man we've had from a grammar school. Most of us are old Carnians ourselves, in fact. Focused when we start. Rode wasn't, and Carne thrilled him. The very name Carne means quality, and Rode loved quality. His wife wasn't like that. She had her standards and they were different, but just as good. I used to watch Rode in the Abbey sometimes on Sunday mornings. Tutors sit at the end of pews, right by the aisle, you know. I used to watch his face as the choir processed past him in white and scarlet, and the Master in his doctor's robes and the Governors and Guardians behind him. Rode was drunk – drunk with the pride of Carne. We're heady wine for the grammar school men, you know. It must have hurt him terribly that Stella wouldn't share any of that. You could see it did. The night they came to dinner with me, the night she died, they argued. I never told anyone, but they did. The Master had preached a sermon at Compline that evening: "Hold fast to that which is good." Rode talked about it at dinner; he couldn't take much drink, you know, he wasn't used to it. He was full of this sermon and of the eloquence of the Master. She never came to the Abbey – she went to that drab tabernacle by the station. He went on and on about the beauty of the Abbey service, the dignity, the reverence. She kept quiet till he'd finished, then laughed, and said: "Poor old Stan. You'll always be Stan to me." I've never seen anyone so angry as he was then. He went quite pale.'

Fielding swept his white hair from his eyes and went on, with something like the old panache: 'I've watched her, too, at meals. Not just here, but at dinner parties elsewhere, when we've both been invited. I've watched her do the simplest things – like eating an apple. She'd peel it in one piece, round and round till the whole peel fell off. Then she'd cut the apple and dice the quarters, getting it all ready before she ate it. She might have been a miner's wife preparing it for her husband. She must have *seen* how people do things here, but it never occurred to her that she ought to copy them. I admire that. So do you, I expect. But Carne doesn't – and Rode didn't; above all, Rode didn't. He'd watch her, and I think he grew to hate her for not conforming. He came to see her as the bar to his success, the one factor which would deprive him of a great career. Once he'd reached that conclusion, what could he do? He couldn't divorce her – that would do him more harm than remaining married to her. Rode knew what Carne would think of divorce; we're a Church foundation, remember. So he killed her. He plotted a squalid murder, and with his little scientist's mind he gave them all the clues they wanted. Fabricated clues. Clues that would point to a murderer who didn't exist. But something went wrong; Tim Perkins got sixty-one per cent. He'd got an impossible mark – he must have cheated. He'd had the opportunity – he'd had the papers in the case. Rode put his little mind to it and decided what had happened: Tim had opened the case and he'd seen the cape and the boots and the gloves. And the cable. So Rode killed him too.'

With surprising energy, Fielding got up and gave himself more brandy. His face was flushed, almost exultant.

Smiley stood up. 'When did you say you'll be coming to London? Thursday, wasn't it?'

'Yes. I had arranged to lunch with my crammer man at one of those dreadful clubs in Pall Mall. I always go into the wrong one, don't you? But I'm afraid there's not much point in my seeing him now, is there, if all this is going to come out? Not even a crammer's will take me then.'

Smiley hesitated.

'Come and dine with me that evening. Spend the night if you want. I'll ask one or two other people. We'll have a party. You'll feel better by then. We can talk a bit. I might be able to help you . . . for Adrian's sake.'

'Thank you. I should like to. Interview apart, I've got some odds and ends to clear up in London, anyway.'

'Good. Quarter to eight. Bywater Street, Chelsea, number 9A.' Fielding wrote it down in his diary. His hand was quite steady.

'Black tie?' asked Fielding, his pen poised, and some imp made Smiley reply:

'I usually do, but it doesn't matter.' There was a moment's silence.

'I suppose,' Fielding began tentatively, 'that all this *will* come out in the trial, about Tim and me? I'll be ruined if it does, you know, ruined.'

'I don't see how they can prevent it.'

'I feel much better now, anyway,' said Fielding; 'much.'

With a cursory good-bye, Smiley left him alone. He walked quickly back to the police station, reasonably confident that Terence Fielding was the most accomplished liar he had met for a long time.

Chapter 17

RABBIT RUN

H e knocked on Rigby's door and walked straight in. 'I'm awfully afraid you'll have to arrest Stanley Rode,' he began, and recounted his interview with Fielding.

'I shall have to tell the Chief,' said Rigby doubtfully. 'Would you like to repeat all that in front of him? If we're going to pull in a Carne master, I think the Chief had better know first. He's just come back. Hang on a minute.' He picked up the telephone on his desk and asked for the Chief Constable. A few minutes later they were walking in silence down a carpeted corridor. On either wall hung photographs of rugby and cricket teams, some yellow and faded from the Indian sun, others done in a sepia tint much favoured by Carne photographers in the early part of the century. At intervals along the corridor stood empty buckets of brilliant red, with FIRE printed carefully in white on the outside. At the far end of the corridor was a dark oak door. Rigby knocked and waited. There was silence. He knocked again and was answered with a cry of 'Come!'

Two very large spaniels watched them come in. Behind the spaniels, at an enormous desk, Brigadier Havelock, O.B.E., Chief Constable of Carne, sat like a water rat on a raft.

The few strands of white hair which ran laterally across his otherwise bald head were painstakingly adjusted to cover the maximum area. This gave him an oddly wet look, as if he had just emerged from the river. His moustache, which lavishly compensated for the scarcity of other hair, was yellow and appeared quite solid. He was a very small man, and he wore a brown suit and a stiff white collar with rounded corners.

'Sir,' Rigby began, 'may I introduce Mr Smiley from London?'

He came out from behind his desk as if he were giving himself up, unconvinced but resigned. Then he pushed out a little, knobbly hand and said, 'From London, eh? How d'you do, sir,' all at once, as if he'd learnt it by heart.

'Mr Smiley's here on a private visit, sir,' Rigby continued. 'He is an acquaintance of Mr Fielding.'

'Quite a card, Fielding, quite a card,' the Chief Constable snapped.

'Yes, indeed, sir,' said Rigby, and went on:

'Mr Smiley called on Mr Fielding just now, sir, to take his leave before returning to London.' Havelock shot a beady glance at Smiley, as if wondering whether he were fit to make the journey.

'Mr Fielding made a kind of statement, which he substantiated with new evidence of his own. About the murder, sir.'

'Well, Rigby?' he said challengingly. Smiley intervened:

'He said that the husband had done it; Stanley Rode. Fielding said that when his head boy brought him Rode's writing-case containing the examination papers . . .'

'What examination papers?'

'Rode was invigilating that afternoon, you remember. He was also doing chapel duty before going on to dinner at Fielding's house. As an expediency, he gave the papers to Perkins to take . . .'

'The boy who had the accident?' Havelock asked.

'Yes.'

'You know a lot about it,' said Havelock darkly.

'Fielding said that when Perkins brought him the case, Fielding opened it. He wanted to see how Perkins had done in the science paper. It was vital to the boy's future that he should get his remove,' Smiley went on.

'Oh, work's the only thing now,' said Havelock bitterly. 'Wasn't the way when I was a boy here, I assure you.'

'When Fielding opened the case, the papers were inside. So was a plastic cape, an old pair of leather gloves, and a pair of rubber overshoes, cut from Wellingtons.'

A pause.

'Good God! Good God! Hear that, Rigby? That's what they found in the parcel in London. Good God!'

'Finally, there was a length of cable, heavy cable, in the case as well. It was this writing-case that Rode went back for, you remember, on the night of the murder,' Smiley concluded. It was like feeding a child – you couldn't overload the spoon.

There was a very long silence indeed. Then Rigby, who seemed to know his man, said:

'Motive was self-advancement in the profession, sir. Mrs Rode showed no desire to improve her station, dressed in a slovenly manner and took no part in the religious life of the school.'

'Just a minute,' said Havelock. 'Rode planned the murder from the start, correct?'

'Yes, sir.'

'He wanted to make it look like robbery with violence.'

'Yes, sir.'

'Having collected the writing-case, he walked back to North Fields. Then what does he do?'

'He puts on the plastic cape and hood, overshoes and gloves. He arms himself with the weapon, sir. He lets himself in by the garden gate, crosses the back garden, goes to the front door and rings the bell, sir. His wife comes to the door. He knocks her down, drags her to the conservatory and murders her. He rinses the clothes under the tap and puts them in the parcel. Having sealed the parcel, he walks down the drive this time to the front gate, following the path, sir, knowing that his own footprints will soon be obscured by other people's. Having got to the road, where the snow was hard and showed no prints, he turned round and re-entered the house, playing the part of the distressed husband, taking care, when he discovers the body, sir, to put his own fingerprints over the glove-marks. There was one article that was too dangerous to send, sir. The weapon.'

'All right, Rigby. Pull him in. Mr Borrow will give you a warrant if you want one; otherwise I'll ring Lord Sawley.'

'Yes, sir. And I'll send Sergeant Low to take a full statement from Mr Fielding, sir?'

'Why the devil didn't he speak up earlier, Rigby?'

'Have to ask him that, sir,' said Rigby woodenly, and left the room.

'You a Carnian?' Havelock asked, pushing a silver cigarette-box across the desk.

'No. No, I'm afraid not,' Smiley replied.

'How d'you know Fielding?'

'We met at Oxford after the war.'

'Queer card, Fielding, very queer. Say your name was Smiley?'

'Yes.'

'There was a fellow called Smiley married Ann Sercombe, Lord Sawley's cousin. Damned pretty girl, Ann was, and went and married this fellow. Some funny little beggar in the Civil Service with an OBE and a gold watch. Sawley was damned annoyed.' Smiley said nothing. 'Sawley's got a son at Carne. Know that?'

'I read it in the press, I think.'

'Tell me – this fellow Rode. He's a grammar school chap, isn't he?'

'I believe so, yes.'

'Damned odd business. Experiments never pay, do they? You can't experiment with tradition.'

'No. No, indeed.'

'That's the trouble today. Like Africa. Nobody seems to understand you can't build society overnight. It takes centuries to make a gentleman.' Havelock frowned to himself and fiddled with the paper-knife on his desk.

'Wonder how he got his cable into that ditch, the thing he killed her with. He wasn't out of our sight for forty-eight hours after the murder.'

'That,' said Smiley, 'is what puzzles me. So does Jane Lyn.'

'What d'you mean?'

'I don't believe Rode would have had the nerve to walk back to the house after killing his wife knowing that Jane Lyn had seen him do it. Assuming, of course, that he *did* know, which seems likely. It's too cool . . . too cool altogether.'

'Odd, damned odd,' muttered Havelock. He looked at his watch, pushing his left elbow outwards to do so, in a swift equestrian movement which Smiley found comic, and a little sad. The minutes ticked by. Smiley wondered if he should leave, but he had a vague feeling that Havelock wanted his company.

'There'll be a hell of a fuss,' said Havelock. 'It isn't every day you arrest a Carne tutor for murder.' He put down the paper-knife sharply on the desk.

'These bloody journalists ought to be horsewhipped!' he declared. 'Look at the stuff they print about the Royal Family. Wicked, wicked!' He got up, crossed the room and sat himself in a leather armchair by the fire. One of the spaniels went and sat at his feet.

'What made him do it, I wonder. What the devil made him do it? His own wife, I mean; a fellow like that.' Havelock said this simply, appealing for enlightenment.

'I don't believe,' said Smiley slowly, 'that we can ever entirely know what makes anyone do anything.'

'My God, you're dead right . . . What do you do for a living, Smiley?'

'After the war I was at Oxford for a bit. Teaching and research. I'm in London now.'

'One of those clever coves, eh?'

Smiley wondered when Rigby would return.

'Know anything about this fellow's family? Has he got people, or anything?'

'I think they're both dead,' Smiley answered, and the telephone on Havelock's desk rang sharply. It was Rigby. Stanley Rode had disappeared.

Chapter 18

AFTER THE BALL

He caught the 1.30 train to London. He just made it after an argument at his hotel about the bill. He left a note for Rigby giving his address and telephone number in London and asking him to telephone that night when the laboratory tests were completed. There was nothing else for him to do in Carne.

As the train pulled slowly out of Carne and one by one the familiar landmarks disappeared into the cold February mist, George Smiley was filled with a feeling of relief. He hadn't wanted to come, he knew that. He'd been afraid of the place where his wife had spent her childhood, afraid to see the fields where she had lived. But he had found nothing, not the faintest memory, neither in the lifeless outlines of Sawley Castle, nor in the surrounding countryside, to remind him of her. Only the gossip remained, as it would while the Hechts and the Havelocks survived to parade their acquaintance with the first family in Carne.

He took a taxi to Chelsea, carried his suitcase upstairs and unpacked with the care of a man accustomed to living alone. He thought of having a bath, but decided to ring Ailsa Brimley first. The telephone was by his bed. He sat on the edge of the bed and dialled the number. A tinny model-voice sang: 'Unipress, good afternoon,' and he asked for Miss Brimley. There was a long silence, then, 'Ah'm afraid Miss Brimley is in conference. Can someone else answer your query?'

Query, thought Smiley. Good God! Why on earth query – why not question or inquiry?

'No,' he replied. 'Just tell her Mr Smiley rang.' He put back the receiver and went into the bathroom and turned on the hot tap. He was fiddling with his cuff-links when the telephone rang. It was Ailsa Brimley:

'George? I think you'd better come round at once. We've got a visitor. Mr Rode from Carne. He wants to talk to us.' Pulling on his jacket, he ran out into the street and hailed a taxi.

Chapter 19

DISPOSAL OF A LEGEND

The descending escalator was packed with the staff of Unipress, homebound and heavy-eyed. To them, the sight of a fat, middle-aged gentleman bounding up the adjoining staircase provided unexpected entertainment, so that Smiley was hastened on his way by the jeers of office-boys and the laughter of typists. On the first floor he paused to study an enormous board carrying the titles of a quarter of the national dailies. Finally, under the heading of 'Technical and Miscellaneous', he spotted the *Christian Voice*, Room 619. The lift seemed to go up very slowly. Formless music issued from behind its plush, while a boy in a monkey jacket flicked his hips on the heavier beats. The golden doors parted with a sigh, the boy said 'Six', and Smiley stepped quickly into the corridor. A moment or two later he was knocking on the door of Room 619. It was opened by Ailsa Brimley.

'George, how nice,' she said brightly. 'Mr Rode will be dreadfully pleased to see you.' And without any further introduction she led him into her office. In an armchair near the window sat Stanley Rode, tutor of Carne, in a neat black overcoat. As Smiley entered he stood up and held out his hand. 'Good of you to come, sir,' he said woodenly. 'Very.' The same flat manner, the same cautious voice.

'How can I help you?' asked Smiley.

They all sat down. Smiley offered Miss Brimley a cigarette and lit it for her.

'It's about this article you're writing about Stella,' he began. 'I feel awful about it really, because you've been so good to her, and her memory, if you see what I mean. I know you wish well, but I don't want you to write it.'

Smiley said nothing, and Ailsa was wise enough to keep

quiet. From now on it was Smiley's interview. The silence didn't worry him, but it seemed to worry Rode.

'It wouldn't be right; it wouldn't do at all. Mr Glaston agreed; I spoke to him yesterday before he left and he agreed. I just couldn't let you write that stuff.'

'Why not?'

'Too many people know, you see. Poor Mr Cardew, I asked him. He knows a lot; and a lot about Stella, so I asked him. He understands why I gave up Chapel too; I couldn't bear to see her going there every Sunday and going down on her knees.' He shook his head. 'It was all wrong. It just made a fool of your faith.'

'What did Mr Cardew say?'

'He said we should not be the judges. We should let God judge. But I said to him it wouldn't be right, those people knowing her and knowing what she'd done, and then reading all that stuff in the *Voice*. They'd think it was crazy. He didn't seem to see that, he just said to leave it to God. But I can't, Mr Smiley.'

Again no one spoke for a time. Rode sat quite still, save for a very slight rocking movement of his head. Then he began to talk again:

'I didn't believe old Mr Glaston at first. He said she was bad, but I didn't believe it. They lived up on the hill then, Gorse Hill, only a step from the Tabernacle; Stella and her father. They never seemed to keep servants for long, so she did most of the work. I used to call in Sunday mornings sometimes after church. Stella looked after her father, cooked for him and everything, and I always wondered how I'd ever have the nerve to ask Mr Glaston for her. The Glastons were big people in Branxome. I was teaching at Grammar School in those days. They let me teach part-time while I read for my degree, and I made up my mind that if I passed the exam. I'd ask her to marry me.

'The Sunday after the results came out I went round to the house after morning service. Mr Glaston opened the door himself. He took me straight into the study. You could see half the potteries in Poole from the window, and the sea beyond. He sat me down and he said: "I know what you're here for, Stanley. You want to marry Stella. But you don't know her," he said, "you don't know her." "I've been visiting two years, Mr Glaston," I said, "and I think I know my mind." Then he started talking about her. I never thought to hear a human being talk like that of his own child. He said she was bad – bad in her heart. That she was full of malice. That was why no servants would stay at the Hill. He told me how she'd lead people on, all kind and warm, till they'd told her everything, then she'd hurt them, saying wicked, wicked things, half true, half lies. He told me a lot more besides, and I didn't believe it, not a word. I think I lost my head; I called him a jealous old man who didn't want to lose his housekeeper, a lying, jealous old man who wanted his child to wait on him till he died. I said it was him who was bad, not Stella, and I shouted at him liar, liar. He didn't seem to hear, just shook his head, and I ran out into the hall and called Stella. She'd been in the kitchen, I think, and she came to me and put her arms round me and kissed me.

'We were married a month later, and the old man gave her away. He shook my hand at the wedding and called me a fine man, and I thought what an old hypocrite he was. He gave us money – to me, not her – two thousand pounds. I thought perhaps he was trying to make up for the dreadful things he'd said, and later I wrote to him and said I forgave him. He never answered and I didn't see him often after that.

'For a year or more we were happy enough at Branxome. She was just what I thought she'd be, neat and simple. She liked to go for walks and kiss at the stiles; she liked to be a bit grand sometimes, going to the Dolphin for dinner all dressed up. It meant a lot to me then, I don't mind admitting, going to the right places with Mr Glaston's daughter. He was Rotary and on the Council and quite a figure in Branxome. She used to tease me about it – in front of other people too, which got me a bit. I remember one time we went to the Dolphin, one of the waiters there was a bloke called Johnnie Raglan. We'd been to school together. Johnnie was a bit of a tear-about and hadn't done anything much since he'd left school except run after girls and get into trouble. Stella knew him, I don't know how, and she waved to him as soon as we'd sat down. Johnnie came over and Stella made him bring another chair and sit with us. The Manager looked daggers, but he didn't dare to do anything because she was Samuel Glaston's daughter. Johnnie stayed there all the meal and Stella talked to him about school and what I was like. Johnnie was pleased as punch and got cheeky, saying I'd been a swot and a good boy and all the rest, and how Johnnie had knocked me about – lies most of it, and she egged him on. I went for her afterwards and said I didn't pay good money at the Dolphin to hear Johnnie Raglan tell a lot of tall stories, and she turned on me fast like a cat. It was her money, she said, and Johnnie was as good as me any day. Then she was sorry and kissed me and I pretended to forgive her.'

Sweat was forming on his face; he was talking fast, the words tripping over each other. It was like a man recalling a nightmare, as if the memory were still there, the fear only half gone. He paused and looked sharply at Smiley as if expecting him to speak, but Smiley seemed to be looking past him, his face impassive, its soft contours grown hard.

'Then we went to Carne. I'd just started reading *The Times* and I saw the advert. They wanted a science tutor and I applied. Mr D'Arcy interviewed me and I got the job. It wasn't till we got to Carne that I knew that what her father had said was true. She hadn't been very keen on Chapel before, but as soon as she got here she went in for it in a big way. She knew it would look wrong, that it would hurt me. Branxome's a fine big church, you see; there was nothing funny about going to Branxome Tabernacle. But at Carne it was different; Carne Tabernacle's a little out-of-the-way place with a tin roof. She wanted to be different, to spite the school and me, by playing the humble one. I wouldn't have minded if she'd been sincere, but she wasn't, Mr Cardew knew that. He got to know Stella, Mr Cardew did. I think her father told him; anyway, Mr Cardew was up North before, and he knew the family well. For all I know he wrote to Mr Glaston, or went and saw him or something.

'She began there well enough. The townspeople were all pleased enough to see her – a wife from the School coming to the Tabernacle, that had never happened before. Then she took to running the appeal for the refugees – to collecting clothes and all that. Miss D'Arcy was running it for the School, Mr D'Arcy's sister, and Stella wanted to beat her at her own game – to get more from the Chapel people than Miss D'Arcy got from the School. But I knew what she was doing, and so did Mr Cardew, and so did the townspeople in the end. She listened. Every drop of gossip and dirt, she hoarded it away. She'd come home of an evening sometimes – Wednesdays and Fridays she did her Chapel work – and she'd throw off her coat and laugh till I thought she'd gone mad.

'"I've got them! I've got them all," she'd say, "I know all their little secrets and I've got them in the hollow of my hand, Stan." That's what she'd say. And those that realised grew to be frightened of her. They all gossiped, Heaven knows, but not to profit from it, not like Stella. Stella was cunning; anything decent, anything good, she'd drag it down and spoil it. There were a dozen she'd got the measure of. There was Mulligan the furniture man; he's got a daughter with a kid near Leamington. Somehow she found out the girl wasn't married – they'd sent her to an aunt to have her baby and begin again up there. She rang up Mulligan once, something to do with a bill for moving Simon Snow's furniture, and she said, "Greetings from Leamington Spa, Mr Mulligan. We need a little cooperation." She told me that – she came home laughing her head off and told me. But they got her in the end, didn't they? They got their own back!'

Smiley nodded slowly, his eyes now turned fully upon Rode.

'Yes,' he said at last, 'they got their own back.'

'They thought Mad Janie did it, but I didn't. Janie'd as soon have killed her own sister as Stella. They were as close as moon and stars, that's what Stella said. They'd talk together for hours in the evenings when I was out late on Societies or Extra Tuition. Stella cooked food for her, gave her clothes and money. It gave her a feeling of power to help a creature like Janie, and have her fawning round. Not because she was kind, but because she was cruel.

'She'd brought a little dog with her from Branxome, a mongrel. One day a few months ago I came home and found it lying in the garage whimpering, terrified. It was limping and had blood on its back. She'd beaten it. She must have gone mad. I knew she'd beaten it before, but never like that; never. Then something happened – I shouted at her and she laughed and then I hit her. Not hard, but hard enough. In the face. I gave her twenty-four hours to have the dog destroyed or I'd tell the police. She screamed at me – it was her dog and she'd damn' well do what she liked with it – but next day she put on her little black hat and took the dog to the vet. I suppose she told him some tale. She could spin a good tale about anything, Stella could. She kind of stepped into a part and played it right through. Like the tale she told the Hungarians. Miss D'Arcy had some refugees to stay from London once and Stella told them such a tale they ran away and had to be taken back to London. Miss D'Arcy paid for their fares and everything, even had the welfare officer down to see them and try and put things right. I don't think Miss D'Arcy ever knew who'd got at them, but I did – Stella told me. She laughed, always that same laugh: "There's your fine lady, Stan. Look at her charity now."

'After the dog, she took to pretending I was violent, cringing away whenever I came near, holding her arm up as though I was going to hit her again. She even made out I was plotting to murder her: she went and told Mr Cardew I was. She didn't believe it herself; she'd laugh about it sometimes. She said to me: "It's no good killing me now, Stan; they'll all know who's done it." But other times she'd whine and stroke me, begging me not to kill her. "You'll kill me in the long nights!" She'd scream it out – it was the words that got her, the long nights, she liked the sound of them the way an actor does, and she'd build a whole story round them. "Oh, Stan," she'd say, "keep me safe in the long nights." You know how it is when you never meant to do anything anyway, and someone goes on begging you not to do it? You think you might do it after all, you begin to consider the possibility.'

Miss Brimley drew in her breath rather quickly. Smiley stood up and walked over to Rode.

'Why don't we go back to my house for some food?' he said. 'We can talk this over quietly. Among friends.'

They took a taxi to Bywater Street. Rode sat beside Ailsa Brimley, more relaxed now, and Smiley, opposite him on a drop-seat, watched him and wondered. And it occurred to him that the most important thing about Rode was that he had no friends. Smiley was reminded of Büchner's fairy tale of the child left alone in an empty world who, finding no one to talk to, went to the moon because it smiled at him, but the moon was made of rotten wood. And when the sun and moon and stars had all turned to nothing, he tried to go back to the earth, but it had gone.

Perhaps because Smiley was tired, or perhaps because he was getting a little old, he felt a movement of sudden compassion towards Rode, such as children feel for the poor and parents for their children. Rode had tried so hard – he had used Carne's language, bought the right clothes, and thought as best he could the right thoughts, yet remained hopelessly apart, hopelessly alone.

He lit the gas-fire in the drawing-room while Ailsa Brimley went to the delicatessen in the King's Road for soup and eggs. He poured out whisky and soda and gave one to Rode, who drank it in short sips, without speaking.

'I had to tell somebody,' he said at last. 'I thought you'd be a good person. I didn't want you to print that article, though. Too many knew, you see.'

'How many really knew?'

'Only those she'd gone for, I think. I suppose about a dozen townspeople. And Mr Cardew, of course. She was terribly cunning, you see. She didn't often pass on gossip. She knew to a hair how far she could go. Those who knew were the ones she'd got on the hook. Oh, and D'Arcy, Felix D'Arcy, he knew. She had something special there, something she never told me about. There were nights when she'd put on her shawl and slip out, all excited as if she was going to a party. Quite late sometimes, eleven or twelve. I'd never ask her where she was going because it only bucked her, but sometimes she'd nod at me all cunning and say, "You don't know, Stan, but D'Arcy does. D'Arcy knows and he can't tell," and then she'd laugh again and try and look mysterious, and off she'd go.'

Smiley was silent for a long time, watching Rode and thinking. Then he asked suddenly: 'What was Stella's blood group, do you know?'

'Mine's B. I know that. I was a donor at Branxome. Hers was different.'

'How do you know that?'

'She had a test before we were married. She used to suffer

from anaemia. I remember hers being different, that's all. Probably A. I can't remember for sure. Why?'

'Where were you registered as a donor?'

'North Poole Transfusion Centre.'

'Will they know you there still? Are you still recorded there?'

'I suppose so.'

The front door bell rang. It was Ailsa Brimley, back from her shopping.

Ailsa installed herself in the kitchen, while Rode and Smiley sat in the warm comfort of the drawing-room.

'Tell me something else,' said Smiley, 'about the night of the murder. Why did you leave the writing-case behind? Was it absent-mindedness?'

'No, not really. I was on Chapel duty that night, so Stella and I arrived separately at Fielding's house. She got there before I did and I think Fielding gave the case to her – right at the start of the evening so that it wouldn't get forgotten. He said something about it later that evening. She'd put the case beside her coat in the hall. It was only a little thing about eighteen inches by twelve. I could have sworn she was carrying it as we stood in the hall saying good-bye, but I must have been mistaken. It wasn't till we got to the house that she asked me what I'd done with it.'

'*She* asked *you* what you'd done with it?'

'Yes. Then she threw a temper and said I expected her to remember everything. I didn't particularly want to go back, I could have rung Fielding and arranged to collect it first thing next morning, but Stella wouldn't hear of it. She made me go. I didn't like to tell the police all this stuff about us quarrelling, it didn't seem right.'

Smiley nodded. 'When you got back to Fielding's you rang the bell?'

'Yes. There's the front door, then a glass door inside, a sort of french window to keep out draughts. The front door was still open, and the light was on in the hall. I rang the bell and collected the case from Fielding.'

They had finished supper when the telephone rang.

'Rigby here, Mr Smiley. I've got the laboratory results. They're rather puzzling.'

'The exam. paper first: it doesn't tally?'

'No, it doesn't. The boffins here say all the figures and writing were done with the same ballpoint pen. They can't be sure about the diagrams but they say the legend on all the diagrams corresponds to the rest of the script on the sheet.'

'All done by the boy after all in fact?'

'Yes. I brought up some other samples of his handwriting for comparison. They match the exam. paper right the way through. Fielding couldn't have tinkered with it.'

'Good. And the clothing? Nothing there either?'

'Traces of blood, that's all. No prints on the plastic.'

'What was her blood group, by the way?'

'Group A.'

Smiley sat down on the edge of the bed. Pressing the receiver to his ear, he began talking quietly. Ten minutes later he was walking slowly downstairs. He had come to the end of the chase, and was already sickened by the kill.

It was nearly an hour before Rigby arrived.

Chapter 20

THE DROSS OF THE RIVER

Albert Bridge was as preposterous as ever; bony steel, rising to Wagnerian pinnacles, against the patient London sky; the Thames crawling beneath it with resignation, edging its filth into the wharves of Battersea, then sliding towards the mist down river.

The mist was thick. Smiley watched the driftwood, as it touched it, turning first to white dust, then seeming to lift, dissolve and vanish.

This was how it would end, on a foul morning like this when they dragged the murderer whimpering from his cell and put the hempen rope round his neck. Would Smiley have the courage to recall this two months from now, as the dawn broke outside his window and the clock rang out the time? When they broke a man's neck on the scaffold and put him away like the dross of the river?

He made his way along Beaumont Street towards the King's Road. The milkman chugged past him in his electric van. He would breakfast out this morning, then take a cab to Curzon Street and order the wine for dinner. He would choose something good. Fielding would like that.

Fielding closed his eyes and drank, his left hand held lightly across his chest.

'Divine,' he said, 'divine!' And Ailsa Brimley, opposite him, smiled gently.

'How are you going to spend your retirement, Mr Fielding?' she asked. 'Drinking Frankenwein?'

His glass still held before his lips, he looked into the candles. The silver was good, better than his own. He wondered why they were only dining three. 'In peace,' he replied at last. 'I have recently made a discovery.'

'What's that?'

'That I have been playing to an empty house. But now I'm comforted to think that no one remembers how I forgot my words or missed an entry. So many of us wait patiently for our audience to die. At Carne no one will remember for more than a Half or two what a mess I've made of life. I was too vain to realise that until recently.' He put the glass down in front of him and smiled suddenly at Ailsa Brimley. 'That is the peace I mean. Not to exist in anyone's mind, but my own; to be a secular monk, safe and forgotten.'

Smiley gave him more wine: 'Miss Brimley knew your brother Adrian well in the war. We were all in the same department,' he said. 'She was Adrian's secretary for a while. Weren't you, Brim?'

'It's depressing how the bad live on,' Fielding declared. 'Rather embarrassing. For the bad, I mean.' He gave a little gastronomic sigh. 'The moment of truth in a good meal! *Übergangsperiode* between *entremets* and dessert,' and they all laughed, and then were silent. Smiley put down his glass, and said:

'The story you told me on Thursday, when I came and saw you . . .'

'Well?' Fielding was irritated.

'About cheating for Tim Perkins . . . how you took the paper from the case and altered it . . .'

'Yes?'

'It isn't true.' He might have been talking about the weather. 'They've examined it and it isn't true. The writing was all one person's . . . the boy's. If anyone cheated, it must have been the boy.'

There was a long silence. Fielding shrugged.

'My dear fellow, you can't expect me to believe that. These people are practically moronic.'

'Of course, it doesn't necessarily signify anything. I mean you could be protecting the boy, couldn't you? By lying for him, for his honour so to speak. Is that the explanation?'

'I've told you the truth,' he replied shortly. 'Make what you want of it.'

'I mean, I can see a situation where there might have been collusion, where you were moved by the boy's distress when he brought you the papers; and on the spur of the moment you opened the case and took out his paper and told him what to write.'

'Look here,' said Fielding hotly, 'why don't you keep off this? What's it got to do with you?' And Smiley replied with sudden fervour:

'I'm trying to help, Fielding. I beg you to believe me, I'm trying to help. For Adrian's sake. I don't want there to be . . . more trouble than there need, more pain. I want to get it straight before Rigby comes. They've dropped the charge against Janie. You know that, don't you? They seem to think it's Rode, but they haven't pulled him in. They could have done, but they haven't. They just took more statements from him. So you see, it matters terribly about the writing-case. Everything hangs by whether you really saw inside it; and whether Perkins did. Don't you see that? If it was Perkins who cheated after all, if it was only the boy who opened the case and not you, then they'll want to know the answer to a very important question: *they'll want to know how you knew what was inside it.*'

'What are you trying to say?'

'They're not really moronic, you know. Let's start from the other end for a moment. Suppose it was you who killed Stella Rode, suppose you had a reason, a terribly good reason, and they knew what that reason might be; suppose you went ahead of Rode after giving him the case that night – by bicycle, for instance, like Janie said, riding on the wind. If that were really so, none of those things you saw would have been in the case at all. You could have made it up. And when later the exam. results came out and you realised that Perkins had cheated, then you guessed he had seen inside the case, had seen that it contained nothing, *nothing but exam. papers.* I mean that would explain why you had to kill the boy.' He stopped and glanced towards Fielding. 'And in a way,' he added almost reluctantly, 'it makes better sense, doesn't it?'

'And what, may I ask, was the reason you speak of?'

'Perhaps she blackmailed you. She certainly knew about your conviction in the war from when she was up North. Her father was a magistrate, wasn't he? I understand they've looked up the files. The police, I mean. It was her father who heard the case. She knew you're broke and need another job and she kept you on a hook. It seems D'Arcy knew too. She told him. She'd nothing to lose; he was in on the story from the start, he'd never allow the papers to get hold of it; she knew that, she knew her man. Did *you* tell D'Arcy as well, Fielding? I think you may have done. When she came to you and told you she knew, jeered and laughed at you, you went to D'Arcy and told him. You asked him what to do. And he said – what would he say? – perhaps he said find out what she wants. But she wanted nothing; not money at least, but something more pleasing, more gratifying to her twisted little mind: she wanted to command and own you. She loved to conspire, she summoned you to meetings at absurd times and places; in woods, in disused churches, and above all at night. And she wanted nothing from you but your will, she made you listen to her boasts and her mad intrigues, made you fawn and cringe, then let you run away till the next time.' He looked up again. 'They might think along those lines, you see. That's why we need to know who saw inside the case. And who cheated in the exam.' They were both looking at him, Ailsa in horror, Fielding motionless, impassive.

'If they think that,' asked Fielding at last, 'how do they suppose I knew Rode would come back for the case that night?'

'Oh, they knew she was expecting you to meet her that night, after the dinner at your house.' Smiley threw this off as if it were a tedious detail, 'It was part of the game she liked to play.'

'How do they know that?'

'From what Rode says,' Smiley continued, 'Stella was carrying the case in the hall, actually had it in her hand. When they arrived at North Fields she was without it; she flew into a rage and accused him of forgetting it. She made him go back for it. You see the inference?'

'Oh, clearly,' said Fielding, and Smiley heard Ailsa Brimley whisper his name in horror.

'In other words, when Stella devised this trick to gratify her twisted will, you saw it as an opportunity to kill her, putting the blame on a non-existent tramp, or, failing that, on Rode, as a second line of defence. Let us suppose you had been meaning to kill her. You had meant, I expect, to ride out there one night when Rode was teaching late. You had your boots

132

and your cape, even the cable stolen from Rode's room, and you meant to lay a false trail. But what a golden opportunity when Perkins turned up with the hand-case! Stella wanted her meeting – the forgotten hand-case was agreed upon as the means of achieving it. That, I fear, is the way their minds may work. And you see, they *know* it wasn't Rode.'

'How do they know? How *can* they know? He's got no alibi.' Smiley didn't seem to hear. He was looking towards the window, and the heavy velvet curtains stirring uneasily.

'What's that? What are you looking at?' Fielding asked with sudden urgency, but Smiley did not answer.

'You know, Fielding,' he said at last, 'we just don't know what people are like, we can never tell; there isn't any truth about human beings, no formula that meets each one of us. And there are some of us – aren't there? – who are nothing, who are so labile that we astound ourselves; we're the chameleons. I read a story once about a poet who bathed himself in cold fountains so that he could recognise his own existence in the contrast. He had to reassure himself, you see, like a child being hateful to its parents. You might say he had to make the sun shine on him so that he could see his shadow and feel alive.'

Fielding made an impatient movement with his hand. 'How do you know it wasn't Rode?'

'The people who are like that – there really are some, Fielding – do you know their secret? They can't feel anything inside them, no pleasure or pain, no love or hate; they're ashamed and frightened that they can't feel. And their shame, this shame, Fielding, drives them to extravagance and colour; they must make themselves feel that cold water, and without that they're nothing. The world sees them as showmen, fantasists, liars, as sensualists perhaps, not for what they are: the living dead.'

'How do you know? How do you know it wasn't Rode?' Fielding cried with anger in his voice, and Smiley replied: 'I'll tell you.'

'If Rode murdered his wife, he had planned to do so long ago. The plastic cape, the boots, the weapon, the intricate timing, the use of Perkins to carry the case to your house – these are

133

evidence of long premeditation. Of course one could ask: if that's so, why did he bother with Perkins at all – why didn't he keep the case with him all the time? But never mind. Let's see how he does it. He walks home with his wife after dinner, having deliberately forgotten the writing-case. Having left Stella at home, he returns to your house to collect it. It was a risky business, incidentally, leaving that case behind. Quite apart from the fact that one would expect him to have locked it, his wife might have noticed he hadn't got it as they left – or you might have noticed, or Miss Truebody – but luckily no one did. He collects the case, hurries back, kills her, fabricating the clues which mislead the police. He thrusts the cape, boots and gloves into the refugees' parcel, ties it up and prepares to make good his escape. He is alarmed by Mad Janie, perhaps, but reaches the lane and re-enters the house as Stanley Rode. Five minutes later he is with the D'Arcys. From then on for the next forty-eight hours he is under constant supervision. Perhaps you didn't know this, Fielding, but the police found the murder weapon four miles down the road in a ditch. They found it within ten hours of the murder being discovered, long before Rode had a chance to throw it there.

'This is the point, though, Fielding. This is what they can't get over. I suppose it would be possible to make a phoney murder weapon. Rode could have taken hairs from Stella's comb, stuck them with human blood to a length of coaxial cable and planted the thing in a ditch *before* he committed the murder. But the only blood he could use was his own – which belongs to a different blood group. The blood on the weapon they found belonged to Stella's blood group. He didn't do it. There's a rather more concrete piece of evidence, to do with the parcel. Rigby had a word with Miss Truebody yesterday. It seems she telephoned Stella Rode on the morning of the day she was murdered. Telephoned at your request, Fielding, to say a boy would be bringing some old clothes up to North Fields on Thursday morning – would she be sure to keep the parcel open till then? . . . What did Stella threaten to do, Fielding? Write an anonymous letter to your next school?'

Then Smiley put his hand on Fielding's arm and said: 'Go now, in God's name go now. There's very little time, for

Adrian's sake go now,' and Ailsa Brimley whispered something he could not hear.

Fielding seemed not to hear. His great head was thrown back, his eyes half closed, his wine glass still held between his thick fingers.

And the front-door bell rang out, like the scream of a woman in an empty house.

Smiley never knew what made the noise, whether it was Fielding's hands on the table as he stood up, or his chair, falling backwards. Perhaps it was not a noise at all, but simply the shock of violent movement when it was least expected; the sight of Fielding, who a moment before had sat lethargic in his chair, springing forward across the room. Then Rigby was holding him, had taken Fielding's right arm and done something to it so that Fielding cried out in pain and fear, swinging round to face them under the compulsion of Rigby's grip. Then Rigby was saying the words, and Fielding's terrified gaze fell upon Smiley.

'Stop him, stop him, Smiley, for God's sake! They'll hang me.' And he shouted the last two words again and again: 'Hang me, hang me,' until the detectives came in from the street, and shoved him without ceremony into a waiting car.

Smiley watched the car go. It didn't hurry, just picked its way down the wet street and disappeared. He remained there long after it had gone, looking towards the end of the road, so that passers-by stared oddly at him, or tried to follow his gaze. But there was nothing to see. Only the half-lit street, and the shadows moving along it.

THE SCREENPLAY

INTRODUCTION

The challenge to convert *A Murder of Quality* into a movie script crept up on me unexpectedly, in the long gorgeous autumn of last year, when my mind was filled with almost anything except the screen possibilities of a novel I had written thirty years before, and had not read since, but which I knew to contain serious structural deficiencies.

I didn't despise the book, or regret it, or hate it. One can no more hate one's own work than hate one's children. I simply remembered it as a necessary stepping-stone to my later stuff, as good as I could get it at the time, given my inexperience and the difficulties under which I was obliged to write. I hadn't re-read it because I am squeamish about revisiting my old books, preferring to live with the ones I have yet to write. They, of course, have no flaws at all!

I was aware – how could I not be? – that, a year or so before, an energetic young producer had bought an option on the novel, and indeed I had spent some time with the screenwriter planning the adaptation. He was, and is, a good friend – which had perhaps been part of the problem, because he and I egged each other down the wrong path.

We had made the mistake of going for a contemporary version of the story, rather than the period piece it had by then become. And we had tried too hard to find a rôle for Ann Smiley, George's wife. We had wanted to build up her connection with the school, which in the novel is only hinted at; and to do something with her lover, for in the novels Ann always has one. We felt, wrongly as it had turned out, that we should make more of George Smiley's intelligence background, and weave in a thread of espionage, and perhaps the lover would be the other end of the thread. The result, as so often when one tries to achieve too many things at once, was that we ended up with none of them: not quite a thriller, not quite a spy story, not quite anything, and too much of everything. A second draft was better, but by then it was virtually an original screenplay – so much so, indeed, that we all three, producer, writer and myself, began to ask ourselves why we were bothering with the novel at all.

Finally we had to admit honourable failure. And thank Heaven we were all secure enough and grown-up enough to admit it and survive as friends and colleagues. Old hands get to know that, when such things happen, the best and cheapest thing to do is swallow your losses, smile and get up from the table.

But since failure is more instructive than success in such cases, we had also learned a lot.

Firstly, that the novel alone didn't offer a sound enough structure to build a film.

Secondly that a contemporary setting, though it was perfectly valid in these Thatcherite times, did not enrich the story, which drew its atmosphere from the more legible hypocrisies of the fifties, where it was originally set.

And thirdly that, since we were dealing with a piece of social comment got up as a murder mystery, we would have done better to stick with it, and not try to graft onto it the apparatus of a spy story.

But these lessons seemed pretty academic, since the producer's option was soon running out and the writer by then had found other and larger fish to fry. So we parted friends, and I dismissed the project from my mind. Yet another nearly-movie, I told myself – what's new?

I was therefore startled, a few months later, to learn that the same producer had renewed his option on the novel and proposed to sign a second writer to make the adaptation. But this time, we would stick to the original period and – as closely as we could – to the original plot as well.

And the new screenwriter – who was as illustrious as the first – did indeed do exactly what was asked of him, improving the plot-line with original material where he had to, and otherwise giving us a faithful, if rather bald version of the original: a country house murder, in other words, where the country house happened to be a school, and George Smiley, in his Hercule Poirot hat, gave us the benefit of his little grey cells where those of the local police superintendent were not up to the job. And after all, that was what the book was about, wasn't it?

140

Or was it?

To find out the answer, I did what I should have done much earlier, and re-read the book. I was actually shocked.

A Murder of Quality, I discovered, had been written in white heat. Period piece or not, it was a spray-gun, frontal assault, not just on the British private educational establishment, but on our whole class structure – religious, social, economic. It was a young writer's act of revenge against the institutions of his childhood. It was downright malicious. But that was also where the entertainment lay, that was the point of the story. What George Smiley had discovered at Carne School was the same root-and-bough corruption that he later unveiled in *Tinker Tailor Soldier Spy*. Carne was the Circus made School. Both were rotten through and through, each had been entrusted with its sacred mission: the one to protect our freedom, the other to educate our children. Both had fallen down on the job. Forget the country-house murder. This was war. If there was anyone at all in the novel with whom I identified, apart from safe old George Smiley, it was the luckless schoolboy, Tim Perkins, the antecedent of little Bill Roach, the boy watcher in *Tinker Tailor Soldier Spy*. Both were the overburdened inheritors of a social system they would never be on terms with, both were doomed. Everyone else, in one way or another, was enemy.

So if the book was to become a film, I reasoned as I read, why should we lose sight of the passion that had informed it? If there was fury in the book, let's have fury in the film; if satire, let there be satire!

And if a moral point was to be scored, let it be the point of the book: that these are the prisons we English build for ourselves; that, as the late Friedrich Dürrenmatt said of the Swiss, we are the prisoners who are also our own warders, since the prison walls are of our own building, and no sooner do we escape them than we consign our children to their darkness; and that the gravest crime a man can commit is to violate the spirit or the body of the children entrusted to his care. Exit poor Perkins. Exit the banalities of just another murder.

I can't be sure how much of all this I confided to the producer and his new writer and director, but I think it was quite a lot.

We certainly talked for a long time, if that's a measure. But it's a delicate business, telling another writer what to write, and it's a delicate business being the writer who's being told. Neither of us was likely to come out of it feeling very comfortable.

And of course I knew very well, as I suppose we all did, that I was asking things of the writer that I should be doing for myself: such as restructuring the story to contain the dynamic that was now gathering on my private horizon; such as inventing new characters and scenes to bear the load of a stronger plot; or kindling, even in the coded mind of George Smiley, such an anger, such an outrage, that he comes as near as he ever comes in his life to an act of calculated revenge against the culprit; such as half pardoning the culprit for the murder of his blackmailer, then furiously consigning him to the noose for the murder of the boy.

So finally I ended up where I most probably should have begun, if I hadn't been so scared of film. I put my pen where my mouth was, and wrote the script myself. If I remember rightly, we had three weeks to go before the first day of shooting, and some of my new characters were not even written, let alone had they been cast. To add to our problems, our leading actor walked out on us when he saw my script. The best children, say old wives, are born in pain. We must hope the same thing applies to this film.

Let me explain why I came so late and reluctantly to my own realisation of the script. All through my writing life, I have had, like many novelists, a love–hate relationship with the film industry, whether we are talking of the big screen or the little one, and hate has most often won the day.

Of the five feature films made of my books, only two – *The Spy Who Came in from the Cold* and now *The Russia House* – are worth crossing the road for.

Of the three television series so far made, *Tinker Tailor Soldier Spy* was the best, and *A Perfect Spy*, though well written, was the saddest disappointment.

Of all of the films – feature or television – only *Smiley's People* bears my name as a screenwriter, although I have given a good slice of my working life to the film industry, and sat through many master-classes in screenwriting.

142

For *The Spy Who Came in from the Cold*, directed by the late Martin Ritt, I was whisked to Ireland to rewrite Richard Burton's lines on set. Burton was in a tantrum, I was cast as the appeaser. The lines weren't all bad and they were used, but the experience was a depleting and unhappy one, and I vowed from then on to stay clear of the movie business and concentrate on my novels.

So it was inevitable, wasn't it, given the consistency we writers are famous for, that six months later I found myself scripting my next novel, *The Looking Glass War* for the British director Jack Clayton. The collaboration was not a success, and a year later Columbia tossed the movie to an American writer-director, with lamentable consequences.

Once more I vowed to stay clear of movies, and I succeeded in doing so until I met Sydney Pollack, who had just made the wonderful *They Shoot Horses Don't They?* and had been signed to direct an Avco-Embassy production of my next novel *A Small Town in Germany*. Sydney is an enchanter. I packed my bags and set off for California, where I lived in Jane Fonda's house on Malibu Beach. But alas Jane Fonda no longer lived in it, and what I remember most is the impotent thunder of the surf that beat itself to death all night and day while it staggered a few feet up and down the sand. The script progressed at much the same pace, though as a matter of fact it wasn't all that bad.

I don't remember what finally went wrong. Perhaps I never really knew. The script, the money, something. Perhaps I have deliberately forgotten. Anyway, it fell apart, and today, I am told, the rights repose in some company liquidator's desk, waiting to be embalmed, or sliced up for bait, or junkbonded to the next loss-seeking entrepreneur. What became of my script is also a mystery. I suppose it grazes in some Hollywood knacker's yard. But what became of Sydney Pollack is history: he made success after success, from *Tootsie* to *Out of Africa*, and his good luck is no surprise to me, for he was a breeze to work with, and one of the most impressive natural intellects you will ever meet.

After Pollack – having first taken further vows of abstinence and celibacy – I worked for six months with Karel Reisz on the film version of *The Naive and Sentimental Lover*, though so far as I remember, nobody ever bought the film rights, and when the book was published, it got such a frightful reception that nobody was inclined to.

And the script? I've never looked at it since. And I suspect I am wise not to.

If you want the rest of it, when Warner's acquired *The Little Drummer Girl* for George Roy Hill, I spent yet more months floating uselessly around the production, escorting the director and screenwriter to Beirut and even doing a version of the script myself. But I'm afraid that, once again, I look back on wasted time – even if it isn't *really* wasted, but more often fallow time between books. And certainly movie time is party time, when for a few blessed days or weeks the novelist doesn't have to brood alone at his desk, but can come out and play 'let's pretend' with the gregarious and often wonderfully entertaining film-makers.

All the same, at fifty-nine you don't like looking back on blank years and wasted writing. You begrudge them, you can't help it. Which I'm afraid is a rather long way round to explaining why I was at first determined not to get caught up with adapting a little novel I had written thirty years before, when I was anyway another person – and how, yet again, I got trapped by my own rhetoric, and my shameful fascination for the medium, and once more departed from my firmly held and repeatedly broken principle not to get mixed up in movies.

I wrote the film script of *A Murder of Quality* over five days at my house in Cornwall, and faxed the pages to the director, Gavin Millar, as I went along. I like to write to particular people when I write, and Millar was not only sympathetic to my purpose but has a fine ear and a graceful way of expressing disagreement. I warned him from the start that I write long, and that didn't bother him. 'Write it all,' he said. I was pleased to imagine him with his felt-tipped pen, inking out the many unnecessary lines and grace notes.

I did not consult the original novel a second time, except to check on the text of key speeches. But I discovered as soon as I started writing that the screenplay had been sloshing around inside me for a long time. I must have been mulling over plot-changes and new characters ever since the first draft over a year back, because they popped out ready-made on to the page, like old friends who had been clamouring to be released during all the time I hadn't been listening.

The problem – more Millar's than mine, I now realise – was to prevent these new or enlarged characters – Mad Janie, Inspector Rigby, D'Arcy, for instance – from stealing the show from the old faithfuls. In the version before you, you can still see how the newcomers are fighting for centre stage before Millar, quite rightly, cut them down to size.

A screenplay is a wretched form of communication, but nobody has so far found a better one to do the job of suggesting to producers and directors how they might make the movie. And at least you need no special knowledge to read one. INT means interior and EXT means exterior and VOICE OVER means you can hear the voice but the speaker isn't in the scene. What follows here is the first version as I wrote it in those turbulent five days, warts and all, before the necessary refining process had begun. The movie itself will be thinner and, I hope, better. Some scenes have already been dropped because they were too expensive, others for lack of time, others because they were indulgences which had the effect of holding up the story rather than advancing it. More refining yet will certainly take place in the cutting room, for the film is still being shot as I write. You will notice, for example, that in this draft, the murdered Stella Rode speaks to us in Voice Over. Gavin Millar went along with this conceit at first, then felt extremely uncomfortable with it and decided to dump it, which was his good right.

It was more than his good right, in fact. It was his duty. Film is, and I hope always will be, the director's medium. The writer provides but one of the dozens of skills on which the director draws to perform his art. In the beginning, it is true, is the word. But after the word come the cameramen (now fatuously called Directors of Photography) the art directors, the musicians, the cast, the make-up artists and the whole mercenary army-on-the-march that a director must command.

In the theatre, it's already different. There the writer still holds sway. In the novel – bless it – he is absolute.

Which is probably why I shall never, never again get involved in writing for the movies. Well – all right – if you insist – just this once.

John le Carré, December 1990

List of Characters

GEORGE SMILEY	Denholm Elliott
TERENCE FIELDING	Joss Ackland
AILSA BRIMLEY	Glenda Jackson
MAD JANIE	Billie Whitelaw
STANLEY RODE	David Threlfall
FELIX D'ARCY	Ronald Pickup
INSPECTOR RIGBY	Matthew Scurfield
TIM PERKINS	Christian Bale
SHANE HECHT	Diane Fletcher
DOROTHY D'ARCY	Fiona Walker
SERGEANT MELLOR	Nick Reding
CHARLES HECHT	Michael Cochrane
SERGEANT TED MUNDY	Charles Pemberton
MR CARDEW	William Armstrong
(Later renamed	
The Reverend Fergus)	
MAJOR HARRIMAN	Moray Watson
MRS HARLOWE	Helen Lindsay
ALICE LAWRY	Samantha Janus
THE PATHOLOGIST	John Grillo
MANDY	Jane Montgomery
SIMON SNOW	Tim Dutton
ANN SNOW	Emily Raymond
MR GLASTON	George Raistrick
DAI	George Winter
STELLA RODE	Joanna Jacobs
PLUM	B. Davis
FRIENDS OF PERKINS	Nick Lewis
	Peter Snelling
HARRY	Thorley Walters

PART ONE

OVER THE TITLES:

1. EXT. CARNE SCHOOL. DUSK TURNING TO EVENING

To the strains of 'Greensleeves' played on a cracked 78 record, we tour the immemorial medieval spires and towers of an ancient Church of England public school.

2. INT. CARNE SCHOOL THEATRE. EVENING

The camera descends to discover boys in black school uniform. The boys are rehearsing a medieval morality play, scripts in hands, while masters and their wives move among them, 'directing'. Some boys already have props: a Tudor hat, a fools' bladder, a belt and a broadsword. TIM PERKINS, *a ginger-haired sensitive boy, is clutching a bow. He is sad faced.* ANN SNOW, *an assistant master's wife, stands behind him, arranging his body as he speaks.*

PERKINS
(*Reading woodenly from script*)
Everyman. Be of good cheer!
(ANN SNOW *lifts his right bow arm in exhortation.*)
I am Good Fellowship. I will go with thee and be thy guide.

The female outbreak of fury from the foot of the steps comes from SHANE HECHT, *a senior housemaster's wife. She is a lantern-jawed, fine built, hunting type of Englishwoman, and tough as boots.*

149

HECHT
Smile, boy! You're *supposed* to be happy, so *be* happy!
God, why don't they smile?

3. INT. CLASSROOM. EVENING

FELIX D'ARCY, *a thin, forty-year-old pedant with a fluting voice, is
painfully rotating the hair of one of his pupils, PLUM, while he instils
learning to his Latin class.*

D'ARCY
Quidquid id est, timeo . . . Go *on* Plum. Go *on*, please
. . . timeo *what?*

PLUM
(*In pain*) I don't *know*, sir.

D'ARCY
Oh, sir, yes you do, sir. (*Twists*) What did I tell you
about fearing Greeks? (*Twists*) Even when they are
bringing gifts, Plum, as I am bringing gifts to you?

4. INT. GYMNASIUM. EVENING

Boxing tuition in progress under the eye of an ex-Marine named COBB.

COBB
Keep your guard up, Mr Selby! Keep it *up*, sir!

*A boxing glove seems to smack us straight in the nose. A boy in boxing
gear peers anxiously into camera.*

BOY
Oh sorry, Selby, did I hurt you?

5. INT. DR STANLEY RODE'S CLASSROOM. EVENING

Boys' laughter. His whole class is standing in a ring, holding hands, laughing. RODE *is a drab, earnest little figure, not at all in the social stamp of* TERENCE FIELDING *(whom we shall meet in a moment).* RODE *teaches maths and science. On the blackboard, drawings of batteries, wires, terminals. And on Rode's desk, a fat black briefcase beside bits of flex, batteries and retorts of coloured water.*

> RODE
>
> *(Addressing first boy)* Go on now. Squeeze. Squeeze his hand . .
> *(To second boy)* . . . go on. Squeeze. Pass it round. On! On! . . . On!

Giggling, the boys pass the squeeze round the ring.

> RODE
>
> Right. So what have we got?

> BOY'S VOICE
>
> An erection, sir.

> RODE
>
> *(Amid more laughter)* Chain reaction! Well done!

RODE *leaps to the blackboard and writes: CHAIN REACTION . . . The laughter wafts us into:*

6. INT. ANOTHER CLASSROOM. EVENING

A completely silent, very eccentric classroom. It is FIELDING's. *Sexy Pre-Raphaelite paintings on the walls, bits of statuary and cultural trophies of all sorts. Pot-pourri on the antique desk, and a large satin cushion with a tassle at the corner.* FIELDING *stands among the boys, not in front of them, and they listen wrapt as he orates wonderfully from* Omar Khayam.

151

FIELDING

And this delightful Herb whose living
   Green,
Fledges the River's Lip on which we lean
Ah, lean upon it lightly! For who knows
From what once lovely Lip it springs
   unseen

Another gust of laughter from next door does not interfere with the
boys' rapture. A Siamese cat, languishing on the satin cushion on his
desk, stretches luxuriously. The boys seem to wake.

FIELDING

(*No longer reading*) No boy is allowed to be bored in my
class. Anyone bored must leave courteously. Those of
you new to my class this Half – we call terms Halfs here
– be advised that I serve boys' sherry in my house every
Sunday evening after prayers. Poets should please bring
their work, and be prepared to read it aloud . . .

7. EXT. ABBEY CLOSE. NIGHT

As FIELDING*'s voice continues, we range the splendid towers of Carne*
by moonlight.

FIELDING

A Flask of Wine, a Book of Verse – and
   Thou
Beside me singing in the Wilderness . . .'
Goodnight sweet laddies. Goodnight. Off you all go.
And create. It's the only thing.

8. EXT. A CORNER OF CARNE'S VAST PLAYING FIELDS. DAY

A squad of boys in Army Cadets' brown uniform and ammunition
boots is force-marched in double time by CHARLES HECHT, *an athletic*
Christian housemaster, and husband to SHANE. *The drill seems to be a*
punishment.

152

HECHT
Hup, hup, *hup*, hup . . . *one*, two, *one*, two . . . *hup*, hup
. . . *hup*, hup . . . Come on, you won't kill Bolshies that
way!

9. INT. ABBEY. CANDLELIGHT. NIGHT

*A processional Lenten hymn as a boy's choir moves slowly down the
aisle past a small evensong congregation including* ANN SNOW, *both*
HECHTS, FELIX D'ARCY *and his sister* DOROTHY, *and* STANLEY
RODE *along with his black briefcase on the floor beside him.*

*The shot-tattered campaign flags of vanished English country regiments
dangle over the mostly empty pews.*

*As the choir proceeds, we begin to hear faintly the crackle of police
radios and the ring of police-car bells. These sounds rise:*

POLICE SERGEANT (*Voice over*)
Jesus Christ!

INSPECTOR RIGBY (*Voice over*)
All available cars close on North Fields, Carey Road,
Carne. Repeat, North Fields . . .

DISSOLVE TO:

10. INT. FIELDING'S HOUSE. NIGHT

The white Abbey candles turn black and become the candelabras on
FIELDING'*s dining table. Dressed in heavy black skirts and clerical
bib,* FIELDING *is checking the preparations for his dinner party: a
carnation for each lady – are the salts and peppers full? – has each
place its correct knives and forks? An Italian maid,* CARMELINA,
watches him. The sounds off continue:

INSPECTOR RIGBY (*Voice over*)
I want those footprints photographed. *Now*. Where's my bloody photographer?

SERGEANT MELLOR (*Voice over*)
On his way, sir!

RIGBY (*Voice over*)
So's Christmas. Call the hospital. I want a pathologist. One with a strong stomach.

FIELDING
(*To* CARMELINA, *handing her a salt cellar*)
Wet salt again, Carmelina. Change it.

11. EXT. ABBEY CLOSE. NIGHT

Evensong is ending. SHANE *and* CHARLES HECHT *emerge from the Abbey and advance side by side without speaking to the railings that border the Abbey Close. Two bicycles are tethered to the railings by thick security cables. Side by side husband and wife stoop to unlock his bicycle. The camera favours their hands unlocking the cables.*

12. INT. D'ARCY'S HOUSE. NIGHT

FELIX D'ARCY, *wearing an apron, is washing up alone while* DOROTHY *sits in the adjoining living-room munching chocolates and watching television.* D'ARCY'*s gaze is fixed on the kitchen window. Through it, across the lawn, we see in the lighted window of a neighbour's kitchen the undressed figure of a nineteen-year-old girl. She is unaware of* D'ARCY *observing her.*

RIGBY (*Voice over*)
Don't mix your flavours, understand? If there's six bloods here, I want six bloods, not a cocktail.

13. EXT. ABBEY CLOSE. NIGHT

In the Abbey Close, the HECHTS *have mounted their bikes and switched on their lights.* SHANE *leading, they set off in single file.*

Titles end as we see the two red tail lights vanish into the darkness, and lead to:

14. EXT. RODE'S HOUSE AT NORTH FIELDS. NIGHT

The interior of the house is partly floodlit. Outside, two police cars, cables, tapes and confusion. Through an open car door we locate the sounds of the police radios that we have been hearing.

15. INT. RODE'S HOUSE. CONSERVATORY. NIGHT

Inside the house, we see Inspector RIGBY, *a shrewd West Countryman, with Sergeant* MELLOR, *as well as a photographer, fingerprint men and medics. They pass slowly from room to room.*

A bloodbath. A covered body, centre. Blood on the walls, floor, furniture. The mayhem of a fight ending in a ferocious bludgeoning. A poster, blood-spattered and awry, appeals for Clothing for the Oppressed of Hungary.

> RIGBY
> (*As he walks,* MELLOR, *a prosaic cockney, aged twenty-eight, takes notes.*)
> Where's the dog? Dog bowl but no dog. Find it. Ever done a murder before sergeant?

> MELLOR
> Not one like this, sir.

> RIGBY
> Those her own teeth?

155

A MEDIC
They were, sir.

RIGBY
Any more word of the husband?

MELLOR
Still under sedation, sir. Sawley Hospital. Doctor says give him a few more hours.

RIGBY
Hullo.

He is no longer listening. Stooping he picks up a blue belt that could belong to a woman's overcoat. Blood has soaked the ends.

RIGBY
Where's the rest of this? She wasn't wearing it. Where is it?

MELLOR
Not known, sir.

RIGBY
Upstairs?

MELLOR
No, sir.

RIGBY
Cupboards, cloakrooms?

MELLOR
Not in the house, or grounds, sir.

RIGBY
Did she wear blue coats?

MELLOR

No, sir. Hers was brown. Wasn't brown when she died,
of course. But it had been. And it would be again if it
was washed. Well, dry-cleaned, I suppose.

RIGBY

(*Moving on, the belt still in his hand*)
Well, that's all we need to do then. Stand in Carne
High Street and wait for a lady in a blue coat without a
belt, with a blackjack in her pocket and a punch like a
heavyweight mule.

MELLOR *and* RIGBY *have reached the drawing-room and now enter the
hall.* RIGBY *still holds the belt.*

MELLOR

Forensic's best guess so far is some sort of chain or –

RIGBY

Or what?

MELLOR

Well something bendy, sir. More a rubber truncheon,
say. Something wangy, if you know what I mean, that
curls round corners.

A young Welsh CONSTABLE, DAI, *guards the front door.*

RIGBY

(*To the young* CONSTABLE)
Foxy weather then, Dai.

DAI

(*Ashen faced, staring at the belt*)
Yes, sir.

RIGBY

Haven't seen a blue coat anywhere, have you?

DAI

No, sir.

RIGBY

Haven't seen a little dog, have you, Dai, dead or alive?

RIGBY *pats his arm.*

RIGBY

Come on, boy. Harden up. – What's that briefcase?

MELLOR *picks up a commodious, Crippen-style black briefcase for Rigby's inspection, the same bag that we have seen in Rode's classroom.* RIGBY *opens it and peers inside. School books, a battery, flex and other visual aids of a science master. Files marked 'Examination Papers Lent Term, 1958'.*

MELLOR

Dr Rode teaches science, sir.

RIGBY *takes the top off a bottle of chemical, sniffs it, pulls a face.*

RIGBY

Wilkins thought he might have seen Mad Janie by the house earlier. You'd better pull her in. She's about due for it anyway.

16. INT. SMILEY'S HOUSE. BYWATER STREET, CHELSEA.
DRAWING-ROOM. EVENING

Dressed in an old cardigan, GEORGE SMILEY *is sitting alone before his fire, a bed-tray across his lap. Shoved to the back of the tray, the remnants of a frugal lamb chop, a glass of Burgundy, a packet of Ryvita, and slimmer's butter substitute. And closer to him, a heap of learned seventeenth century German-bound volumes, flagged for reference, which he consults as he writes precisely on a ruled pad. On the wall, German prints and sixteenth century French drawings, notably one by Callot of nymphs and shepherds. A simple gramophone is playing Mahler.*

158

The telephone rings. It is across the room, on a long flex. SMILEY
*scowls at it, lets it ring. The phone is his enemy. Finally he gets up,
lifts the arm off the record and, bracing himself, picks up the phone.*

SMILEY

(*Into phone*) Ann, for heaven's sake – why don't we both
just go to sleep? – hullo?

MISS BRIMLEY (*Voice over*)

George? George? is that you?

SMILEY

(*A long wait, a slow smile*)
Ailsa Brimley, as I live and breathe! Brim, darling, how
are you? Whatever do you want?

17. INT. EDITOR' OFFICE, CHRISTIAN VOICE. EVENING

A tacky, idiosyncratic little press den in a great building. AILSA
BRIMLEY *sits at her desk, telephone in hand. She is a bobbed,
formidable, tweedy woman, once pretty, falsely severe, warm-hearted
and coarse-spoken. She is smoking like a chimney.*

BRIMLEY

You, George. And your furtive little mind. Stay just
where you are. I'll be round in fifteen minutes.

SMILEY

You can't. I'm going to bed!

BRIMLEY

Then I'm in luck, aren't I?

18. INT. CARNE. A BOY'S STUDY. EVENING

TIM PERKINS, *alone in his tiny kingdom, is practising 'Lazy Sheep' on
his violin. He's not very good. He stops and listens to the deep silence.
Far away, the earnest, indistinct voice of one boy lecturing another,*

159

ending with something like 'Put your head in here'. Silence again.
Then the thwack of a cane. Then another.

19. INT. CARNE. A BOYS' WASHROOM. EVENING

A glimpse of a formal beating. One boy has his head in an empty
washbasin and is clutching the taps. The Head of House beats him
with a cane walking-stick while the House Prefects look gravely on.

20. INT. SMILEY'S DRAWING-ROOM. EVENING

SMILEY *and* BRIMLEY *sit opposite each other, whiskies at their elbows,*
as BRIMLEY *reads from a handwritten letter.*

BRIMLEY
(*Reading*) '. . . I don't know who else to turn to. I told
Mr Cardew at the tabernacle but I don't think he
believed me. But I'm sure you will, and you'll know I'm
normal. I am so afraid of the long nights. I can't go to
the police and I'm not mad and I know my husband is
trying to kill me, the same as he killed the dog. Yours in
Jesus, Stella Rode. R–O–D–E.
(SMILEY *seems to have dozed off.*)
Address, North Fields, Carne. Her husband teaches at
Carne School. George, are you awake?

SMILEY
How do you know he teaches at Carne?

BRIMLEY
What else is there to do at Carne? She's a
schoolmaster's wife. Obviously.

SMILEY
(*Reproachful*) Brim . . .

BRIMLEY

All right, I snooped. North Fields is a school property, let to new staff. A Doctor Stanley Rode is the new tenant.

SMILEY

How did you snoop?

BRIMLEY

I had my girl ring the post office and check the voters' list. What does it matter how I snooped?

SMILEY

Just interest. Why *Jesus*?

BRIMLEY

She's a *Christian*, George. Low Church.

SMILEY

So why did she write to you? Why not to Jesus direct?

BRIMLEY

(*Tetchy*) I'm her *Aunt*, George! 'Let Auntie Barbara solve your problems.' I run a little weekly mag for pious housemaids, called the *Christian Voice*! – Not that anyone's got a housemaid anymore, they all work at tills in supermarkets. But they still have problems.

SMILEY

And husbands . . . How do you *kill* a dog? Shoot it? So why didn't she say *shoot*? Or *drown*? Or *poison*? You'd think she'd be more graphic. Odd.

BRIMLEY

I *owe* her, George! I owe them all. They're like the agents we ran in the war, except they're called readers. They're maddening and contrary and unpredictable and totally real, and there's not one of them I'd drop down a hole. Stella Rode included. She's a Glaston. The Glastons have been subscribers since the rag was

161

founded. They're pottery owners, Godthumpers from the North, pious as hell. Her old Dad's a hammer in the local tin tabernacle and Stella's the last of the line.

SMILEY *takes the letter from her and studies it.*

BRIMLEY
How's that fool wife of yours? Wandering again?

SMILEY
(*Reading the letter*) She usually does at the start of the Spring.

BRIMLEY
Who's she got this time?

SMILEY
I understand he intends to act.
(*He holds the letter to the light to examine the watermark.*)
Perhaps she should put her troubles to Barbara Fellowship. Doctor what of, I wonder?

BRIMLEY
Chemistry. Hull University 1956. Still spying, are we, George?

SMILEY
(*Handing back the letter*)
Well, they've given me a sort of sabbatical, as a matter of fact. Honoris causa . . . Whatever are the 'long nights'? Some Nonconformist rutting ritual, I suppose.

BRIMLEY
I want you to go and see her, George.

SMILEY
Ann?

BRIMLEY

Stella! Don't play games with me, I know you *far* too
well. I want you to go to Carne and see her and find out
why she thinks she's going to be topped by her old man.
Then report back to me.

SMILEY

(*Indicating his books*) Dammit, Brim, *you* go. Leave me to
my seventeenth century German poets. They're far
more reliable than Mrs Rode.

BRIMLEY

I can't. You know that.

SMILEY

Why on earth not? Let someone else bring out your
beastly newspaper for once.

BRIMLEY

I'm not clever, that's why. Not *your* clever. When could
I ever disappear into the woodwork? I'd be a cow in a
china shop down there. You know how I am.

SMILEY

(*Sincerely*) You're the salt of the earth, Brim. If you
don't know it, I do. So did our agents.

BRIMLEY

Well then, don't argue. Terence Fielding's down there.
Did you know that?

SMILEY

Who?

BRIMLEY

George! Terence Fielding – brother to our late wartime
colleague – *Adrian*, George! – is a housemaster at Carne
School!

SMILEY

Oh my dear Lord, so he is. Yes, yes, I remember about Terence. Too many appetites. We turned him down.

BRIMLEY

Well Carne didn't. And he's the senior housemaster, and you have a line to him.
(*She picks up the telephone, plonks it down beside him and lifts the receiver and dials 0.*)
So use it. Tell him you're coming down on the morning train –
(*Into phone*) Carne 251 please, this is Primrose 2829 – sound him out.

SMILEY

(*While the telephone rings out.*)
Why didn't she go to the police?

BRIMLEY

Would *you*? If Ann was trying to knock *you* off?

21. INT. FIELDING'S STUDY. EVENING

Over a bottle of claret, FIELDING *is preparing three of his boys for Confirmation, the morose* TIM PERKINS *included. Bibles and notebooks among the glasses. An air of conviviality.*

FIELDING

So that's God's problem. On the one hand He's totally consistent, which we, thank God, are not. And on the other hand, what on earth is the point of praying to someone who's so perfect He never changes his mind? – Bugger!

The telephone is ringing. Making a long arm, FIELDING *puts the receiver to his ear. It occurs to us that he is slightly tipsy – and that the boys may be too.*

FIELDING
(*Into phone*) Gas, Light & Coke Company!
(*Pause.*) Come out, come out, whoever you are!
(*He is playing to the boys.*)

SMILEY (*Voice over*)
Is that Mr Terence Fielding?

FIELDING
(*Playing Scrooge*) Jacob Fielding's been dead these seven
years.

The boys in fits of swallowed laughter.

SMILEY (*Voice over*)
My name's George Smiley, I was a colleague of your
brother Adrian's in the war.

FIELDING
(*No longer funny*) I know who you are. What do you
want?

22. INT. SMILEY'S DRAWING-ROOM. EVENING

BRIMLEY *has her ear bent to Smiley's phone. Their heads are touching.*

SMILEY
It's an odd matter really. I thought I might pop down
to Carne on the morning train and we could talk about
it –

FIELDING (*Voice over*)
About my brother?

At a loss, SMILEY *glances to* BRIMLEY *for advice. She mouths 'tell
him!'.*

SMILEY
Well, it's about a letter a friend of mine has had from
one of the Carne wives. It's rather disturbing.

165

FIELDING (*Voice over*)
What's her name?

23. INT. FIELDING'S STUDY. EVENING

The Confirmation boys, now tense, eyes on FIELDING.

24. INT. SMILEY'S DRAWING-ROOM. EVENING

SMILEY
Rode. Stella Rode.

FIELDING (*Voice over*)
(*Very deliberate*) Mrs Rode is dead.

25. INT. FIELDING'S STUDY. EVENING

FIELDING
. . . bludgeoned by an unknown assailant, for unknown
reasons. We're all desolated. The *boys* are especially
desolated.
(*He rings off.*)
Aren't you? She's cast a dark shadow over my last
glorious term at Carne.

Favour the sad PERKINS *as we:*

26. INT. SMILEY'S DRAWING-ROOM. EVENING

SMILEY *has replaced the receiver. Now he lifts it again and is dialling.*
BRIMLEY *is still stunned.*

BRIMLEY
Dead? Stella.

SMILEY
Not shot, not drowned, not poisoned. Bludgeoned.

BRIMLEY

What are you doing?

SMILEY

Phoning Ben Sparrow at Special Branch. He'll put me on the map with the Carne police. I'll need you to help me pack. I'm not very good at it.

BRIMLEY

You never were.

27. EXT. CARNE. D'ARCY'S HOUSE. MORNING

A pack of King Charles spaniel puppies are screaming at a wall of chicken wire as DOROTHY D'ARCY *in slacks and Wellingtons approaches with their feed pail. As she does so, a lower window of the house opens and* FELIX D'ARCY *looks out.*

D'ARCY

(*Calling*) Breakfast, Dorothy!

DOROTHY

(*To the puppies*) Oh, shut up!

28. EXT. CARNE. WOODED HILLTOP. DAY

A remote wooded hilltop overlooking the waking town. A police car noses along the lane. Seated in the front, two uniformed policemen, MUNDY *and* DAI, *scan the hedgerows and side turnings. Suddenly* DAI *spots something.*

DAI

(*Pointing*) On your left now, Ted –

*The police car turns quickly into a track in pursuit of the ragged figure of a woman (*MAD JANIE*) as she scurries away. They pull alongside her.* MUNDY *lowers his window.*

MUNDY

Wher're you going, Janie? Want a lift then? Bloody hell!

MAD JANIE *has smashed a rock against the windscreen, starring it.*
The two policemen leap from the car to run after her but she has
disappeared into the woods. MUNDY *wipes blood from his cut face,*
looks at it on his hand, looks after her.

MUNDY

That's how you do it, then. Now we know.

29. INT. POLICE STATION. OPS ROOM. DAY

Crisis mode. RIGBY *in command. Police in plain clothes and uniformed*
constables, secretaries, ringing phones, grisly relics. Copies of the day's
press piled on the desk. A girl is taking cuttings from them, and
stapling them on to pages of foolscap. MELLOR *hands* RIGBY *a phone,*
his hand over the mouthpiece.

MELLOR

Special Branch, sir. Commander Sparrow.

RIGBY

You joking, Mellor?

MELLOR

No, sir.

RIGBY

(*Taking phone*) So she was a spy too, was she?
(*Into phone*) Rigby . . . yes, sir. I see, sir. Who, sir? . . .
I'll write that down.
(*Writes*) I'll see he gets all reasonable facilities, sir.
(*Rings off, hands phone back to Mellor.*)
That's very nice. I'm blessed.
(*He's furious.*)
They're sending a funny, Mr Mellor. Name of *Smiley.*
(*He grabs a report from a secretary, reads it, signs it, hands it*
back.)

168

Had a nasty war, looks like a frog, dresses like a bookie and a brain the Commander of Special Branch would give his eyes for. Give me a bloody cigarette.

RIGBY *looks up.* FELIX D'ARCY *is standing in the doorway, still in sub fusc. (Gown, dark suit, white tie, mortar board.)*

RIGBY
Hullo, Mr D'Arcy, sir. Can I help you?

D'ARCY
Yes, Inspector. I rather hope you can. It's about my sister's gold necklace. She reported it missing two weeks ago. She's heard nothing at all since.

RIGBY
Maybe you should ask the Chief Constable. He may know.

D'ARCY
However, that is not what I came for. One of your officers has asked me whether I wear galoshes. I consider his intrusion gratuitous.

RIGBY
Do you wear galoshes?

D'ARCY
Certainly not.

RIGBY
I'll see he's disciplined.

But D'ARCY *still has not gone.*

D'ARCY
There's something else I feel I should mention.

RIGBY
Oh.

asked him impertinent details. Afterwards the boy was
upset so I wrote to her. I was intemperate. I warned her
not to meddle. Such a letter, taken out of context, could
be misunderstood.

RIGBY
Warned her?

D'ARCY
I said that such behaviour could prejudice her
husband's career.

RIGBY
And that's all it said: 'Don't meddle or your husband's
career will suffer?'

D'ARCY
I was not so crass.

RIGBY
Forgive me. I'm not very educated, you see. But that
was the drift?

D'ARCY
Crudely, yes.

RIGBY
Well you've nothing to worry about then, have you?

D'ARCY
I am merely anxious to avoid unfounded speculation.

Long silence.

RIGBY
Anything else you want to tell me?

D'ARCY
Nothing, thank you.

Well, then.

RIGBY opens the door for D'ARCY *as* MELLOR *advances on it from the other side.*

RIGBY

You're always welcome, Mr D'Arcy. Drop in any time. Yes, William.

MELLOR

They lost her, sir.

RIGBY

Who lost who?

MELLOR

Ted Mundy and Dai, sir. Mad Janie, sir. She's gone to ground in Carey forest. She was wearing an overcoat, sir. Could have been blue.

RIGBY

Belt?

MELLOR

They think string, sir. Couldn't be sure.

RIGBY

I don't want her. I know I don't. Bloody hell! . . . get on to Criminal Records. I want an immediate check on Mr Felix D'Arcy, Assistant Master, Carne School . . . Find out why he writes threatening letters to ladies who get themselves killed. And don't tell the Super.

MELLOR

Maybe she heard about Alice Lawry, sir.

RIGBY

Who the hell's Alice Lawry?

MELLOR

She's a raver, sir actually. Works for the vet. Nineteen years old and always keen to oblige. They say Mr D'Arcy is giving her a right seeing to.

RIGBY

D'Arcy is? He's a fairy! Lives with his sister and a bunch of poodles.

MELLOR

They're King Charles spaniels, actually.

RIGBY *is turning away when an afterthought strikes him.*

RIGBY

Did you say vet?

MELLOR

Major Harriman, sir, over at Oak Drive. Miss D'Arcy uses him for her dogs.

RIGBY

So where's Rode's dog?

MELLOR

Dead, sir. Put down.

RIGBY

Who put it down?

MELLOR

The vet, sir. Major Harriman.

RIGBY

Says who?

MELLOR

Neighbours, sir. Dr Rode was cut up rotten. So was his missus.

MELLOR *and one or two others are staring at Rigby oddly.* RIGBY
catches himself, shakes his head, bewildered by his own line of enquiry.

RIGBY
I've gone soft. Why am I looking for a dog? I'm looking
for a murderer.

A CLERK *is holding out a fingerprint report.* RIGBY *accepts it,
examines it. Silence.*

CLERK
From Forensic, sir.

Mounting tension as everyone in the room waits for RIGBY *to react.*

RIGBY
(*Studying report*) Smudges. Beautiful. Give me a
cigarette.

31. INT. SAWLEY HOSPITAL, CARNE. DAY

*A uniformed female nurse walks down a long green Victorian corridor,
carrying a tray of tea and biscuits. She stops before a closed door
guarded by a policeman and enters without knocking. In a private
ward,* STANLEY RODE, *fully dressed, sits on the edge of the bed, his
head between his fists. The nurse sets the cup beside him with two
yellow pills.*

NURSE
(*Brightly*) That's the way then.

RODE
Where's my watch?

NURSE
You're wearing it, silly. Drink your tea.

32. EXT. CARNE SCHOOL MAIN QUAD. DAY

The Abbey clock strikes eleven. Five hundred boys in drill lines are doing their daily physical training. They wear their suits and trousers and braces, and have removed the stiff collars from their white shirts. On a trestle platform before the assembled school, CHARLES HECHT, *a splendid, bullish, close-cropped figure of fifty, wearing a tightly fitting white gym vest, long white trousers and perfectly whited gym shoes, conducts physical training with his own body, while the boys heave and sweat below him, among them* PERKINS, *who exercises as though he would kill himself.*

> FIRST BOY
> (*Sotto voce to his neighbour as they do their press-ups*)
> Dippy D'Arcy killed her.

> SECOND BOY
> Bollocks. Spartacus did. Look at him up there. All that wasted energy.

Beside them, PERKINS *continues to flail himself with effort.*

Another angle, close on HECHT *on the platform as he continues to press up and down. Suddenly he glimpses the apologetic face of* MELLOR *in plain clothes staring up at him from ground level. Effortlessly,* HECHT *freezes in mid-movement.*

> MELLOR
> Very sorry, sir. Police, sir. Just routine, only it's slightly urgent. We're asking everyone, you see.

> HECHT
> (*Huge yell*) Carry on! No slacking!

HECHT *springs trimly from the platform to land face to face with* MELLOR. *As the two men head briskly for the cloisters, the five hundred press-ups become ragged, then cease altogether.*

33. EXT. D'ARCY'S HOUSE. DAY

King Charles spaniels scream at the wire as SERGEANT TED MUNDY *presses the front door bell. Leaning against the porch, two bicycles, a man's and a woman's.*

DOROTHY D'ARCY *flings open the door.*

DOROTHY
Yes?

MUNDY
Police Sergeant Mundy, madam, regarding the late Mrs Rode. There's one or two questions we're asking everyone . . .

DOROTHY
(*Admitting him*) There is a back door, you know.

34. INT. EMPTY CLASSROOM, CARNE SCHOOL. DAY

As if alone, RODE *sits correcting boys' exercise books. We pull back to see* RIGBY *at a boy's desk, watching him. Open at* RODE*'s feet, the black Crippen bag.*

RODE
Nice of you to bring my bag back. I was a bit lost without it. I'm new, you see.

RIGBY
Yes, sir.

RIGBY
When you're new, you have to wait for a classroom. You're a sort of gypsy. So much junk you have to cart around. Specially if you're a science man. It's all right in the lab, when you get one.

RIGBY

Do you happen to own a bicycle, by any chance, sir?

RODE

Never bothered, really.

RIGBY

Ever borrow one?

RODE

Not really. Rather walk or take a bus . . . I like correcting when I'm a bit low. It's soothing. Like crosswords.

RIGBY

You'll have to get another dog soon, won't you. Company.

RODE*'s pen runs faster.*

RODE

I'll never get another dog in my life. I don't deserve one.

RODE *continues correcting and* RIGBY *continues watching him. A distant bell clangs. At Carne, a bell is always clanging. As the bell ceases, we hear:*

MALE VOICES (*Voice over*)

Henry! marvellous! . . . Jack . . . Cyril, you old devil, *you've* put on a bit! . . .

35. EXT. CARNE RAILWAY STATION. DAY

Open on MR CARDEW *the Methodist Minister in the station fore-court on his bicycle. A train has just arrived from London. On the platform, a group of Church of England dignitaries in an impressive array of purple shirt fronts and clerical collars and gold crosses receives an arriving group of similar port-and-pheasant clergymen of the same class. Congratulations, backslapping, rugby-playing laughter. We are watching a reunion of old Carnian clergy, and a fair selection of the people who ruined England. Porters and other passengers must move round them, including the unobtrusive* GEORGE SMILEY *who wears a shabby suit and carries his own suitcase.* SMILEY *blinks round, and finally spots* CARDEW *peering at him from the shadow of the station awning. They greet uncertainly.*

CARDEW
Christian Voice?

SMILEY
(As they shake hands)
How very clever of you. How did you guess? Smiley.

36. EXT. CARNE. STREETS. DAY

CARDEW *pushes his bike,* SMILEY *walks behind him, balancing his suitcase precariously on the bike's carrier. They pass the local secondary school. Boys and girls romp cheerfully on the concrete playground.* CARDEW *is about thirty, thin and unsmiling and Welsh.*

SMILEY
We thought we'd make rather a splash of it. Get some old photographs of her family.

CARDEW
Her father was a fine man. Still is. His money never turned his head. That's for sure.

SMILEY
Play up her work for the Church. What we call a feature article.

36A. EXT. METHODIST TABERNACLE. DAY

A tin tabernacle has come into view, huddled beneath the great hulk of Carne Abbey. CARDEW *leans his bicycle against the porch. Business with the suitcase. They enter to the sounds of very small children singing 'There is a green hill far away . . .' .*

37. EXT. CARNE OUTSKIRTS. MRS HARLOWE'S COTTAGE. DAY

Riding his bicycle like the wind, the fraught TIM PERKINS *arrives at a pretty country cottage, and all in one movement, detaches his violin from the bike's carrier, leans the bike against the porch, and hauls on the chain of the front door bell. From inside the cottage, we hear the uncertain sounds of another pupil playing.*

38. INT. METHODIST TABERNACLE. DAY

The sweet disorder of the charitable poor pervades the split-level drill hall that is also the Chapel. There is no altar, just a Lord's Table and pews shoved higgledy piggledy against the walls. Missionary posters, a framed reproduction watercolour of Jesus among children of all races, a noticeboard littered with prayers, such as 'Gentle Jesus, please heal my child' and signed 'Pat Easton, 9 Castle Road'.

CARDEW *and* SMILEY *sit at the Lord's Table with cups of tea.* SMILEY *has his notebook open. On the lower level,* MRS CARDEW *and her young* ASSISTANT *are managing a playschool. Their singing over, the kids are sitting two at a desk making woolly dolls out of old-style milk-bottle tops, threading the wool round and round the paper ring, then (with assistance) cutting it with scissors. Someone is always crying, someone always needs the loo.* MRS CARDEW *is a serious, pious, good-hearted red-haired woman of twenty-five.*

SMILEY
I can surely say that she was universally loved.

As CARDEW *continues to consider his reply,* MRS CARDEW *approaches them with a child on her way to the loo.*

CARDEW
I don't hold too much with that kind of talk, as a matter of fact. Nobody's universally loved, not even when they're dead. Look at Christ.

179

SMILEY

Well, what about Dr Rode? Did he worship here? What could I say about him?

CARDEW

Oh no, he's gone over long ago. He's School. Anglican Popery.

SMILEY

(*Rueful*) Well I can say he's a dog lover, can I? That always touches readers' hearts.

CARDEW

(*Wooden*) I think the dogs are more in her line, actually.

SMILEY

I heard they lost their dog shortly before Mrs Rode died. A double tragedy as it were.

CARDEW

Did they, now?

SMILEY

Well what *can* I say?

Overhearing, MRS CARDEW *pauses at the Table.*

MRS CARDEW

Tell them about her Hungarian refugee work. She did a lot for *them*. There's plenty round here could do with cast-off clothes, as a matter of fact, but the School knew better, naturally.

MRS CARDEW *and the* CHILD *disappear into a door marked 'Toilet'.*

SMILEY

I do have one more question that bothers my editor. Mrs Rode wrote a very strange letter to us just before her death. It named the person she thought was going to kill her.

*Stanley Rode
(David Threlfall)*

Terence Fielding (Joss Ackland)

Sergeant Mellor (Nick Reding), Inspector Rigby (Matthew Scurfield) and policemen

George Smiley (Denholm Elliott) with Inspector Rigby, Sergeant Mellor and the Pathologist (John Grillo)

Mad Janie (Billie Whitelaw)

Alice Lawry (Samantha Janus) and Felix D'Arcy (Ronald Pickup)

◀ *George Smiley*

George Smiley

Mandy (Jane Montgomery) and Ailsa Brimley (Glenda Jackson)

Mad Janie and Sergeant Ted Mundy (Charles Pemberton)

George Smiley and Ailsa Brimley in the Sawley Tap

Terence Fielding

Ailsa Brimley, George Smiley and Sergeant Mellor

CARDEW
(*Dead calm*) Who's that then?

SMILEY
Her husband.

CARDEW
Oh, I don't think your editor should pay too much attention to that.

SMILEY
And she never said anything like that to you, for instance?

CARDEW
I would tell her to burn it, actually.

39. EXT. HECHTS' HOUSE. DAY

HECHT, *still in his whites, and* SHANE HECHT *stand before their bicycles, while* MELLOR *painstakingly examines their tyres.*

MELLOR
Now that's a Firemaster 3-ply, right, front and back the same, part worn but still a few miles left to go, I will say. And what's this lot . . . 'Treadsure'. Amazing the way they think up the names. These your own invention, sir?

SHANE HECHT
(*Acid*) Seventeen and six at Drew's, Constable.

MELLOR *is fingering the security cable of Hecht's bike, noticing its frayed edge and red-brown specks.*

MELLOR
What's inside here? (*He feels*) The normal chain by the feel of it. And the cloth round the outside to keep off the mud. I call that really ingenious.

SHANE HECHT
And you're so wonderfully observant, Constable.

MELLOR
Sergeant, actually.

SHANE HECHT
What *was* she killed with, by the way? I'd have thought
one needed something a bloody sight heavier for a head
like hers.

MELLOR
(*Unfazed*) You don't own a blue overcoat, do you, by
any chance, madam?

SHANE HECHT
I wouldn't be seen dead in blue.

40. EXT. HARRIMAN HOUSE. DAY

*A vet's surgery, kennels, sheds, broken cars, a sprawling rural slum. A
notice saying 'Dogs Boarded'. Ponies in the paddock and dogs of all
descriptions barking in their kennels or charging up and down their
runs. It is feeding time. Pretty Alice Lawry is taking round the food as*
D'ARCY *drives up in a Morris Oxford Estate with a King Charles
spaniel bitch in the back.* ALICE *puts down her pail and walks over to
the car.*

*They confer out of earshot. They walk quickly together towards the
shed. We have an impression of something conspiratorial or
prearranged.*

41. INT. POLICE STATION. RIGBY'S OFFICE. DAY

SMILEY *sits in an armchair,* RIGBY *at the desk. The strains of the
investigation are already showing in* RIGBY'*s features. A constable is
serving tea.*

RIGBY
You still, er, doing what you do?

SMILEY
Oh well, sort of, yes, I dare say, in a manner of speaking. Oh yes.

The phone rings on RIGBY*'s desk.*

RIGBY
(*Into phone*) I said, wait!

He rings off.

SMILEY
I've brought a – uh – letter for you.

RIGBY
It's all right, sir. I know you're important. It's just I haven't got a lot of time for small talk at the moment, sir.

SMILEY *hands him Stella Rode's letter.*

SMILEY
. . . and this is the envelope.

SMILEY *hands* RIGBY *the envelope in a cellophane container. He reads the letter.*

SMILEY
Barbara Fellowship is actually Miss Brimley, the editor of the magazine. She doubles as the Agony Aunt. She received the letter on Monday evening.

RIGBY
Why did she bring it to *you*?

SMILEY

We worked together in the war. We're sort of . . .
buddies.

The phone rings again. RIGBY *lifts it.*

RIGBY

I said *wait!* . . . What sort of cable? Spell it.

RIGBY *writes on a block and rings off.*

RIGBY

Have you ever heard of *coaxial* cable?

SMILEY

It means having a common axis. It's cable with a
copper rod at the centre, and a lot of fine wires round
the rod.

RIGBY

Oh yes.

SMILEY

It's used a lot in telephone communication. For
example, under the Atlantic. The density of the wires
produces extra fields that circle round the same axis.

RIGBY

Oh.

SMILEY

So you can have many more telephone calls going than
you've wires to carry them. If you see what I mean.

RIGBY

Could you murder somebody with it?

SMILEY

Oh I think so. Yes. I'm sure you could. A piece of it.
Yes, it would do rather well.

RIGBY
Could you kill a dog with it?

SMILEY
I'm sure.

RIGBY
You on the technical side of your lot then?

SMILEY
Oh no. God forbid.

RIGBY *goes back to the letter.*

RIGBY
Where did *you* go to school?

SMILEY
Oh, here and there. A bit in Germany.

RIGBY
That was before the war then?

SMILEY
More or less.

RIGBY
(*Back to the letter again.*)
I'll have to keep this, if you don't mind. What's next on
your agenda, Mr Smiley?

SMILEY
Oh, I'd just like to be useful.

RIGBY
You're not, well, reporting to someone, are you?

SMILEY
Well only to you really. And Miss Brimley when the
time comes.

RIGBY
We're not fond of amateurs in our profession, you see.

SMILEY
Oh, nor are we in ours. They're an absolute pest.

RIGBY
He travels fastest who travels alone, I say.

SMILEY
Oh, I do so agree.

42. EXT. SAWLEY HOSPITAL. DAY

Rigby's police car arrives at Sawley Hospital. MELLOR *drives,* SMILEY *and* RIGBY *sit in the back. They enter the hospital.*

43. INT. SAWLEY HOSPITAL. DAY

We are in the bowels of the hospital, a cellar morgue. A shrouded body lies on a slab. The PATHOLOGIST *holds a clip board with a human body printed on it, and expounds to* RIGBY *in a murmur while* SMILEY *looks on from a distance. The* PATHOLOGIST *is dry and middle class.*

PATHOLOGIST
I make it thirty or forty blows. I could be a liar. I'm assuming the first salvo was the hardest, after that the murderer began to run out of puff. First blows seem to have come from the left, so probably a right hander, but you never can really tell. Some people prefer backhand. Then of course the victim does tend to wriggle around, not many of us stay still when a maniac is walloping us with a chunk of cable. We get fidgety. Fragments of copper here, more there, bits of coloured rubber coating stuck in the bone here. Some lacerations on the shoulders, but that's probably when he bished . . .

While the PATHOLOGIST *runs on, Rigby's gaze moves round to*
SMILEY *in mute astonishment.* SMILEY *has pulled back the sheet and is*
staring at the battered face of Stella Rode.

SMILEY
Am I right in thinking that he went on hitting her after
she was dead?

PATHOLOGIST
Couple of times. Looks like it.

SMILEY
Or *she* of course. It could have been a woman. Using
both hands.

PATHOLOGIST
If she was an Amazon. Just.

44. INT. SWIMMING POOL, CARNE SCHOOL. DAY

SHANE HECHT *alone swims a length superbly.*

45. EXT. SCHOOL PLAYING FIELDS. DAY

Huge roar of a large dog as DOROTHY D'ARCY *beats off an Alsatian*
that is worrying her King Charles spaniels. The Alsatian slinks away
in disgrace.

46. INT. SAWLEY HOSPITAL. DAY

RIGBY *and* SMILEY *descend the staircase to the hospital entrance lobby*
where STANLEY RODE *sits alone, at attention, correcting books.* RIGBY
goes to him.

RIGBY
Dr Rode. How are you today, sir? I thought you were
back teaching.

RODE

I came to see whether I could have her yet. I've got the certificate from the doctor saying life's extinct.

RIGBY

Yes, well I'm sorry about that, sir. Can I ask you a question, sir? It's just routine. When you're doing your teaching sir, do you have any occasion to use coaxial cable?

RODE

Oh yes. I had a demonstration sample of it somewhere.

RIGBY

So where might we put our hands on that?

RODE

I don't know. It went missing.

RIGBY

When did you first notice it was missing, sir?

RODE

Ten days ago. Five. You lose your sense of time when a thing like this happens. It's the valium, I suppose.

RIGBY

Did you advise anyone it was missing – at the time, I mean? Ten days ago . . . five?

RODE

Perhaps I told Stella, I don't know. I'm thinking about Perkins actually.

RIGBY

Who's Perkins then, Dr Rode?

RODE

He's in Science 4. They're dunces, really. He never got more than thirty per cent in his mock certificates. Now suddenly he's got seventy-eight. Young Simon Snow must have been dreaming when he corrected that paper.

RIGBY

The other question is going back to something we've discussed. You very sadly lost your dog recently. How did that happen exactly?

RODE

(*At last*) Well, I suppose my wife thought it had to go. So she took it to the vet.

RIGBY

She did? Plucky of her.

RODE

Oh she was never short of courage.

SMILEY *has moved forward and he is speaking in a lowered tone to suit the humble role he has assumed.*

SMILEY

Dr Rode? My name is Smiley, I'm representing the editor and staff of the *Christian Voice*. Your wife was a very loyal subscriber to our journal, what we call one of our faithfuls. She won first prize for kitchen hints a few years back.

RODE

She never told me that.

SMILEY

There you are. Modest to the end. My magazine is planning a small celebration of her life, you see, sir, mentioning her family and the old connections. I've had a word with the Minister already, but I'd very much like the chance to ask you a few questions, when you feel able. Nothing personal, if you're willing. We could talk about her work for the Hungarians. Where will I find you, sir?

189

In the background, RIGBY *is visibly impressed by* SMILEY'*s footwork.*

RODE
They've all offered me hospitality. Shane. Dorothy. Even Fielding. I didn't feel able to accept. 6 Sawley Avenue. Mrs MacFarlane's.

SMILEY
I'll drop by then. If I may.

RODE
(*Vaguely, looking at his watch*)
It's not like the school at Mrs MacFarlane's. We have tea at six. More like home . . . so many people, all so kind. You wonder who she was.

47. INT. SHED. HARRIMAN'S KENNELS. DAY

In the afterglow of their lovemaking ALICE *and* FELIX D'ARCY *are lying on an old army blanket.* ALICE *is wearing a gold chain and locket round her neck.*

D'ARCY
(*Fingering the chain*) I thought I told you never to wear this in Carne.

ALICE
I wear it under my blouse, don't I? Feels nice against my skin.

D'ARCY
I love you.

ALICE
I love you too.

D'ARCY
And you haven't told anyone else? Not any more?

ALICE

Not after Stella. I only told her because I trusted her and she was Chapel. She said I looked happy, so I told her why. She said she was happy for me. I liked her, didn't I? There's nothing wrong in liking people. Just because *you* haven't got any friends, doesn't mean I can't, does it?

D'ARCY

(*Kissing her*) Just never tell anyone else. Promise. We can't let scandal come between us. Ever.

48. INT. RIGBY'S CAR. CARNE TOWN. DAY

SMILEY *and* RIGBY *in the back,* MELLOR *driving. They are passing the Abbey. The police radio is chattering all the time.*

RADIO

(*A West Country voice.*) All right then Abel Two, but don't forget it's milking or you'll never get home –

MELLOR

Back to the station, sir?

RIGBY

Turn that damn thing off.
(*To* SMILEY *as* MELLOR *obliges*)
You wouldn't have a cigarette, by any chance, would you?
(*To* MELLOR *as* SMILEY *delves in pocket*)
North Fields.

49. EXT. RODE'S HOUSE. DAY

RIGBY*'s police car drives slowly round the perimeter of the garden.*

RIGBY

She was murdered between ten past eleven and a
quarter to twelve. Her husband found the body. They'd
been out to a school dinner. Dr Rode had to stay behind
and talk some point of business. Mrs Rode, well she was
bored or tired, so she went home ahead, walked, by
herself.

50. INT. FIELDING'S HOUSE, HALL/FRONT DOOR. NIGHT

FIELDING *is ushering* STELLA RODE *out of the front door. We do not
see her face. (In all flashbacks we never see her face.)*

51. EXT. RODE'S HOUSE. DAY

RIGBY

There's nothing to that round here . . . it's a safe little
town. He comes home, there she is, still warm
naturally. You never saw blood like it. Travelled blood,
straight from the arteries. Clothes, hands, face, he must
have been literally a bloody nightmare.

51A. EXT. RODE'S GARDEN. DAY

They have left the car, and are walking in Rode's garden.

RIGBY

Blood in the footmarks. Wellingtons probably, could
have been rubber overshoes, size ten and a half, part
worn. From the spacing of the prints we'd say six feet
tall and running, but that's guesswork. It could have
been five feet tall and walking like Groucho Marx. He
came in through the back garden and went God knows
where. Everything vanishes in this case. People,
clothing, weapons. There's no footprints out, of course.
There's bicycle marks in the lane but just about
everyone round here has a bicycle.

51B. INT. RIGBY'S CAR. DAY

They are back in the car, driving through the poor part of town.

RIGBY

There's a piece of coaxial cable missing from Dr Rode's possession, and there's a piece of coaxial cable that did her in. That doesn't make Dr Rode a murderer unfortunately. There's not a motive in sight that's worth a French kiss on Putney Bridge, there's a Carnian Superintendent who'd like to sweep Stella Rode under the carpet. And there Mr Felix D'Arcy, the distinguished sexual athlete, who seems to have written Stella a threatening letter about something he's not letting on. All we need to wrap it up is a weightless six foot psychopath in Wellingtons who can fly through the air and take his clues with him on his broomstick.

51C. EXT. PLAYING FIELDS. DAY

They pass playing fields. A school rugby match is in progress. Boys, staff and wives yell for the home side.

RIGBY

Stella wore a necklace. It's missing. Nothing else is, except a blue woman's overcoat with no belt that doesn't belong to anyone.

SMILEY

A valuable necklace?

RIGBY

Piece of junk. Boring bunch of green beads on a bit of string. God I hate women sometimes. Like bloody Hottentots.
(*This in part for the Carne wives on the touch line who are still yelling for bloodthirsty victory in the field.*)

SMILEY

Who saw the beads last?

RIGBY

Fielding. Mr Terence Fielding. Senior housemaster at Carne. It was his dinner party. That's his house too.

SMILEY

(*Surveying* FIELDING's *house*)
Is Fielding married?

RIGBY

Very much not.

SMILEY

Is he anything else?

RIGBY

(*Evasive*) No, no . . . Just a capon, I expect. You know these English intellectuals.

SMILEY

No appetites, you mean.

RIGBY

(*Innocently*) No appetites, no criminal record. Not for outsiders.

SMILEY *continues to survey the house as they pass it slowly by.*

SMILEY

What's this Hungarian refugee story that Stella was mixed up in?

RIGBY

She was a do-gooder. The senior wives got an appeal going for unwanted clothing for the oppressed of

Hungary. Stella made the clothing into bundles and sent it up to London – thanks to the generosity of Carne! – What's up, Mellor?

MELLOR *has hastily switched the police radio back on as a* POLICE MOTORCYCLIST *cuts in front of the car and beckons* MELLOR *to follow him.*

RIGBY
Who the devil's that?

MELLOR
Peter Hoskins, sir, from Carey Town.

RIGBY
Hell's he doing in our parish? . . . Oh my God, not another one.

53. EXT. CARNE COUNTRYSIDE. A LANE. DAY

Two police cars and several motorbikes are parked in the opening to a field. Two constables stand in the ditch, several more policemen above them, looking down, including MUNDY. *Gruesome expectation of another corpse as* SMILEY *and* RIGBY *hurry towards the ditch.*

A length of coaxial cable lies in the mud. Blood and human hair are stuck to it.

RIGBY
(*Very pleased*) Who found this horrible object?

MUNDY *throws up his arm.*

MUNDY
Me, sir. Mundy. Just happened to be passing on my bike, sir. Looked down, there 'un was. Well, I thought –

RIGBY
Just passing *backside*, Ted Mundy! You were poaching.

Much laughter as RIGBY *clambers into the ditch. Accepting a pair of rubber gauntlets, he begins easing the cable from the mud.*

RIGBY
My God, she's some weight, I'll tell you! Forty blows, he said. I can't hardly pick her up.

SMILEY *is investigating bicycle tyre marks in the mud.*

54. INT. HECHT BEDROOM. NIGHT

Two strong bare forearms, a man's and a woman's, are locked fiercely against each other as the HECHTS *arm-wrestle face to face. Suddenly* SHANE *gives in, grinning and panting from the exertion.* HECHT *falls on top of her and they embrace hungrily after their bedroom game.*

55. INT. FIELDING'S HOUSE. SERVANTS' CORRIDOR. NIGHT

A powerful hand lays a chisel against a wooden packing case. A well aimed hammer blow shatters the wood. TERENCE FIELDING, *looking remarkably sturdy in old corduroys and a shirt, is opening a case of claret.*

56. EXT. MRS MACFARLANE'S B & B. BACK GARDEN. CARNE.
    EVENING

A humble house near the railway station. STANLEY RODE *is chopping firewood, on and on. The camera closes on him to reveal the tears pouring unchecked down his cheeks.*

57. EXT. MRS HARLOWE'S COTTAGE. NIGHT

TIM PERKINS *mounts his bike to leave the house of his violin teacher,* MRS HARLOWE, *who waves him off.*

MRS HARLOWE
Go carefully now, Tim. You know what they say at Carne. 'Go carefully in the long nights.'

PART TWO

58. INT. SAWLEY ARMS, CARNE. SMILEY'S BEDROOM. EVENING

SMILEY*'s bedroom,* SMILEY, *dressing for the evening, is trying to polish his shoes and study German literature at the same time. His bound books and manuscript notes crowd the tiny washing table. A knock at the door. He opens it and expresses delight.*

SMILEY
Ah! Luigi. How *very* kind.

A tubby Italian waiter of roughly Smiley's build is offering a tail suit, dickey and – his greatest pride – a white tie.

SMILEY
You think of everything.

SMILEY *accepts the suit and, after a hunt, gives* LUIGI *a pound note from the washstand drawer. Alone again,* SMILEY *holds the tail suit against himself in the long mirror. It is filthy, stained with soup and grease. The trousers are six inches too long.*

59. INT. POLICE STATION. RIGBY'S OFFICE. EVENING

A huge thwack of something solid hitting something soft. Again and again.

PULL BACK *to show* RIGBY, *watched by* MELLOR, *assaulting a cushion with a length of coaxial cable.* RIGBY *is already flagging.*

MELLOR
Twenty-one . . . twenty-two . . .

RIGBY
Bloody hell.

Massaging his wrist, RIGBY *accepts a cigarette from* MELLOR, *returns to his chair, the cable in hand. On the deck stands a brown replica of Rode's briefcase, open. Thoughtfully,* RIGBY *lays the coaxial cable inside the briefcase among a stack of police manuals and loose paper. He closes the case, lifts it, sets it down again.*

RIGBY
Try it.

MELLOR *picks up the case and registers its considerable weight.*

60. INT. FIELDING'S HOUSE. DINING-ROOM. EVENING

A Fielding dinner party has reached the dessert stage. The conversation is at its height. FIELDING *heads the table,* DOROTHY D'ARCY *has taken the other end.* SMILEY *sits on her right,* SHANE HECHT *on* FIELDING'*s right. Other guests are* ANN *and* SIMON SNOW, *a personable, decent young teaching couple,* FELIX D'ARCY, HECHT, *and two of the High Church clergymen we saw at Carne railway station, named* HARRY *and* TEDDY. *Also a weasely-looking Franciscan monk named* BROTHER ALGY. SMILEY *is conspicuous as the only person – apart from* BROTHER ALGY – *not in evening dress. He wears a battered suit. The Italian maid* CARMELINA *serves. Black candles, cut glass, an air of barely affordable splendour, and* FIELDING *in his element. The talk is scattered and animated. Several conversations at once, till one or other soloist breaks through.*

SHANE HECHT
(*To* HARRY) Dreadful about the murder, wasn't it? we're still recovering.

HARRY
Appalling. In the midst of life . . .

DOROTHY D'ARCY
It's everywhere. Some bastard stole my gold necklace a month ago. Been in the family for ages. Police don't

take a blind bit of notice. Probably pinched it themselves.

SHANE
Stella was such a *nice* person. One's so grateful for the adjective. And so *unusual*. She did such clever things with the same dress.

HARRY
Oh, you bad girl!

SMILEY
Was she popular at Carne?

SHANE
Oh, my darling, we're not *popular* at Carne, I hope. But I think she was popular with the *populace* of Carne. She was a Christian Scientist or something.

ANN SNOW
She was a Methodist actually.

SHANE HECHT
Darling. How sweet.

SMILEY
Didn't she do rather good work for the refugees?

SIMON SNOW
Terrific. She really got the thing going. She had the boys behind her too. A real groundswell.

SHANE HECHT *ignores this. Her eyes are on* SMILEY *and they are not kind.*

DOROTHY D'ARCY
Who *are* you?

SMILEY
Oh, nobody really. A very dull civil servant I'm afraid.

FIELDING
(*Down the table*) Knew my brother during the war.
Adrian. They spied together. Adrian was the white
sheep of the family.

D'ARCY
Why do you know so much about Stella?

SMILEY
Well I suppose we all do at the moment.

SHANE HECHT
Only Smiley I ever heard of married one of Lord
Sawley's cousins, a tart called Ann Sercombe. *He* was a
civil servant. Don't know what he served. No one said.

SMILEY
Oh, I'm afraid there are a lot of us about.

TEDDY
Are you a spy *now*? Do say you are! Except you
wouldn't, would you. You're not allowed.

DOROTHY D'ARCY
(*Joining battle with* SHANE HECHT)
Simon's right. Stella did a jolly good job on my
refugees. She didn't mind rolling up her sleeves. Good
form isn't everything in life.

SMILEY
How did it work, actually?

DOROTHY
Pick up points. My idea. North, South, East, and us.
Yellow bins. One in the front of each house.

SMILEY
And Stella?

DOROTHY

We called her our baglady.
(*Huge laugh from Shane.*)
She was the assembly point. Absolutely dependable.
First class.

SHANE

I found her insufferable. One of those tiresome little
snobs who think only the humble are virtuous. Algy,
you're glowering.

BROTHER ALGY

It was your conscience, Shane. I never glower. I can't.

TEDDY

Not allowed to, you mean!

Huge laughter round the table.

SMILEY

(*To* DOROTHY) So they were *your* refugees.

DOROTHY

I'm Area Organiser. Stella was Regional Officer.

SMILEY

Right up to when she died?

DOROTHY D'ARCY

Absolutely. Parcels to London practically every day.
HQ gave us a pat on the back only last week.
Marvellous little worker.

SMILEY

She must have been.

ANN SNOW

(*Pink and indignant from the wine.*)
We've only been here two Halfs. Stella was kinder to us
than anyone. She was happy to be herself. So people

sneered at her. Just because she was simple about the things she liked.

SNOW
(*Placating*) All right, darling. . . .

The embarrassed silence is saved by FIELDING.

FIELDING
Blessed are the meek! Well, I'm meek as hell. And I haven't inherited the earth. I used to regard the roadsweeper as a person inferior to myself. These days I rather doubt it. Something's dirty, roadsweeper makes it clean, state of the world advanced. What have I done? Entrenched a ruling class that, present company excepted, is possessed of neither talent nor culture. Opening young minds to wonders they'll never be able to enjoy. Faked. Pretended. Postured. Dreamed. What did La Rochefoucauld say? Hypocrisy is the tribute vice pays to virtue? Well, my God, I paid. Carne's not a school. It's a sanatorium for dying souls. Every day our minds atrophy and rot. You see before you a dead soul and Carne's the body I inhabit. Or did. (*Drinks.*) God bless us all.

DOROTHY D'ARCY
(*Angrily to her brother*) I think Terence is suffering from a very bad case of last term blues. Don't you, Felix?

D'ARCY
(*With innuendo*) Lucky to have made it this far, if you ask me, Terence. Carne's been good to you. Better not to forget it.

SHANE HECHT
You were always a little too rich for Carne's blood, weren't you, Terence?

Enter TIM PERKINS, *breathless, wearing a Duty Prefect's gown and carrying a staff. He takes two steps into the room, stands to attention,*

202

*beats the staff on the floor for silence, and bellows an exhortation in
Latin while those who know the form, which is everyone but* SMILEY,
grin at their plates and listen. Then, as he finishes, everyone stands,
SMILEY *a little after them, so that he is able to witness:*

FIELDING
(*To* PERKINS) My dear Perkins, have you just won the
marathon?

PERKINS
Bicycling from Mrs Harlowe's, sir. Extra violin.

FIELDING
(*A pat*) You did very well, Tim. Well done.

60A. INT. FIELDING'S HOUSE. HALLWAY & CORRIDOR. NIGHT

Placing himself in front of FIELDING, PERKINS *leads the whole
company in line ahead, down the corridor to the boys' dining room.*
SMILEY *goes last with* SIMON SNOW.

SMILEY
Is that the same Perkins who did so well in his science
exam?

SNOW
Good Heavens, how on earth did you know that?

SMILEY
I was talking to poor Stanley Rode. He was mystified.

SNOW
So was I. I couldn't help wondering whether he'd – well
– had a little help. My God, you do remember things.

The Head Prefect is calling 'Adsum'. At the raised table sit FIELDING *and his dinner guests, facing the boys,* FIELDING *presiding. As each boy's name is called, the boy flings up his arm and shouts 'Adsum'.*

PREFECT

Swire.

SWIRE

Adsum!

PREFECT

Tower!

TOWER

Adsum!

PREFECT

Wadham Major!

WADHAM MAJOR

Adsum!

PREFECT

Wadham Minor!

WADHAM MINOR
(*Very squeaky voice*) Adsum!

Laughter.

PREFECT
(*Affecting not to hear*)
Wadham Minor!

WADHAM MINOR
(*A tiny boy, pink with anger.*) Adsum! Adsum!

FIELDING *stands. Everyone else puts his face in his hands in prayer.*
SMILEY *is following suit as he catches sight of* PERKINS, *seated on a*
stool before an upright piano, staring blankly ahead of him, lost to
everything but his own thoughts.

FIELDING
(*Praying*) Oh Lord, bless this school and us who teach
here, and the boys entrusted to our care. May your
good heart so guide our minds and tongues that we may
rest each night in peace with Thee. Amen . . .

A hiatus before PERKINS *wakes to his task. Then with extra energy he*
strikes up on the piano. Bouncing to their feet, the boys at once burst
into a lusty rendering of the School Song as they turn and start their
processional exit:

BOYS
Rulers all on bended knee,
Bow to thy humility!
God of Gods
And King of Kings,
Blessed the School, Thy praises sing!

As the music continues into the last lines.

62. EXT. HILLTOP. NIGHT

MAD JANIE *is in what seems to be a cave, and is lighting a fire to keep*
her warm.

MAD JANIE
I knowed a man who rode on the wind. I see'd a man
fly clear at the moon. 'Ere' I said. 'You'm a penny short
of a pound, you are, same as me.' But he don't stop to
answer. He'm too damn busy riding on the wind.
'Come on, Janie, get aboard,' he says. 'There's room for
two up here! Get aboard, Janie, can't you damn fly?'
No, sir, Janie can't fly. There's other things Janie can
do. But she'm got an impediment, see, in her head, that

205

hinders her flying . . . Janie's a penny short of a pound, same as you, sir.

A darting shaft of light catches her. In the same moment MAD JANIE *screams, turns and dives into the undergrowth as a police car, with bells ringing, tears down on her.*

63. INT. FIELDING'S STUDY (OR DINING-ROOM). NIGHT

SMILEY *and* FIELDING *sit alone before the fire over a last whisky and soda.* FIELDING *is down and dangerous: an actor after the show.*

SMILEY
Delightful party. Nice people.

FIELDING
I hate them all. Worth the journey?

SMILEY
Very much so.

FIELDING
Why come otherwise?

SMILEY
Indeed.

FIELDING
So why come?

SMILEY
Oh, bullied into it by an old friend who couldn't come down herself and felt something should be done. You know how it goes.

FIELDING
You said on the phone something about a letter from Stella Rode.

206

SMILEY

Did I? Oh yes . . . She'd gone in for some competition the magazine was running. She'd complained rather aggressively that she'd been discriminated against. All water under the bridge now.

FIELDING

(*Still suspicious*) But you thought you'd come all the same.

SMILEY

Yes. What was Stella really like?

FIELDING

She was common. As you heard. We're all common. Middle class bores with upper class pretensions and third class degrees. She dragged us down, they said. We're down already. Flat on the ground, some of us. Flat, flatulent, flatulentest. Flat broke.

SMILEY

What are you going to do with your retirement?

FIELDING

(*Hollow laugh*) Retirement? Without a pension? Oh, Cipriani's in Venice for a few months. Buy a little place in the Dordogne. Find a gorgeous boy to ease my declining years.

SMILEY

No pension?

FIELDING

I'm a temporary master here. Permanently temporary. In 1940 I happened to be cottage crawling in tasteful Hull while I was examining for Higher Certificate. Do you know what that means? Cruising gentlemen's lavatories in search of temporary consolation. Mine turned out to be a very charming young policeman. Fielding's a common enough name, I thought I might

get away with it. I reckoned without the D'Arcys – the eyes
and ears of Carne. The Governors took a lenient view. 'Stay
on sufferance, but don't expect a pension.' I don't tamper
with little boys. I am not a monster. They understood that at
least. Why am I telling you all this? Because you know, don't
you. Adrian tried to help me out, but your bloody office
chose to turn me down. I can't think why, considering how
many of us you took. Perhaps I wasn't pretty enough.
Another whisky?

> SMILEY

So what will you do?

FIELDING *is mixing the drinks.*

> FIELDING

I've been lucky. There's a charming little National
Trust house near Salisbury, Manor Court. Some nice
eighteenth century portraits, a decent staircase, some
slightly suspect furniture, a reasonable flat on the top
floor and six hundred a year for the curator. I think it
rather appropriate to die in a museum. I shall miss the
warmth of human contact, naturally. You might tell me
how my brother died. He was always such an example.
I'm sure he did it wonderfully.

> SMILEY

Yes. He did.

> FIELDING

You're snooping. I can feel it. What do you want?

The door bell rings. FIELDING *frowns and goes to answer it.*

63A. INT. FIELDING'S HALLWAY & FRONT DOOR. NIGHT

RIGBY *enters, carrying his lookalike version of Rode's briefcase.*

RIGBY
Sorry about this. Just routine.

His eye catches SMILEY *who has drifted into the hall from the study (or dining-room). He is looking totally blank.*

FIELDING
(*Introducing*) Mr Smiley. Friend of mine.

SMILEY *nods.*

RIGBY
Evening, sir. First time in Carne?

SMILEY
Yes, I'm afraid it is.

RIGBY
(*To* FIELDING) I can always tell an old boy. They've got the confidence. Now sir, just one question if you don't mind.

(*He glances questioningly at* SMILEY.)

FIELDING
(*With edge*) Don't worry about him. He's family.

RIGBY
Well sir, this briefcase here, is by way of being a rough approximation to Mr Rode's. I believe I'm right in saying that Mrs Rode on the night of the murder, she left early after your dinner party.

64. INT. FIELDING'S HOUSE, HALL/FRONT DOOR. NIGHT

As previous flashback (Scene 50). Different angle. Again, back view of STELLA RODE'*s head. Favouring* FIELDING *and* GUESTS.

STELLA RODE'S VOICE
Oh, I'll be all right, thank you. I'm quite happy leaving you men to swap your little secrets.

STELLA *leaves and walks off into the darkness.*

RIGBY

But *Mr* Rode, he left later, and he took . . . the lane home.

FIELDING

He took the path across the fields. He always does.

RIGBY

Bit dark though, wasn't it?

FIELDING

I lent him a torch.

RIGBY

I thought he had one.

FIELDING

He gave it to his wife. I lent him mine.

RIGBY

So you saw him to the door, I dare say.

FIELDING

Yes.

RIGBY

And he took his briefcase with him?

FIELDING

Yes.

RIGBY

Did you watch him to the field path.

FIELDING

Yes, I did as a matter of fact. It was a nice night. I stood outside and took a breath of fresh air.

RIGBY *digs in the briefcase and extracts a torch.*

RIGBY

This the torch, sir?

FIELDING

Yes.

RIGBY

It's all yours, sir. I should get you to sign a receipt but I shan't bother. Now, sir. During dinner, where was this briefcase situated?

FIELDING

In the front porch, on the marble shelf. He takes it with him everywhere. Rather silly of him. Makes him a figure of fun. When he arrived, he put it on the shelf. When he left –

RIGBY

And when he left – ?

SMILEY *and* RIGBY *are watching* FIELDING *intently.*

FIELDING

I handed it to him.

RIGBY

Yourself? Physically handed Mr Rode the briefcase?

FIELDING

Yes. I always see people off.

RIGBY

Put it in his hand.

FIELDING

Yes.

RIGBY

And the briefcase was *light*, was it – Just a few exam papers, I understand, couple of exercise books.

FIELDING

It was heavy as lead. I made a joke to him. Forget what I said. No, I don't. 'Christ, what do you keep in here, Stanley? You doing a bit of plumbing on the side?'

RIGBY

(*Grimly satisfied*) Very funny.

A tap on the door. PERKINS *enters.*

FIELDING

(*Angry*) Have you been standing outside that door all the time?

PERKINS

No, sir.

FIELDING

What do you want?

PERKINS

Permission to sound Senior Boys' Bell, sir.

FIELDING

Sound it, Tim. Sound it.

PERKINS *exits.*

RIGBY

Well I mustn't keep you gentlemen. Goodnight, Mr Fielding.
Goodnight, Mr –

SMILEY

Smiley. Goodnight.

RIGBY

You staying here or can I give you a lift somewhere, sir?

SMILEY

Oh, it's only the Sawley Arms. I think the walk will do me good, thank you. After such a lavish dinner.

RIGBY
(*Jocular*) Well, mind how you go now, sir. These are tricky times.

RIGBY *leaves.*

FIELDING
Want one? For the road?

SMILEY
No, I must be off.

FIELDING
Policemen are so bloody obvious. No wonder all the best murderers are at large. Better take the torch, hadn't you?

They are suddenly face to face.

FIELDING

Shall I come with you?

SMILEY
Oh, I shall be fine.

FIELDING
Take care, it's not like London here. Country people take the law into their own hands.

SMILEY
You mean they break it?

FIELDING
Good night.

66. EXT. CARNE. NIGHT

SMILEY *alone in the lane. His mood is brisk and operational. A public footpath sign points across moonlit fields.* SMILEY *glances back at*

FIELDING's *house. A bicycle is chained to the railings. Shining the torch on his watch,* SMILEY *checks the time exactly, then strikes out across the field.*

67. EXT. RODE'S HOUSE. NIGHT

A little breathless, SMILEY *arrives at the back door and looks again at his watch: twenty-one minutes.*

Another angle as SMILEY *peers round for a way to enter the house. He shines the torch into the back door keyhole. The end of the key protrudes: it is in the lock, inserted from the inside.* SMILEY *casts round again, sees a stuffed dustbin, extracts an old newspaper.*

Another angle. SMILEY *is feeding a double sheet of newspaper under the back door. When it is three-quarters through, he stands up, takes a propelling pencil from his pocket and pokes the keyhole till the key falls on to the newspaper on the other side of the door. He slides the newspaper out from under the door. The key lies on it. He picks it up and inserts it in the lock.*

68. INT. RODE'S HOUSE. NIGHT

SMILEY *prowls, flashlight in hand. From the kitchen he passes to the living-room, peers into the blood-spattered conservatory and spots a bare door at the far end. He goes to it and opens it. It gives on to an old scullery, now a packing room for Stella's refugee work. A small pile of old clothes, perhaps not good enough to send, lies in a corner.* SMILEY *turns them with his foot. On the centre table, a large set of postal scales. On shelves above them, piles of jute sacks with draw strings round the throat and packs of printed tie-on labels. He examines a label. It reads:*

> Clothes for Hungary
> 27, Wilton Street
> London, SW1

And on the back: Station 19, Area 3, Dorset.

He puts a label in his pocket, passes through the drawing-room, enters a small study containing a single bed with science books on the bedside table.

He moves upstairs, enters a single-bedded room. Beside this bed, a Bible, tracts. Then a Methodist prayerbook with a folded piece of paper in it. He scans the paper by torchlight.

Does he hear a sound? He is fast but very calm. Putting the paper in his pocket, he goes silently to the landing, listens. In his hand he holds a plaster head of Lloyd George.

He tiptoes down the stairs, the bust in his hand, slips to the living-room and stands just inside the door.

68A. INT. CONSERVATORY. NIGHT

In the conservatory, a muffled ragged figure stands with her head lifted attentively to the sky, something in her hand.

SMILEY
(*Softly*) Janie.

MAD JANIE *turns abruptly to stare at him. She holds a sprig of holly.*

MAD JANIE
I thought you was the Devil, Mister, but you'm got no wings to fly.

SMILEY
I'm not the Devil, Janie. I'm a friend.

MAD JANIE
You can't do nothing by me, Mister, 'cos I got the holly for to hold yer! You bide there, Mister!
(*She starts backing away from him*)
There's some do laugh at Janie. But I've see'd the Devil, I 'ave. Silver wings, he had. I see'd him flying, riding on the wind, and the moon behind him lightin'

up the way! They'm close as sisters, Moon and Devil.
And they've got blood to 'em you wouldn't not *believe*!

On the last word SMILEY *ducks, but only just in time, as* MAD JANIE
spirits a rock from the recesses of her tattered dress and flings it at
SMILEY *with all her strength, smashing a mirror behind him. She is*
gone.

69. INT. RIGBY'S OWN CAR. OPEN HILL COUNTRY ABOVE CARNE.
   NIGHT

RIGBY *driving fast up a hill.*

RIGBY
(*Heavily sarcastic*) Thank you for your help. I've just
founded Trespassers Anonymous. Next time you feel
the urge, phone me first, do you mind, I'll come round
with a bottle and talk you out of it.

SMILEY
It takes twenty-one minutes exactly.

RIGBY
What does?

SMILEY
To walk from Fielding's house across the fields to
Rode's house.

RIGBY
Fascinating.

TED MUNDY *has appeared in the lane, flagging them down.* RIGBY
slows, but doesn't stop, to let MUNDY *hop into the back seat.*

RIGBY
Which way?

MUNDY

Straight on. One and a half miles. You'll see a sign to
Mallow's Pool
(*To* SMILEY) Evening, sir.

SMILEY

Good evening.

MUNDY

(*Hospitable to* SMILEY) There's four to five of these
villages up here. On a plateau like, sir. More
settlements than villages, they are: Pontis Vallum,
Miser's Cord, Pylle . . . Pylle's where the local idiots
come from. Incest it is, probably. They're inbred as a
barnful of cats.
(*To* RIGBY) That's the light. Go slow now. Left in one
hundred yards. In the field there, on its own. Easy
now.
(*To* SMILEY) A Plague church, Pylle is. When the plague
came, the villagers left their dead and burned their
houses and moved away, you see, sir.

RIGBY

Shut up, Ted.

MUNDY

(*To* SMILEY) I saw the light, you see, sir. There's only
one person lights a light in Pylle church these days.

70. EXT. NEAR PYLLE CHURCH. NIGHT

*A windswept hilltop, racing clouds, a fugitive moon, screaming night
birds, drifting veils of mist and driven snow.*

RIGBY

(*To* SMILEY) You better stay back here. Last thing we
need is you to look after.

217

MUNDY

Come behind me, sir. Just look out for badgers, they'll
go for you this time of year.

71. INT. PYLLE CHURCH. NIGHT

*Two candles and an oil lamp on a bare altar, either side of a crudely
fashioned cross. Before the altar, on the sanctuary step, sits* MAD
JANIE, *her face daubed with brown mud. She is surrounded by the
bodies of small animals, and she is performing a ritual of exorcism.
From* SMILEY'S *point of view we close slowly on the altar. A string of
green beads hangs from the cross.*

MUNDY

Come along, my lovely. Time for a nice car ride. Where
d'you get that pretty coat from, Janie?

A shaft of torchlight. MAD JANIE *is wearing a blue coat like a cape
over her shoulders.*

72. INT. RIGBY'S CAR. DESCENDING HILL. NIGHT

MAD JANIE *sits in the back between* SMILEY *and* MUNDY. *She is quiet
and composed.*

MUNDY

You gone and quarrelled with someone, Janie?

MAD JANIE

I don't quarrel with 'ee. I don't like 'ee. Dear God.

MUNDY

You do something for him, did you, Janie? What' you
do for him?

MAD JANIE

He gave me a necklace. He gave me a coat to keep me
warm. I'm scared, Ted Mundy. You'd better bloody be
scared too.

MUNDY

He talk to you too, did he?

MAD JANIE

She did.

MUNDY

What she say then, Janie?

MAD JANIE *opens her mouth and lifts her eyes like a dying woman. She begins to whimper in short tense jerks.*

MAD JANIE

No . . . don't . . . stop . . . don't . . . no . . . don't . . .
please . . . please . . .
(*She is rolling her head from side to side, more and more hysterical.*)
. . . God, don't . . . Don't . . . *don't* . . . !

73. INT. ABBEY. DAY

Sunday Matins. School and staff are giving a lusty rendering of Blake's 'Jerusalem'. We recognise TIM PERKINS *in the choir. The* HECHTS, D'ARCYS , SNOWS, FIELDING *and* RODE *are among the congregation.*

Another angle. Up in the 'hencoop' on the balcony, SMILEY *sits unobserved, reading a work of seventeenth century German literature. The hymn ends. He hears the final blessing and softly closes his book.*

74. EXT. CARNE TOWN. DAY

SMILEY *and the* SNOWS *strolling together after the service.*

SIMON SNOW

He just got everything right. Tick, tick, tick, straight down the column. Seventy-eight per cent. No question.

SMILEY

It *was* Perkins' writing?

SIMON

Oh sure. Blobs everywhere.

SMILEY

Perhaps he cribbed.

SIMON

The two boys he was sitting next to both got twenty-five.

ANN SNOW

I think it was just Simon's brilliant influence. He's doing poor Stanley's teaching for him while he's off.

SMILEY

I'm sure it was.

75. EXT. MAJOR HARRIMAN'S HOUSE. KENNELS. DAY

SMILEY *and* HARRIMAN *walk among the barking dogs. In the background,* ALICE *is attending to a pony.* HARRIMAN *is a shrewd, gung-ho ex-professional soldier.*

HARRIMAN

So Felix sent you, did he? Good on Felix. What do you want? Guard dog? Big dog, small dog, long hair, short hair? Go for short hair, if I were you, unless you want to be cleaning off their rear ends all the time.

SMILEY

Well something fairly robust. If I'm settling in the country. I suppose everyone's saying that at the moment.

HARRIMAN

Bitches are more loyal, as a rule. Depends on whether you trust Alsatians. I don't. But then I don't trust any

of 'em. She's a good 'un. Come here, Sophie!
(*He cursorily fondles an Alsatian.*)
Put a notice up. 'Fierce Dog'. Starve her one day a
week. Just keep on the right side of her, that's all.

SMILEY
They say Mrs Rode's dog let her down completely. Ran
away.

HARRIMAN
Absolute bloody nonsense! Pack of lies, start to finish.
Rumour factory, this place is, worse than a regiment.
Bloody wives at the root of it. What ruined India.

SMILEY
So what happened?

HARRIMAN
Dog wasn't even there!
(*He turns into another pen.*)
Not in evidence. Not within *miles* of the house. Hadn't
been for – oh, a week or more. Sally, Sally, Sally, come
here! Come here!

SMILEY
So where was it?

HARRIMAN
(*Fondling Sally*) Here. This is her. Very dog. Been here
for – Alice!

ALICE *approaches*.

HARRIMAN
How long have we had Sally here?

ALICE
(*Giving* SMILEY *the glad eye*)
A week. We're going to keep her if we can. She's my
favourite.

SMILEY

But what a tragedy. She might have saved Mrs Rode's life.

As HARRIMAN *is talking,* D'ARCY's *Morris Oxford van is approaching.* ALICE *turns quickly and scampers over to it.* FELIX D'ARCY *climbs out. There is no greeting, but there is complicity as, together,* D'ARCY *and* ALICE *walk round to the back of the car and unload a couple of King Charles spaniels. Then walk with them side by side towards the house. Meanwhile:*

HARRIMAN

There you are. There's your chum. Some of his sister's puppies for jabs. Alice can look after 'm . . . Yes, she brought it in herself one afternoon. Said her husband was sick of the sight of it. Wanted it out of the house for a while. Said he'd threatened to drown it. She was scared.

SMILEY

But no talk of putting it down.

HARRIMAN

No, no, just one of his moods, she said. Wait till it blew over, best thing. Said if her husband rang, I should say the dog was dead. I wouldn't have said any such thing, of course. Lot of human nature in this business. You get to know the types.

SMILEY

What was her type?

HARRIMAN

(*Laughs*) Trouble. I've had a few of *them* in the regiment in my time too. Butter-wouldn't-melt. Holier-than-thou, then all of a sudden, *Wallop!* I'd say she was the hysterical type. Self dramatising. Weeping all over the house for days on end. Drive their husbands to drink. Or worse. Sunday virgins, we used to call 'em. ODs most of 'em. Other Denominations.

222

76. INT. TIN TABERNACLE. AFTERNOON

CARDEW *is addressing a dark-clothed congregation of townspeople and relatives. Among them,* RODE, SMILEY, RIGBY *and the* SNOWS. *And old* MR GLASTON, *Stella's father, a venerable, iron-jawed northerner of sixty-five.*

> CARDEW
> And so we may use this occasion to . . . honour the dead . . . and to offer our heartfelt sympathy, love and fellowship and understanding . . . to those who endure the shock and grief of Stella's going . . . her husband, Stanley, . . . her father, Henry Glaston . . . her fellow workers here in the Chapel. Oh God, who gave His Son to us, and understands our pain, please comfort these people in their distress. Amen.

77. INT. TABERNACLE. VESTRY. DAY

SMILEY *and* MR GLASTON *sit alone at a tiny table with sandwiches and tea before them. Through the open door to the Chapel, we see the congregation having their own stand-up tea.* SMILEY *has his notebook open.*

> GLASTON
> Are you Chapel yourself?

> SMILEY
> No.

> GLASTON
> Why do you write for a Chapel paper, then?

> SMILEY
> It's a job.

GLASTON *nods in approval.*

GLASTON

Stanley was Chapel, when they married. Then he went
over. Where I come from, Chapel was something we'd
stood up for and won. Same as the vote. She was a great
one for chatter.

SMILEY

I'll put that. Loved to pass the time of day with people.

GLASTON

Busybody, more like. Bearing tales. She'd never have
married poor Stanley, if he hadn't got his Doctor of
Chemistry.

SMILEY

I wonder if there's a phrase we might agree on –
something that best sums up how you like to remember
her best.

GLASTON

Maybe she got what she deserved.

78. EXT. THE SAWLEY GARDENS. EVENING

The formal gardens of Carne. SMILEY *and* RODE *sit on a bench,
staring at the empty bandstand. Behind them, the Abbey and the Carne
skyline.*

SMILEY

So what was in the briefcase exactly, when you walked
home across the fields?

RODE

Nothing much, exam papers mainly. A few exercise
books.

SMILEY

You mean, exam papers for correction?

RODE

No. Papers I'd set. Papers for the exam the next day. I
have to carry it all with me. If I sit in the Common
Room and set a paper, I've still to carry the paper
home . . .

SMILEY

Nothing heavy – no heavy samples – visual aids –
you're sure?

RODE

Of course I'm sure. What's it to you anyway?

SMILEY

It's called exploring every avenue. It's what the police
are doing. I'm afraid you're one of the avenues.

RODE

That's stupid.

SMILEY

What happened to your dog, Sally?

RODE

She killed it.

SMILEY

Why did she do that?

RODE

To hurt me – why d'you think? I came back home, it
wasn't there. She said she was sick of seeing all my love
going on a dog. 'Now you can love me instead,' she
said. She'd taken it to Harriman's to be put down.
That's when I moved downstairs. I couldn't sleep with
her after that. I hated her. There. I've said it now.

SMILEY

Well, don't say it to anyone else.

79. INT. SAWLEY ARMS. LOBBY. EVENING

SMILEY *in a phone box, inserting huge coins, then pressing button A.*

SMILEY
Ailsa, I want you to do me a little favour. Have you got
a pencil? It's called the Clothes for Hungary Campaign,
27 Wilton Street, SW1. Just be your sweet, innocent
self. Can you still do that.

80. INT. SAWLEY ARMS. SMILEY'S BEDROOM. NIGHT

SMILEY *sits alone in his cardigan among his academic books. But he is
not reading them. He has Stella Rode's handwritten prayer beside him
on the bed, and he is earnestly studying the slip of paper he took from
Stella's prayer book.*

STELLA RODE'S VOICE
'Oh God, make me better than I can be on my own,
because I know I'm bad without you. Stella.'

PART THREE

81. EXT. SAWLEY ARMS. DAY

In the forecourt of the hotel, LUIGI *is lending* SMILEY *a bicycle.*
SMILEY, *frantically patting his pockets, tips* LUIGI *a couple of green
pound notes.*

82. EXT. WILTON STREET, SW I. DAY

AILSA BRIMLEY *alights from her cab and approaches a noble
eighteenth century house with steps rising to a portico.*

83. EXT. RODE'S HOUSE. DAY

SMILEY *sits on his stationary bicycle. He looks at his watch, braces
himself, and as the second hand reaches twelve:*

SMILEY

Go!

He begins pedalling like mad.

84. INT. 27, WILTON STREET. DAY

BRIMLEY *is finding her way down some stairs to the basement. A
rather superior secretary hovers, having given her directions.*

85. EXT. FIELDING'S HOUSE. DAY

Overtaking boys on their way to class, SMILEY *pedals furiously past the house, looks at his watch as he does so, but keeps pedalling till he is round the corner, where he gratefully dismounts, breathing heavily. From the bay window of the Spinning Wheel coffee house* SHANE HECHT *and two other Carne wives stare at him in perplexity.*

86. INT. BASEMENT. WILTON STREET. DAY

This is where the real work is done. In a vast unhygienic boiler room with pipes running along the ceiling, and big wicker baskets stacked against the walls, three volunteer upper class English girls in overalls are tipping out the contents of sacks from all over England, then sorting them into piles of coats, gloves, hats, shoes. The head girl is MANDY.

> MANDY
> (*As she and her helper hump a basket across the floor.*)
> Oh well I mean, gosh, no, any way we can help you.

> BRIMLEY
> Well, my dear, it's too silly and I hate to interrupt you. There's this friend of mine who lives in Carne –

> MANDY
> Gosh, how frightfully grand.

> BRIMLEY
> More a sort of cousin, really, but it's simpler to call her a friend – she's a *bit* scatty.

> MANDY
> Oh dear.

> BRIMLEY
> And what she did, last week, if you can believe it, is give her cast-offs to the refugee people, which is absolutely fine, including a rather old cashmere cardigan she's had since the *Flood*.

MANDY
Still, it is cashmere. Jolly nice of her really.

BRIMLEY
– leaving pinned to it, if you can credit this, a really
rather scrumptious diamond brooch that had belonged
to her maternal aunt –

MANDY
Oh my hat, oh how simply awful – I mean for you too,
having to sort of cope – I mean, imagine it going to
Hungary.

MANDY *grabs a log book from a desk and opens it.*

MANDY
Carne, you said . . . Now the absolutely crucial thing is,
which day would it have been posted to us?

87. INT. BASEMENT DELIVERY ROOM. DAY

*An adjoining basement room with an improvised wooden chute from
pavement level to receive heavy postal packages. At the top of it, steel
doors open to the London sky. At its foot, a dozen sacks with the
familiar printed labels.* MANDY *examines each in turn.*

MANDY
Marlborough . . . Exeter . . . Edinburgh . . .
Winchester . . . Here we are, *Carne!* Gosh let's hope
we're in luck. Postmark last Thursday, when did she
hand in her cardigan, that's the point? Sometimes they
take simply ages to turn stuff round – specially in the
country –

Between them they are pulling the sack away from the pile. MANDY
sets to work untying the drawstring.

MANDY
We can tell a lot of our regulars by their knots.
Extraordinary what you can learn about people from

knots. Carne's are usually *frightfully* neat . . . This one's an absolute pig – (*pulling at the string*) Crikey. . . .

BRIMLEY

Here. Let me help.

MANDY

Oh, I *do* hope. Let's pray to Saint Anthony. He's super at finding things.

BRIMLEY *has loosened the string and opened the throat of the sack. They look inside.*

Their heads rise and their eyes meet. BRIMLEY*'s face is iron hard, but* MANDY *is opening her mouth to scream.* BRIMLEY *gently puts her hand to* MANDY*'s lips.*

BRIMLEY

You're not to scream. You're not to be sick. This is a police matter. You're to say nothing to anybody. Do you understand, dear?
(*As she reties the throat of the sack*)
When I've gone, you're to sit on a chair and count to a hundred. Then go and make yourself a cup of sweet tea.

88. INT. CARNE POLICE STATION. INTERVIEW ROOM. DAY

Over cups of tea, MAD JANIE *sits beside a policewoman while* TED MUNDY *gently questions her, a notebook before him. She is distraught and almost mute.*

MUNDY

So he's got a hump on his back now, has he?

MAD JANIE *nods.*

MUNDY

So he's riding on the wind with a hump on his back. Sounds more like Father Christmas to me. Big hump?

MAD JANIE *nods.*

> ### MUNDY
> Big as me?

MAD JANIE *shakes her head.*

> ### MUNDY
> What d'e do with the hump then, Janie?

MAD JANIE *shakes her head.*

> ### MUNDY
> Nothing. He carried it. Over his shoulder like? Did he have to hold it on or did it sit there by itself, I wonder. Wasn't a coat was it, like yours?

MUNDY *sighs and glances at the policewoman, indicating that further questioning is over.*

> ### MUNDY
> Janie, you're going to have to bide here a few days, see. Have some more nice baths and a few square meals and clean yourself up.

MUNDY *is leaving the room.*

> ### MAD JANIE
> I got to 'ave sky. I'm no damn dog in a kennel, bugger you, Ted Mundy!

> ### MUNDY
> I got to 'ave sky too, my love. But sometimes indoors is that bit safer. Not just for you.

89. INT. SAWLEY TAP PUB. CARNE. DAY

SMILEY *and* STANLEY RODE *drinking beer in a corner.*

RODE

I don't understand you any more. You said you were a journalist.

SMILEY

You're lucky I'm not, after what you told me yesterday evening.

RODE

I feel better now I've said it.

SMILEY

Did you ever hit her?

RODE

No. I'm not the kind.

SMILEY

Perhaps you saved it all up for one big jamboree.

RODE

Don't think I didn't think of it.

SMILEY

What did she have on D'Arcy?

RODE

(*Mimicking his wife's voice*)
'I've got another of them for you, Stan. That fine Mister Felix D'Arcy's putting his hands up Alice Lawry's skirts. You thought he was a nancy boy. That's not what Alice said. Not just his hands either.' Then she showed me his letter. 'I must remind you that your husband is still on probation and that I am a senior member of the Board of Administration.'

SMILEY

Where's the letter now?

RODE

She burned it. She was crafty. 'There,' she said. 'It never happened. Now it's all in my mind again. That's where they all a.e. Locked up in my head. Prisoners serving out their punishment in my head.'

SMILEY

Who else did she have locked up?

90. INT. CARNE SCHOOL. HECHT'S CLASSROOM. DAY

CHARLES HECHT *is teaching geography to a bunch of obtuse athletes. His subject today is Rhodesia, as the map shows. Utter boredom, shared by* HECHT.

MARSH

Sir, Cecil Rhodes, sir.

HECHT

(*Addressing map*) One of the greatest Englishmen ever born. Inland country, bounded in the south and south-west by Transvaal, Bechuanaland and South West Africa, formerly German, now in the right hands. Ours. What's this river, Plum? Name the river, Plum, that divides the British Colony of Rhodesia into two unequal halves.

PLUM

Sir, Tiber, sir.

HECHT

(*Still addressing map*) Abercrombie?

ABERCROMBIE

Zambesi, sir.

HECHT

(*Still to map*) Stay behind after school, Plum. One of the most marvellous countries in the world and if any of you are ever bright enough to pass the Colonial Office exam., which I doubt, you can go out there and run it.

91. INT. SAWLEY TAP. DAY

RODE *and* SMILEY *drinking.*

> RODE
>
> He stole. That's what she said.

> SMILEY
>
> What did he steal.

> RODE
>
> The Expedition money. That's what she said. He got a School Expedition together to Alaska. Launched an Appeal to the Old Boys. Shane was treasurer. The Expedition came back, big spread in the School Magazine, everyone very proud. Then one of the parents didn't like the look of the accounts. There was two thousand pounds not accounted for. It was swept under the carpet. 'Pardonable incompetence.'

> SMILEY
>
> How did she find this out?

> RODE
>
> The school secretary told her. Chapel. It wasn't ill-meant. Just chat really. But there was no such thing as just chat for Stella. It was all poison to be stored away. 'There you are, Doctor. The bigger they are, the worse they are. That's what life's about.' She loved calling me Doctor. 'Heal thyself,' she'd say. You don't meet evil a lot in life. Not real evil. I married it.

> SMILEY
>
> Did she tease Hecht?

RODE
Both of them, I expect. I don't know. I tried not to
listen.

SMILEY
I suppose one way not to listen would have been to
close her mouth.

92. EXT. CARNE COUNTRYSIDE. DAY

*The same spot where the piece of coaxial cable was found by Ted
Mundy. His bike propped against the gate, SMILEY stands and stares,
first at the ditch, then up the lane, where the outlines of Carne Abbey
are just visible.*

93. EXT. D'ARCY'S HOUSE. DAY

*The Morris Oxford van is in the driveway. To the barking of spaniels,
SMILEY rides slowly by, glancing at his watch as he does so. Unseen
by SMILEY, FELIX D'ARCY eyes him maliciously from behind the lace
curtains. There is a yellow refugee clothing bin evident at the front.*

94. EXT. HECHT'S HOUSE. DAY

*SMILEY rides slowly by, checking his watch. A sailing dinghy is
parked in the driveway, attached to the rear of a senile Rover. SHANE
HECHT is bent over the boot. She is wearing Wellingtons. As SMILEY
passes, she too lifts her head to watch his departing back.*

95. EXT. CARNE SCHOOL, CLOISTERS. DAY

*FIELDING and TIM PERKINS walk side by side. FIELDING is being
'capped' by boys: a slight lifting of the right hand and a muttered
'sir'. PERKINS wears rugby gear and carries a pair of walking shoes,
and his violin in a case. FIELDING wears Wellingtons. Among the
passers by, one or two wear plastic rain capes.*

FIELDING

Is it home?

PERKINS

No, sir.

FIELDING

Is it work?

PERKINS

Don't know, really.

FIELDING

Is it me? It could be. I can be a monster when I feel like it. The Vampire of Carne.

PERKINS

No, sir, honestly, sir, it's not you, really.

FIELDING

Is it a boy? Love isn't a beatable offence. Not in my house, at least. Unless it gets out of hand. Well?

PERKINS

No, sir.

FIELDING

So it's a girl. I admire you, Tim. You've beaten Alcatraz.

PERKINS

(*Weak giggle*) No, sir. It's not a girl, sir.

FIELDING

Another master?

PERKINS

(*At the edge of tears*)
It's all right, sir, honestly. I don't know. It's only me, sir. It's really all right. I'm just being wet.

FIELDING

You have reason to celebrate, *actually*. Seventy-eight in science. That's not to be sneezed at. You seem to have confounded your elders. Mr Rode and Mr Snow are both bemused. However did you do it? Did you crib?

PERKINS

Not in school, sir.

FIELDING

What does that mean, Perkins?

PERKINS

I couldn't, sir. There wasn't any point. We sit in alphabetical order in exams. Palfrey and Phillimore are worse at science than I am.

FIELDING

So where did you crib?

PERKINS

(*Desperate*) I didn't! I didn't crib! I just did it by myself.

96. INT. SAWLEY ARMS. EVENING

SMILEY *enters, goes to the porter's desk to collect his room key. The ancient* PORTER *extracts a scrap of paper but no key from* SMILEY*'s pigeonhole. Looks at paper, throws it away.*

PORTER

Your wife's got it, sir. She's gone up to the room.

SMILEY

My what?

PORTER

Your wife, sir. You are married, I take it. Only they're quite tight about that here.

SMILEY

(*Recovering*) Of course I'm married. Thank you. I'm sorry. Yes, of course.

97. INT. SAWLEY ARMS. UPSTAIRS CORRIDOR. EVENING

SMILEY *appears at the top of the stairs and walks to his bedroom door and taps on it. He stands back as if out of the line of fire.*

SMILEY

(*Cockney accent*) Porter, sir. Parcel for you.

Again he stands clear. The door opens. It is AILSA BRIMLEY. *Behind her on the floor of Smiley's bedroom, her sack from Wilton Street.*

BRIMLEY

George! Don't be so stupid! Come in at once.

98. INT. SAWLEY ARMS, SMILEY'S BEDROOM. EVENING

SMILEY *and* AILSA BRIMLEY *are huddled in their overcoats by a small popping gas fire. They are contemplating the grisly contents of the refugees' sack: a full-length transparent plastic 'pac-a-mac' with hood, a pair of rubber overshoes, a pair of old leather gloves. They are all heavily blood-stained. At the bottom of the sack, cast-off clothes make up the bulk.*

SMILEY

(*Softly*) 'Silver wings he had. I see'd him flying, riding on the wind.' On a bicycle. Down the lane. Four minutes ten seconds from Fielding's house, three minutes fifty seconds from the Hechts but they're very muscular Christians so I'm sure they'd have set their own record. The only person who's off the hook is Rode. Apart from Mad Janie, naturally.

BRIMLEY

Why Rode?

SMILEY

Because he didn't arrive on a bicycle, he didn't come down the lane, and he didn't go anywhere afterwards.

BRIMLEY

(*Looking at label*) And Stella's batch. No question?

SMILEY *fishes in his pocket and produces the label he took from the Rodes' house.*

SMILEY

(*Matching labels*) None. He must have dropped off the sack at a pick up point. (*He shrugs.*) *She* must . . . What the murderer didn't reckon with was Janie interrupting. He or she gave Janie Stella's beads – I imagine they had become detached from their owner – and a coat to keep her warm. Stella was a blackmailer. Not for money. For fun.

BRIMLEY

Don't you think it might be time to go public George?

99. INT. CARNE POLICE STATION. RIGBY'S OFFICE. EVENING

RIGBY

(*A sullen outburst. He is very tired.*)
The Super's going to murder *me* now. You know that, don't you. He wants the lid kept down, not taken off! There's no proof Janie didn't do it.

BRIMLEY

In English law one's supposed to think the other way, if you don't mind.

RIGBY

Don't you tell me my law, thank you, madam! All right, someone posted the parcel, and the parcel contained the murderer's apparel and this is the murderer's apparel, no question. Doesn't mean who posted the parcel killed Stella Rode!

(*Silence.*)
God damn it!, so who the hell *did* do it? The
headmaster? The whole blasted Common Room?

BRIMLEY

And their wives.

RIGBY

Heaven protect me from amateurs. I'm sorry, Miss
Brimley, now I didn't mean that. I ought to be
thanking you. I may be a trifle tired. I am. (*Shouts*)
Sergeant Mundy!

MUNDY *appears, buttoning up his tunic.*

RIGBY

(*To* MUNDY) Take Mad Janie up the hill. Put her back in
her nest. No charges. Give her a couple of quid out of
the charity box. Tell her to go out and get drunk.

100. INT. THE SAWLEY TAP. NIGHT

SMILEY *and* AILSA BRIMLEY *drinking at a corner table.*

BRIMLEY

Hecht?

SMILEY

Could be Hecht. He's got the muscles. Don't know
about the nerve. She's got the wrists. So has D'Arcy. So
has his sister.

BRIMLEY

What's his sister like?

SMILEY

Caligula.

BRIMLEY

Do you think she *is* his sister?

240

SMILEY
Perhaps she's his brother. Fielding's a dead cert. Plenty of motive. He'd kill every woman in the world if he had his way, from what I remember.

BRIMLEY
I don't think he'd confine himself to women, necessarily.

They drink.

101. EXT. CARNE QUAD. NIGHT

Heavy rain is falling. We identify the school theatre, all its windows lit.

102. INT. CARNE SCHOOL THEATRE. NIGHT

The morality play has gone indoors for its 'Tech Run' which is being played before a substantial audience of boys and staff, including FIELDING, *the* HECHTS *and* D'ARCY. *The* SNOWS *are co-producing with* SHANE HECHT. *The production has advanced since our last sight of it. More props, more fluency. On stage,* EVERYMAN *is being prepared for his journey.*

EVERYMAN
But who shall be my friend? Let there be one who takes my hand, and guides me through this foreign land!

Hiatus. Grins. Everyone looks round.

SHANE HECHT
(*Beating her script on her lap*)
Good Fellowship, you're the bloody end! Where's Tim Perkins again?

Unobserved, AILSA BRIMLEY *slips into the back stalls.*

A BOY
Extra violin, Mrs Hecht.

SHANE HECHT

It was *firmly* understood at the last staff meeting, by *all* staff, that the play had precedence over absolutely everything. *You* know it, *I* know it, Tim Perkins knows it, his housemaster knows it –

FIELDING

(*Unabashed, from the auditorium, raises his hand*)
My fault, Shane. Mea culpa. Sorry, sir, I forgot.

SHANE HECHT

Right. In that case, since I've got no Good Fellowship, *no* clown, and a Devil with *mumps*, there is no *earthly* point in carrying on tonight. The Tech Run will take place at this time next Saturday.

Over the thunder of departing people:

SHANE HECHT

(*Bellowing*) Will you please make sure you all know your lines perfectly! Discord! I'm thinking of you particularly.

103. INT. CHAPEL/SOMEWHERE TO BE DETERMINED. EVENING

SMILEY *and* STANLEY RODE *sit side by side in a pew, like passengers travelling in the same direction.*

SMILEY

Fielding?

RODE

She hated him.

SMILEY

What for in particular?

RODE

She said he'd ruined England.

SMILEY

Single-handed?

RODE

His sort had. All the vanity and privilege and decadence. She said we ought to knock him off his perch.

SMILEY

Do you agree with her?

RODE

I'm beginning to wonder whether I killed her after all. That's what's happened to me now. I seem to hate her more when she's dead than when she's alive. She's unfinished business to me still.

104. INT. MRS HARLOWE'S HOUSE. EVENING

Under MRS HARLOWE*'s kindly but pained eye,* TIM PERKINS *is attempting the last bars of a simplified passage of Mozart.* MRS HARLOWE *is a fifty-five-year-old retired musician. Suddenly* PERKINS *stops playing and stares at the fire instead. Cocoa mugs on the table.*

MRS HARLOWE

Tim?

PERKINS

Yes?

MRS HARLOWE

Why don't you go home and get a good night's sleep?

PERKINS

I'd like some cocoa if I could.

MRS HARLOWE

You've just had some, Tim. You've forgotten. Would you like to sleep here? I could ring Mr Fielding.

243

PERKINS

It's all right.

MRS HARLOWE

Would you like me to drive you back? It only takes ten minutes.

PERKINS *shakes his head.*

MRS HARLOWE

Tim? When we're young, we sometimes accuse ourselves of terrible things. That's because we think we're responsible for everything that happens in the world. It's rather vain of us really. We don't realise how innocent we are. I shan't tell a soul what you've told me tonight. Unless you want me to. Do you? No? All right then. Off you go. Come here.
(*She gives him a big hug, which, though embarrassed, he doesn't resist.*)
You can leave your fiddle here if you like.

PERKINS

I'd better take it thanks, Mrs Harlowe. It's a House rule.

104A. INT. A BOY'S WASHROOM. NIGHT

The smallest boys are preparing for bed.

FIRST BOY

She did it for herself, I'll bet you. She rammed her head against a wall to spite everyone. I feel like doing that sometimes.

SECOND BOY

She was bonkers.

THIRD BOY

You're not allowed to be disrespectful about staff wives. She's dead. That's jolly serious.

105. EXT. CARNE COUNTRYSIDE. NIGHT

TIM PERKINS *riding hard through the night, raincoat billowing behind him, his violin strapped to the rear carrier of his bike.*

106. EXT. CARNE COUNTRYSIDE. NIGHT

A car is approaching down the lane. PERKINS *pulls right into the curb and stops to let it pass. A sickening thud.*

107. EXT. CARNE COUNTRYSIDE. NIGHT

PERKINS *kneels in a ditch, dazed and injured, but struggling to get up. He raises his head and seems to see help. We glimpse Wellingtons and a pair of gloved hands grasping a length of fence post, and hear the sound of ringing police bells, accompanied by ambulance and police voices and flashing lights.*

108. INT. CARNE POLICE STATION. RECREATION ROOM. NIGHT

RIGBY *and* MELLOR *have been playing darts. The phone rings.* RIGBY *on the phone, registering alarm. He shouts to* MELLOR:

RIGBY
Get Smiley and that woman of his now!

109. INT. CARNE POLICE STATION. ENTRANCE LOBBY VIEW OF
     OPS ROOM. CHAOS. NIGHT

SMILEY *and* AILSA BRIMLEY *arrive running.* BRIMLEY *is shepherded towards a weeping and broken* MRS HARLOWE *in the Ops room.* SMILEY *is stopped in the doorway by* RIGBY *running out. He grabs him and pulls him towards the exit:*

RIGBY
Smiley, with me.

110. INT. CARNE POLICE STATION. NIGHT. OPS ROOM OR
INTERVIEW ROOM

A policewoman is giving MRS HARLOWE *a cup of hot sweet tea. She's still weeping.* BRIMLEY *sits by her, comforting.*

MRS HARLOWE
I tried to tell him it didn't matter.

BRIMLEY
What didn't?

PART FOUR

111. EXT. CARNE COUNTRYSIDE. NIGHT

The spot where Tim Perkins died. MELLOR *has parked a police car above the embankment, lights trained on the scene. Observe the litter left behind by emergency teams: tyre tracks, cigarette butts and papers, bandage wrappers, sand tossed around to soak up blood. Armed with torches* RIGBY *and* MELLOR *tread gingerly among the garbage.* SMILEY *accompanies them.*

> RIGBY
> Wonderful. Police work at its bloody best.
> (*Stooping to examine something*)
> . . . What's this then?

MELLOR *stoops beside him.*

> RIGBY
> Who wore Wellingtons? Do ambulance boys wear
> Wellingtons?

> MELLOR
> Gym shoes, mostly. Pretty little lace-ups.

> RIGBY
> Do traffic policemen wear Wellingtons? Who the hell
> wears Wellingtons round here?

Holding out an arm for MELLOR *to grab,* RIGBY *lowers himself down the slope towards the sandpatch.*

RIGBY

You don't. I don't. So who does? Or are we talking
about rubber overshoes?

SMILEY *is examining a broken fence.*

SMILEY

Hit the fence with his head. How? He had to climb out
of the ditch and hurl himself at high speed up a bank
. . . The car didn't hit a fence. The car *stopped*. So it
wasn't hit and run, Inspector. It was hit, *stop*, and run.
Or was it stop, *hit* and run?

RIGBY *picks up a piece of fence, perhaps the murder weapon. It is
caked in mud and sand.*

RIGBY

I know what. The fence started it. The boy was cheeky
so the fence hit him.
(*Handing* MELLOR *the piece of fence*)
Get on the radio, Mr Mellor. Wake up that dozey
pathologist. Tell him I've got work for him.

112. INT. FIELDING'S STUDY. NIGHT

The time is 10.15 p.m. FIELDING, *wearing a housecoat over his school
day clothes, sits broken at his desk. Telephone in evidence. A large
Scotch at his elbow.*

FIELDING

I killed him. I told the parents. Can you imagine telling
the parents? First the mother. Then the father. 'Well
thank you very much for letting us know.' My God, we
English! Drink?

SMILEY

No thank you. How did you kill him?

FIELDING

He was distraught. I knew he was. I thought it was his twilight time. The storm-clouds of adolescence. I thought he'd discovered his body. I wanted him to tell me himself. So I made opportunities for him to talk to me. That's what I do. Then I began to realise I was on the wrong track. He'd cheated in his science exam. Cribbed somehow. Smuggled a bit of paper. Written formulae on the back of his hand . . . Whatever they do. They have criminal minds at that age. But not the criminal consciences to go with them. I should have wormed it out of him. Punished him. Given him his absolution.

SMILEY

Do you mean you drove him to suicide.

FIELDING

To distraction. To utter carelessness. To self-hate. Have you ever done that?

SMILEY

Killed somebody?

FIELDING

Stared at an oncoming train. A bus. The lights of a car. And wanted to throw yourself in its path? Good God, man, have you no feelings at all?

SMILEY

Was Perkins duty prefect here the night Stella Rode died?

FIELDING

(*Distracted*) I suppose so . . . yes, yes he was.

SMILEY

The night Stanley Rode left his briefcase in the front porch?

FIELDING *is at the drinks table, topping up his Scotch. He swings round angrily and starts to reply. But after the first few words we do not hear his voice any more . . .*

FIELDING

Do you mind not playing the detective at a time like this! How can you be so cheap? A boy – a precious life entrusted to my care . . .

STELLA RODE'S VOICE

With a past like yours, you don't deserve a future, I'm afraid, Terence. A man like you, ending his days in that pretty museum, showing off to the public. Do they know your little secret?

STANLEY RODE (*Voice over*)

(*Imitating Stella*) 'That's what they all are. Locked in my head. Prisoners serving out their punishment in my head.'

FIELDING

. . . dead on a slab, and all you think of is that vulgar little woman.

SMILEY

Do you own a car?

FIELDING

I'm not a complete pauper.

SMILEY

Have you taken it out tonight?

FIELDING

(*Tears*) I drove it to the Sawley Hospital to identify the body of somebody I loved.

113. INT. HOSPITAL MORGUE. NIGHT

PATHOLOGIST, RIGBY, MELLOR, *the covered body of* PERKINS *on the slab.*

PATHOLOGIST

Do you want it straight or shall I mince my words to spare your sensitivities?

RIGBY

I think we can take it.

PATHOLOGIST

I don't know. Head injuries, inflicted by a chunk of wood. I'd need a couple of days at a microscope.

RIGBY

Did the car hit him?

PATHOLOGIST

Yes, but he didn't die of it.

RIGBY

So what did he die of?

114. INT. CARNE SQUASH COURTS. NIGHT

Alone in one of half-a-dozen partly open squash courts, SHANE *and* CHARLES HECHT *are playing ferocious squash. Seconds of violent combat before the players' door leading into the back of the court flies open and* SMILEY *enters, wearing the same shabby suit and walking shoes as in his last scene.*

HECHT

(*Furious*) What in the name of – ? Your shoes man! What the hell do you think you're doing? Are you drunk?

SMILEY

(*Attempting to take off his shoes*) Unfortunately not. Tim Perkins is dead.

HECHT

Who?

251

SHANE HECHT
Oh my God. How?

SMILEY
Perkins. In Fielding's house. Your pupil, I believe, for geography. Inspector Rigby thought you should be told at once.

SHANE HECHT
How did he die?

SMILEY
Well not like Stella. Not quite. He sort of fell off his bicycle and got crushed. Have you been playing long?

HECHT
What crushed him? A horse? A bus? Tell us what happened.

SMILEY
It's not really known. Have you been playing long? You don't look exactly exhausted, either of you.

HECHT
Couple of sets.

SMILEY
Did you come by car?

HECHT
Hell's it got to do with you?

SHANE HECHT
How dare you suggest something like that.

The camera favours their hands clenching their racquets.

SMILEY
I don't think manners are very important just at the moment. Perkins was Carne's ward. Your sacred trust.

He died in your care, as Stella did. I wondered whether you'd killed him. Or perhaps you know who did. Then I could pass it on to Inspector Rigby.

As the camera moves between the furious, stunned faces of the HECHTS:

114A. INT. FLASHBACK FIELDING'S HALLWAY. NIGHT

HECHT *and* STELLA *(same as Scene 60).*

STELLA RODE'S VOICE

You're a perfect marriage, aren't you? You even steal together. They'll need to know that, won't they, next time you apply for a headmastership somewhere? They'll need to know they're hiring thieves . . .

114B. INT. SQUASH COURT. EVENING

HECHT

You tell Rigby – no . . . let me tell you . . . you're a meddling little man. Get out of here before I . . .

His squash racquet has lifted from his side.

SMILEY

Before you beat my head in?

115. EXT. D'ARCY'S HOUSE. NIGHT

SMILEY *in the forecourt, testing the temperature of the bonnet of* FELIX D'ARCY'*s Morris Oxford. The dogs start barking.* DOROTHY D'ARCY *opens the door.*

DOROTHY

(*Yells*) Who's that?

SMILEY

Ah. You're back.

DOROTHY

Been in all evening. What do you want? Who is that?

SMILEY

Smiley. George Smiley.

He walks past her into the house.

116. INT. D'ARCY'S HOUSE. NIGHT

FELIX D'ARCY, *sitting at a desk, correcting, stares up in astonishment.*

SMILEY

How about him? Has he been in all evening too? Have you?

D'ARCY

This is a most extraordinary intrusion! Dorothy! Throw him out!

SMILEY

Where did you go? Your car's warm.

D'ARCY

I refuse to say! How dare you interrogate me in my own house? You're an intruder, sir. Get out! Dorothy!

SMILEY

Where have you been?

DOROTHY

Tell him.

D'ARCY

To the kennels.

SMILEY

Harriman's?

D'ARCY

Yes.

SMILEY

Why?

D'ARCY

To take a dog. It had been vomiting. Dorothy thought the matter could wait until morning, but I thought it more prudent to see to it now.

SMILEY

Can you prove it! Perkins is dead! Tim Perkins, your pupil, has died in a ditch in what the police are pleased to call suspicious circumstances. Prove it!

In the silence, DOROTHY *vaguely picks up the phone then puts it down, bereft.* FELIX D'ARCY *stares at* SMILEY . . .

116B. INT. FLASHBACK. FIELDING'S HALLWAY. NIGHT

STELLA RODE'S VOICE

Who's been a naughty boy, then? Playing touch wee-wees with Alice Lawry while his big sister's back is turned? Do you play touch wee-wees with your sister too? They say you do?

STANLEY RODE (*Voice over*)

(*Imitating Stella*) 'You thought he was a nancy-boy, that's not what Alice says.'

116C. INT. D'ARCY'S HOUSE. NIGHT

(*As before.*)

D'ARCY

(*Head in hands*) Harriman wasn't there. I went to see his kennel maid. I've been having an affair with her.

SMILEY

Oh, I think that's pretty well-known already. I think what people are really asking is whether you killed Stella Rode. The two deaths are connected, you see. We don't know quite how, yet. But they surely are.

D'ARCY

Of course I didn't.

DOROTHY

(*In utter contempt*) It wouldn't be seemly, would it, darling?

SMILEY

(*To Dorothy*) But *you* could have done it. Couldn't you? She was blackmailing him. You're his big sister.

DOROTHY

Oh, I expect I'd have done her in if it had helped. But I didn't *know*, did I? I couldn't have killed the boy though. I couldn't have done that.

The phone rings in front of D'ARCY. D'ARCY *at his desk remains inert before it, head in arms.*

DOROTHY

(*To* D'ARCY) Pick it up, you little coward!

D'ARCY

(*Into phone*) . . . what? Yes . . . He's here . . .
(*To* SMILEY) Rigby. For you.

He hands the receiver to SMILEY, *then puts his head back in his arms.*

117. INT. POLICE CAR. NIGHT

MELLOR *driving.* RIGBY *and* SMILEY *in the rear.*

> **RIGBY**
> He's been in all evening. Not stirred. The boys have
> spoken to his landlady. Ate a hearty tea, watched a bit
> of TV, took no phone calls, made none. Sat in front of
> the fire correcting. He doesn't own a car and he hasn't
> got a driver's licence.

> **SMILEY**
> Perhaps he flew then.

They pull up at the house of RODE*'s landlady.*

118. INT. MRS MACFARLANE'S BOARDING HOUSE. NIGHT

RIGBY *and* SMILEY *sit on Rode's bed.* RODE, *in his dressing gown,
has been writing on a block in bed before going to sleep.*

> **RODE**
> Perkins? Who would do such a terrible thing as that?

> **RIGBY**
> Wouldn't be his first time, necessarily, would it? Could
> be somebody you know, I suppose. Could be a friend of
> yours. Doing you a favour. Somebody under pressure.
> Blackmail. Who are you writing to?

> **RODE**
> Nobody.

> **RIGBY**
> Writing to yourself, are you?

> **RODE**
> Yes.

RIGBY *picks up the block and reads.*

RODE

Mr Cardew said write it all down. Get it out of myself once and for all.

SMILEY

Will you tell me something?

RODE

If I can.

SMILEY

On the night Stella was killed, you took your briefcase to Fielding's house, didn't you. Where did you put it during dinner?

118A. INT/EXT. FLASHBACK. FIELDING'S HALLWAY. NIGHT

RODE (*Voice over*)

In the porch. Well, gave it to the boy actually. The duty boy opened the door, I handed him my coat and case. He put the coat on a hook. And the case, well, he put it on a shelf. I'd have done it myself except Fielding likes to teach them manners. So I let the boy . . .

He dries.

118B. INT. RODE'S BEDROOM. NIGHT

(*As before.*)

SMILEY

And the boy was . . . ?

RODE

Yes. He was. Perkins.

SMILEY

And when you left?

RODE

It was there. I just took it. I picked it up. And took it. Across the fields. Fielding lent me his torch.

RIGBY

Fielding didn't hand it to you?

RODE

No. He just stood there watching me. He was sullen. He gets like that after dinner parties. He's disappointed. Things are never as good as he wants them to be. Not afterwards.

RIGBY

He never picked it up and felt the weight of it? On oath Rode!

RODE

Why should I lie about a thing like that? I don't lie. You know that, Mr Smiley.

SMILEY

Was it locked? The briefcase?

RODE

Of course not. Ask him.
(*Pointing at* RIGBY) He knows that. It doesn't lock. Even if it did, I wouldn't lock it. I live out of the damn thing. Till I get my classroom.

SMILEY

So the science examination paper you had set for the following day – the 4C science paper, is that right? – was inside the briefcase all through dinner?

RODE

Yes.

SMILEY

And Perkins is in 4C.

A Carne clock strikes.

119. INT. SAWLEY ARMS, FOYER. MORNING

SMILEY *on the phone,* BRIMLEY *is leaning close. We don't know who he's talking to.*

SMILEY

Well, no. No. In the circumstances, we were all a little
overwrought . . . and so we should have been.
(*Pause.*)
Well, listen. If you're coming up this week, why don't I
make amends and give you dinner? May we say
Thursday? Eight for eight-fifteen. Don't bother to dress.

120. INT. SMILEY'S HOUSE, BYWATER STREET. DINING-ROOM.
EVENING

AILSA BRIMLEY *is setting the dinner table for four. Much attention to
detail.*

SMILEY (*Voice over*)

You wouldn't know where Ann keeps her pot-pourri
would you?

121. INT. SMILEY'S DRAWING-ROOM. EVENING

SMILEY *is polishing the silver.*

BRIMLEY (*Voice over*)

Cut an apple into it. That'll help.

122. INT. SMILEY'S HOUSE. DINING-ROOM. NIGHT

Dinner in progress. FIELDING *at the head,* SMILEY *on his right,*
BRIMLEY *on his left. The fourth place, at the other end of the table, is
set but unoccupied.* FIELDING *is in splendid form.*

FIELDING

God, I hate London! I only have to be here half a day
to rush back to my Cobbett and my country pleasures.
'A wen on the face of nature.' How right he was.
(*To* SMILEY) Is your wife always late?

SMILEY

Sometimes she never appears at all.

FIELDING

Divine claret.
(*To* BRIMLEY) So you worked with Adrian in the war.
Are your lips as tightly sealed as George's? Tell me
general things, then. Was he ever a fake? Was he ever
the tiniest bit like me?

BRIMLEY

One does see a resemblance, of course. But I fear it's
only skin deep.

FIELDING

So unfair. He was an athlete. He was a scholar. He was
straight. He got all the good genes. I got all the dregs. I
talked to an impertinent Westminster boy today. I was
supposed to be interrogating him about Swinburne and
I got carried away. He said he'd been taking tea with
the headmaster's wife. And how was *that*? I said. 'Oh
you know the kind of thing, sir. Milk in first and
Indian.' I gave him an Alpha naturally. How could I
resist? Gorgeous salmon. Did you cook it yourself? I
always think it's a mark of discernment to serve claret
with salmon. The lower classes wouldn't dare.
(*A mocking, genteel voice, reminiscent of Stella's.*)
'Red meat, red wane. *Whate* meat, *whate* wane.' Why am
I doing all the talking? I must be happy, I suppose.
Always good to get out of Carne. I should do it more
often.

SMILEY

(*As if he is talking of the weather*)
You killed Stella Rode. We found all the stuff you used.

The plastic cape, the rubber overshoes, gloves. Ailsa went to the Hungarian place and dug them out. Rigby's got them.

BRIMLEY
(*The same matter-of-fact note*)
She was blackmailing you. She was a bitch. That's a very strong defence plea, actually. If you can prove blackmail, judges lend an awfully sympathetic ear.

SMILEY
The irony is, you'd still have got away with it if you hadn't panicked and killed Tim Perkins too. And for that, of course, there is no mitigation at all. Not in law, and not in life. Aren't you going to protest your innocence? Yes, you are. You're about to tell me I'm joking or I'm out of my mind. Or is it that you've never been so insulted in your life? Let me spare you the formalities.

123. INT. FIELDING'S HOUSE. ENTRANCE HALL. NIGHT

Flashback. The dinner party of the night of the murder is ending. FIELDING *is in the hall, waving his dinner guests into the night: the* HECHTS, *the* D'ARCYS, *the* SNOWS.

SMILEY (*Voice over*)
Stella had left early. That was already a help. But you needed to keep Rode back, so you invented a piece of shop – what was the topic, I forget?

124. INT. FIELDING'S HOUSE. ENTRANCE HALL. NIGHT

Time lapse. FIELDING *and* RODE *before the fire.* FIELDING *admonishing,* RODE *listening.*

FIELDING (*Voice over*)
The Babel coming out of his science lessons. I was merciful, of course. I didn't want to hurt his feelings. Why should I?

125. INT. FIELDING'S HOUSE, HALL. NIGHT

RODE *picks up his briefcase from the marble shelf,* FIELDING *puts a torch in his hand and sees him to the door.*

> SMILEY (*Voice over*)
> You made sure he had taken the field path as usual, then slipped into your murderer's uniform. Then you raced down the lane on your bicycle in order to get there ahead of him. You'd already stolen his piece of cable. You had your victim and you had your culprit. What could be simpler?

125A. EXT. CARNE, THE LANE. NIGHT

FIELDING *is racing through the Carne night on his bicycle, his plastic cape billowing.*

> SMILEY (*Voice over*)
> The only person with whom you hadn't reckoned was Mad Janie. Well no one can blame you for that.

A flash shot of MAD JANIE *in the bushes, watching the apparition of* FIELDING *fly by.*

> SMILEY (*Voice over*)
> The least a murderer is entitled to is a little privacy, after all.

125B. INT. RODE'S HOUSE, CONSERVATORY. NIGHT

FIELDING *is murdering* STELLA. *Finished, sated and near exhaustion he straightens up. Some noise or movement from outside frightens him. Feverishly he starts to tear off his bloodstained clothing and backs into the packing room between the conservatory and the house. He looks round, panicking, for somewhere to hide the dripping cape and spies one of Stella's refugee sacks. Gasping he starts to stuff the cape, gloves and the galoshes into the sack.*

263

126. EXT. RODE'S HOUSE. GARDEN. NIGHT

In the bushes something is moving towards the conservatory.

127. INT. RODE'S HOUSE, PACKING ROOM. NIGHT

FIELDING *hurriedly finishes knotting the tie-on label of the sack and looks up just as* MAD JANIE *shuffles into the conservatory. She stares first at Stella's body, then at* FIELDING. *She catches sight of the green necklace. Her hand reaches out towards it as it lies near Stella's bludgeoned head. She seems more fearful that* FIELDING *will stop her from taking it. She grins at him, trying to placate him.* FIELDING *stoops, pulls an old blue overcoat from the pile of unsent clothes and tosses it to her. She grabs that and the necklace and flees, dropping the belt on the floor, soaking up the blood.*

FIELDING, *sweating and panting, considers his next move. He makes as if to leave, then remembering, turns back, picks up the sack and disappears. He exits by the front door.*

128. EXT. RODE'S HOUSE, FRONT. NIGHT

FIELDING *hurries round by the front path to his bicycle in the lane and cycles off into the darkness. In the hedgerow* MAD JANIE *watches the devil with a hump on his back flying towards the moon.*

129. EXT. DITCH. NIGHT

FIELDING *cycles furiously past, flinging the cable, the murder weapon, into the ditch.*

130. EXT. THE WOODS. NIGHT

MAD JANIE, *wearing the blue coat like a lady of leisure and fingering the green necklace luxuriously, wanders off into the darkness.*

131. EXT. HECHTS HOUSE. NIGHT

FIELDING *passes by the front gate and with great care he silently drops the sack into the yellow ;efugees clothing bin.*

132. EXT. RODE'S HOUSE. NIGHT

STANLEY RODE *returns home up the front path, and lets himself in.*

133. INT. RODE'S HOUSE/FOOT OF STAIRS. NIGHT

RODE
Stella! I'm back.
(*Silence. He calls up the stairs.*)
Stella? Are you there?

RODE *walks down the corridor opening doors and calling his wife's name. Puzzled, he finally turns into the passageway towards the conservatory, out of sight. After a moment we hear a chilling, almost animal scream.*

134. INT. FIELDING'S HOUSE/STUDY. NIGHT

FIELDING *is wearing his dinner-jacket again. He enjoys a nightcap in front of the fire. Sibelius on the gramophone.*

SMILEY (*Voice over*)
And so home for a nightcap and bed. Leaving nature to take her course.

135. INT. BYWATER STREET, DINING ROOM. NIGHT

FIELDING
It was a necessary work of art! You've been in situations, don't tell me you haven't. You're an expediency man. You must be in your profession. You

believe in the appearance of things. So do I. What else is there, in the end? We're artists, both of us. Artists of expediency. We're the last of the Romans, for God's sake. Are we supposed to sit there and watch the Barbarians steal away our empire? You're a scholar! You believe in excellence! She was blackmailing me. *Me!* That little slut was blackmailing *me!* I've more quality in my little finger than that woman had in –

BRIMLEY
'In her entire body,' is how it goes on.

SMILEY
You did frame the husband too, of course. You'd have sent him to the gallows. All the same, I do see a shadow of a case for you this far. Ailsa can't. But I can. Just. You were provoked. You had to act. One of you had to die. Stanley Rode – well, he'd have been the innocent bystander who caught a stray bullet. And after all, no bystander is ever completely innocent, is he?

FIELDING
Then let me go. You've got influence. You know people. You loved Adrian. You're a snob in your way, just as I am. I'll disappear. You'll never hear of me again. I swear.

SMILEY
You killed Tim Perkins too.

FIELDING*'s head has fallen on to his chest.*

SMILEY
And that was the crime of crimes. It's also what narrowed the field to *you.*

136. INT. CARNE SCHOOL, FIELDING'S HOUSE. PERKINS' STUDY. NIGHT

TIM PERKINS *sits at his desk,* RODE*'s briefcase open at his feet. He is copying out exam questions from* RODE*'s science examination paper.*

SMILEY (*Voice over*)

He'd seen inside Rode's case. He'd borrowed the case while you were all having dinner, and he'd copied out the questions. He was being blackmailed too, in his way. You might have had a little sympathy for him, but you didn't.

FIELDING (*Voice over*)

I loved him!

SMILEY (*Voice over*)

He might even have to leave the school if his work didn't improve. So he turned his hand to crime.

The boys are all in bed. In his study, PERKINS *returns the papers to the briefcase.*

137. INT. CORRIDORS AND STAIRS, FIELDING'S HOUSE. NIGHT

We follow PERKINS *down the corridors, briefcase in hand, as he tiptoes.*

137A. INT. FIELDING'S HALL & FRONT DOOR. NIGHT

The 'private side' of FIELDING*'s house.* PERKINS *replaces the briefcase on the marble shelf.*

SMILEY (*Voice over*)

. . . but his real crime was not what he didn't know, but what he *did* know. He knew what there *was in the briefcase. And above all, what there wasn't*: no coaxial cable, no murderer's workclothes. Nothing that incriminated Rode at all.

FIELDING (*Voice over*)

Smiley, I forbid you to say this. You can't put things like that into words! 'They're the other side of the door!' Not *here*, not –

137B. EXT. CARNE COUNTRYSIDE. NIGHT

FIELDING *in Wellingtons seizes a piece of fencing and drives it into something at his feet. There is revulsion in his face, fastidiousness, even shame.*

> FIELDING (*Voice over*)
> There are two sides to our heads, Smiley. *You've* done unspeakable things too, I know you have . . . sabotage, silent killings . . .

138. INT. BYWATER STREET, DINING-ROOM. NIGHT

> FIELDING (*Voice over*)
> . . . My brother told me. The garotte, the hands, the knife. It was to preserve, Smiley! To preserve what we believe in. *Us. Our* kind. People like us! The best of England. Ailsa – you too! You worked with him. You're as guilty as any assassin with a knife. Both of you. Guilty! You can't judge me! I'm one of *you!*

FIELDING *stares from one face to the other, but sees no mercy.*

> FIELDING
> You've no proof. The boy's dead.

138A. EXT. SMILEY'S HOUSE. NIGHT

A police car and a Black Maria have pulled up outside 9 Bywater Street. The doors of the Black Maria fly open. We stare into the cavernous darkness as into a grave. Footsteps . . .

139. INT. SMILEY'S HOUSE/DINING-ROOM. NIGHT

FIELDING *has his head in his hands.*

> FIELDING
> The weapon *was* in the briefcase. I felt the weight of it myself. If Rode says otherwise he's lying. He's a liar. A

common little liar and a murderer. He killed the woman, then he killed the boy. I deny everything, you're ridiculous.

During this speech, SMILEY *leaves the room.*

140. INT. HALLWAY. NIGHT

SMILEY *opens the door to* RIGBY. *On the front steps,* RIGBY *puts out his cigarette.*

141. INT. SMILEY'S DINING-ROOM. NIGHT

During his speech, FIELDING *has got up, and now towers menacingly above* BRIMLEY.

BRIMLEY
Better tell that to Mrs Harlowe, Terence. Mrs Harlowe, the lady who taught Tim Perkins extra violin. The police talked to her. I was there. Tim made what we might call a deathbed confession to her, though he didn't know he was about to die, of course.

RIGBY *has now entered the room,* SMILEY *and* MELLOR *behind him.*

RIGBY
We've also been looking at your car rather carefully. You made a good job of washing it, but we did find a spot of blood on the front axle, and I've a suspicion it's not rabbit. Transport outside, sir, if you don't mind . . .

FIELDING
(*Screaming*) Smiley! Save me, damn you! For my brother's sake, save me!

142. INT. CARNE SCHOOL. FIELDING'S CLASSROOM. DAY

A college servant is removing some of the 'objets' which decorate Fielding's classroom.

143. EXT. CARNE PLAYING FIELDS. DAY

A rugger match is approaching its dramatic climax. Boys and staff are cheering frantically from the touchlines.

> CROWD
> School! . . . School! . . . School! . . . School! . . .

As the cheers mount in savagery we see RODE *taking a solitary walk at the far end of the playing fields. His dog Sally scampers gratefully at his feet.*

144. EXT. ST JAMES'S PARK. DAY

In long shot, SMILEY *and* BRIMLEY *walking beside the lake.*

> BRIMLEY
> We could go to the Tate if we hurried.

> SMILEY
> No, I don't think I feel like the Tate.

> BRIMLEY
> All right, then, let's get some tickets for the theatre.

> SMILEY
> No, I don't think I feel like the theatre.

> BRIMLEY
> (*Remonstrating*) George!

THE END

Credits

A Portobello Film for Thames Television

Producer	Eric Abraham
Director	Gavin Millar
Music by	Stanley Myers
Production Designer	Grant Hicks
Costume Designer	Anne Sinclair
Make-up Designer	Louise Fisher
Director of Photography	Denis Crossan
Film Editor	Angus Newton
Executive Producer Thames Television	Brian Walcroft
Production Associate	Vanessa Lees
Production Supervisor	David Barron

Filmed on location at Sherborne School and in the town of Sherborne, Dorset, and at Shepperton Studios.